THE MAPMAKERS

TAMZIN MERCHANT
Illustrated by PAOLA ESCOBAR

PUFFIN

PUFFIN BOOKS

UK | USA | Canada | Ireland | Australia
India | New Zealand | South Africa

Puffin Books is part of the Penguin Random House group of companies whose addresses can be found at global.penguinrandomhouse.com.

www.penguin.co.uk
www.puffin.co.uk
www.ladybird.co.uk

First published 2022
This edition published 2023
001

Set in 12.1/16.38 pt Bembo Book MT Std
Typeset by Jouve (UK), Milton Keynes
Printed and bound in Great Britain by Clays Ltd, Elcograf S.p.A.

The authorized representative in the EEA is Penguin Random House Ireland, Morrison Chambers, 32 Nassau Street, Dublin D02 YH68

A CIP catalogue record for this book is available from the British Library

ISBN: 978–0–241–42634–0

All correspondence to:
Puffin Books
Penguin Random House Children's
One Embassy Gardens, 8 Viaduct Gardens, London SW11 7BW

MIX
Paper from responsible sources
FSC
www.fsc.org
FSC® C018179

Penguin Random House is committed to a sustainable future for our business, our readers and our planet. This book is made from Forest Stewardship Council® certified paper.

For Mum and Dad

List of illustrations

1 Blackfriars Bridge

2 Sargasso Chocolate House

3 Compass and Main

4 Tower of London

5 Tyburn

6 Storm-Eye Hall

7 Vauxhall Pleasure Gardens

Cordelia Hatmaker was following a star.

The North Star hung above the dark jostle of night-time London – just out of reach but never out of sight. Even the smudges of smoke rising from the city's chimneys could not dim Polaris's brightness.

Cordelia felt like she was trying to catch a song in her hand. She had followed the star from her home, Hatmaker House on Wimpole Street, to the wharves near St Katherine's by the Tower. All around her, seagoing galleons creaked and swayed in their sleep, rigging like black lace against the sky.

In the lapping waters of the River Thames, Polaris's reflection gleamed like a coin dropped to the bottom. And on the map in Cordelia's hands, the same star winked at her in silver ink.

Between the three versions of the same star, Cordelia could feel a secret being whispered in a language she didn't speak.

'Where am I meant to go next?' she asked, in plain English.

It was not the first time she had asked that question, and not the first time the North Star had simply twinkled mysteriously down at her in reply.

But it *was* the first time that a guttural voice rasped from the dark, 'Pretty bit of treasure you got there, missy.'

A shadow lurched towards her. Cordelia sprang back, almost toppling off the quay. A hand shot out – she was jerked forward – suddenly a snarling mouth was an inch from her nose.

'Gimme it.'

Cordelia gagged as stale ale-breath wafted into her face. It was a sailor, stinking of drink, his yellow teeth bared in a grin. He was so close that the bristles of his beard scratched her chin.

'Ugh!'

She tried to push past him, but he grabbed her arm.

'Gimme that,' he slurred.

'It's just a bit of paper!' Cordelia gasped, flapping the map. 'It isn't worth anything!'

She was lying. The map was one of the most valuable things she owned. Although she hadn't yet worked out what it was a map of, she knew that maps generally led to treasure.

In this case, she hoped the treasure it led to was her father. Captain Hatmaker had hidden the map inside a telescope as his ship was sinking and given it to a cabin boy, Jack Fortescue – the only known survivor of the shipwreck.

For you. From him, the wreck-shocked Jack had whispered as he'd handed Cordelia the telescope.

The *Jolly Bonnet* had sunk almost two months ago and Cordelia's father had disappeared with it. Most of the Hatmaker family believed he had gone down with his ship, but Cordelia would not – could not – believe it.

It had taken Cordelia several days to find what looked like a blank piece of paper hidden inside the telescope. And it had taken her several more days to discover that it was actually a map, drawn in ink that could only be read by starlight. This discovery had made her even more determined: her father was alive, and he needed her help.

But the map was very puzzling. For a start, normal maps had helpful place names on them. *This* map showed a circus with eight roads leading off it, surrounded by a maze of lanes, but none of them was named. *Thames* was the only place name on the entire map, and it was surrounded by little swirls of silver ink to symbolize the river, with an *X* marked just beside it in the bottom-right corner. In the crook of the lane cutting across the opposite corner, there was a tiny drawing of a face with wide eyes, a curly beard and wisps of wind blowing out of his round mouth: the North Wind.

Beside him, Polaris glimmered at the tip of the Ursa Minor constellation.

At least she knew that the Thames was the right river. But it was miles long, and though Cordelia had been methodical in her search – she had started at Westminster Bridge and worked her way slowly eastwards, keeping the North Star in view at all times – she had found no sign of the circus, nor the crook in a lane where the North Wind blew. Westwards, the Thames stretched all the way to Oxford. Eastwards, it went all the way to the sea. Finding the place she was looking for would take years at this rate.

There was also a riddle, written in curling letters around the edge of the paper:

At the sign of the Rose and Sea
Runs the Fast River secret beneath.
Face the North Wind and follow him south,
There you'll find the hidden mouth.

Then there was a line of writing scrawled on the back, in her father's energetic handwriting:

Look to the stars.

Every starlit night since discovering the map, Cordelia had slipped out of Hatmaker House, quiet as a shadow, and gone hunting around London, trying to find the place shown on the map.

She had been lucky: she had managed to avoid trouble. She hadn't come up against the pointy end of a knife.

Until tonight.

The sailor's eyes slid over the map. Drinking too much grog had made him somewhat groggy.

'*Paper?*' he muttered. 'Thass not gonna get me any money.'

'Exactly,' Cordelia said, hoping she sounded confident and not as if her legs were made from Tremulous Elver tentacles and might jiggle out from under her at any moment. 'K-kindly release me and be on your way, sir.'

'Woss this, though?' The sailor squinted at the pendant hanging around her neck, and his eyes came alive with greed.

'No!' Cordelia gasped.

The pendant was a delicate shell. Painted on the inside was a portrait of Cordelia's mother – small as a snowdrop blossom but so detailed it was possible to see the individual freckles on her nose. Cordelia had only been a few weeks old when her mother died in a storm at sea. Her father had always told her she looked like her mother, but this portrait was the only proof that it was true.

The necklace, along with the map, was by far the most precious thing Cordelia had ever possessed. Both her parents had been lost at sea, years apart, their ships gathered into the crushing arms of storms and turned to driftwood. She would not let a drunk sailor rob her of either of the treasures that linked her to her mother and father.

She curled her fingers into claws and swiped at the sailor's face. There was a yowl of rage and a wild struggle, at the end of which Cordelia found herself suspended over the Thames.

'Shuddup or I'll drop ya,' the sailor hissed.

Only his finger, hooked in the chain of her necklace, was keeping Cordelia from plunging into the black slick of the river. She gripped the edge of the quay with her tiptoes.

'Please –' She could barely breathe.

The sailor pulled out a short knife. It glinted wickedly, like it had a hard question to ask. For a moment Cordelia thought it might all be over – then the sailor started sawing at the chain.

It severed in seconds. Cordelia grabbed the pendant with one hand and the sailor's beard with the other. She yanked, glad to find that the beard was strong enough to take the weight of an eleven-year-old.

The sailor bellowed in confusion as his beard dragged him downwards. Cordelia dived sideways, like a woodsman dodging a falling tree.

She threw herself belly-down on to the quay, felt her legs kick the air.

'That was close!'

Two seconds later –

SPLOSH!

Caws of laughter, like the shrieks of strange nightbirds, rang in the rigging above her.

'That's right, miss!'

'He needed a wash!'

Cordelia scrambled to the edge and peered into the river. The reflection of the North Star jumped in the ripples. Then a selection of swear words announced the sailor's arrival back at the surface.

'Best be away – before he gets 'imself out!' a voice from the rigging, gasping with laughter, advised her.

Cordelia opened her fist to check, and the steady eyes of her mother gazed at her from the shell pendant. She let out a shuddery sigh of relief.

She fled from the wharves, faster than a Lunar Hare at full moon, and did not stop running until she reached London Bridge.

The sky in the east was pale by the time Cordelia staggered to a stop. When she was certain that the sailor wasn't following her, she tucked the shell pendant with its broken chain carefully into an inner pocket. Then, making sure there was nobody else around, she unfurled the map again. The lines gleamed like threads of silver as the stars above sprinkled their light.

She studied it carefully.

If only she could solve the riddle – she was certain it would narrow down her search. But, no matter how many times she read it, she could not decipher the meaning.

At the sign of the Rose and Sea
Runs the Fast River secret beneath.
Face the North Wind and follow him south,
There you'll find the hidden mouth.

She assumed that the first part of the riddle was the name of an inn, and yet there did not seem to be a tavern, coffee house or tea parlour anywhere in London called the Rose and Sea. She had investigated an inn called the Rose and Crown, loitered near an establishment full of jaunty, cooing ladies called the Roses and Thorns, and had been shooed away from the window of the Rambling Rose chocolate house. But she had not found a place that went by the name of the Rose and Sea.

'And a *fast river* that's a *secret*?' Cordelia said aloud for the thousandth time, hoping to find new sense in the riddle.

She peered over the stone balustrade of London Bridge. The Thames below gave a slow shrug on its way past.

'You're not a fast river,' she said to the water. 'And you're definitely not a secret. I see you here on the map – the only thing I'm actually sure of.'

And how did you face the North Wind but follow it south? Did it blow you south? How far? Should she wear a billowy cloak that would catch the wind and carry her along?

She turned the map over and frowned at the line of writing scrawled on the back:

Look to the stars.

She watched the words fade as the stars above faded too. Another night was gone and the map remained as mysterious as the first time she had unfurled it. Her heart, which had been blazing with hope when she slipped out of Hatmaker House hours earlier, now felt like a spent match.

She padded home in the grey dawn, footsore and heartsore.

The map was a question from her father – and she had to find the answer.

'Where ya bin goin' at night?' a voice, brighter than the sunlight, chimed.

Cordelia woke to find a pair of brown eyes twinkling down at her.

'Aaah!' she cried, jerking upright.

Sam Lightfinger sprang to the end of the bed. She surveyed Cordelia, grinning suspiciously.

'What on earth makes you think I've been going out at night?' Cordelia asked, pulling the blanket up to her chin to hide the fact that she was still wearing yesterday's clothes.

'Fer a start, yer still wearin' yesterday's clothes,' Sam said. 'And I heard ya sneaking in just after dawn – *again*.'

Cordelia had been delighted when Aunt Ariadne had said Sam could live with them, but it was sometimes inconvenient to have such a keen-eared person sleeping in the bedroom below hers; her comings and goings were always noticed, no matter how softly she trod. Before moving into Hatmaker House, Sam had lived on the streets, having to fend for herself after her brother was sent away on a prison ship. Cordelia and Sam had become firm friends, Cordelia happily sharing everything she had with Sam. But the one thing she *wasn't* ready to share was the truth about her nightly searches along the Thames . . .

'You must have been dr-dreaming,' she declared, but halfway through the word 'dreaming', she was overcome by an enormous yawn, which was slightly undermining.

'I'm serious, Cor,' Sam said. 'Yer not savvy. There's people out there that could do ya harm.'

In a rush, Cordelia remembered: the quay, the sailor, the necklace!

She scrabbled through blankets and clothes to get to her inner pocket. She pulled out the necklace: it was safe. She sobbed a little sigh of relief seeing her mother's face, tiny, in the palm of her hand.

'What 'appened to that?' Sam asked, nodding at the broken chain.

'Nothing.'

But Sam was quick; she swiped the necklace.

'Cut with a blade,' Sam said gravely. 'Next time, the blade could be on yer neck.'

'Don't say that!' Cordelia cried. 'That's horrible!'

'Yes,' Sam said seriously. 'It *is* 'orrible. Ya shouldn't go out by yerself.'

Sam handed back the necklace, eyeballing Cordelia. There was a long moment of scrutiny, during which Cordelia unsuccessfully tried to arrange her face into an innocent expression.

Then Sam grinned. 'Fine, don't tell me. But when yer slow gettin' up in the mornings, I get ta eat all the toast!'

She bounded across Cordelia's bedroom and disappeared down the trapdoor into the house.

'Wait!' Cordelia leaped out of bed. 'Leave a slice for me!'

She tucked the shell necklace safely under her pillow. Pulling off yesterday's clothes and grabbing some fresh ones, Cordelia hurried after Sam.

She was more or less dressed by the time she reached the kitchen.

Cordelia's family were sitting round the big oak table and Sam had already tucked into a stack of toast piled as high as her nose. Aunt Ariadne was finishing her porridge and Great-aunt Petronella, perched by the fire in her large armchair, was singeing a crumpet she had speared on a toasting fork. She ate like a bird – in pecks.

Uncle Tiberius took his last gulp of tea as Cordelia tumbled into the room.

'Have you sewn Schlafen Grass into your nightcap, Dilly?' he teased. 'You're sleeping so late these days!'

Cordelia smiled sheepishly as Cook poured her a big cup of Honeymilk tea.

'Don't forget lessons with your great-aunt this morning, Cordelia,' Aunt Ariadne said. 'And we'll need you in the workshop soon. There's lots to be done before the shop opens.'

Cordelia nodded, helping herself to eggs.

'And remember Sam's lesson,' Aunt Ariadne added. 'You're teaching her the most important magic of all.'

'Reading and writing's magic?' Sam asked through a mouthful of toast.

'Indeed it is! Learning to read is like learning how to make a fire: it will light your way through life.'

Leaving Cordelia and Sam chewing that over, Aunt Ariadne hurried upstairs after Uncle Tiberius to begin working on the hats they planned to make that day.

Sam swallowed the last bite of toast, but Cordelia didn't really mind. It had been two months since Prospero had gone missing in the shipwreck. Without Sam's merry presence, Hatmaker House would have been full of shadows. But Sam's sunshine chased the shadows away.

Since moving in with the Hatmakers, Sam had cheerfully refused to wear a dress, but she had never said no to a single meal. It made Cordelia happy to see the new dimple appearing in Sam's cheek when she smiled.

Cordelia had not told her family about the starlight map her father had sent her. She did not want to raise their hopes only to disappoint them if the map led to a dead end. They'd given up hope, believing Prospero Hatmaker had drowned. But Cordelia daydreamed about finding her father and bringing him home, pictured him stepping in through the front door, imagined her aunt's joyful face, her uncle's happy tears . . .

'Jones! To the Alchemy Parlour!' Great-aunt Petronella cried, waving her toasting fork like a sword. 'Time for today's lesson!'

Jones poked his head through the kitchen window. Jones was the Hatmakers' coachman, and also, as Great-aunt Petronella impishly called him, 'Conveyor of the Ancient Maid'. She hadn't left her armchair for as long as Cordelia could remember, and was simply carried from room to room by Jones, often assisted by other members of the household.

Today, Cordelia and Sam each took an arm (of the armchair, not the great-aunt), to help Jones carry her up the spiral stairs.

The Alchemy Parlour was alive with tiny lights, as though someone had scattered a handful of Elysium Seeds across the room. A collection of crystals hung in the wide window, casting diamonds of sunlight over everything.

'Ah! Excellent!' Great-aunt Petronella cawed as they set her chair down by the flickering lilac fire. 'The Empyrean Crystals are refracting the sunshine nicely!'

Jones slipped away as Cordelia settled Sam at a table with a quill and ink. She wrote out the alphabet on a clean sheet of paper for Sam to copy. Sam began her work, with one eye closed and her tongue sticking out.

'Helps me concentrate,' she explained. 'But my tongue does get a bit cold.'

Great-aunt Petronella picked up a tall jar of grey water that stood on her workbench. She held it up to the light and Cordelia saw pearl-bright ripples in the water.

'Blimey!' Sam said, looking up from writing a rather wobbly *f*. 'What's that shiny stuff?'

'It is joy,' Great-aunt Petronella croaked. 'Today's lesson is on extracting Essence of Joy from this rainwater, which I collected yesterday. All water contains joy. But there is a special kind to be found in rain. It is a gentle joy if the rain is soft, and a fiercer joy when the rain is harder. It also gathers at the edges of clouds to make silver linings. Even just by letting raindrops fall on your face, you can feel the joy they hold.'

She dipped her gnarled fingers into the jar and flicked droplets at Cordelia and Sam. Sam giggled, and Cordelia felt little dashes of happiness where the drops landed. Her great-aunt dabbed a little rain behind her ears as though it was perfume.

'Come winter, we will work with snowflakes,' she said. 'A single snowflake can contain a large quantity of wonder. But today: rain!'

Following careful instructions from Great-aunt Petronella, who pointed at things from her chair using the toasting fork (to which she seemed rather attached), Cordelia set up the distillation equipment, while Sam carried on with her letters.

Cordelia poured the jar of pearly rain carefully into a large bulbous bottle set on a trivet above a small stack of wood. She fetched a bowl from a high shelf and fixed a twisty glass tube to the mouth of the bottle.

'Distillation is a method of extracting something pure from water,' Great-aunt Petronella explained. 'Put the bowl under the lip of the pipe, ready to catch the joy – good. Now we are ready to light the fire.'

She turned her bird-bright eyes on Sam. 'Come here, little Lightbringer, I think you should do it.'

Sam looked up, forgetting to put her tongue back in her mouth. 'My name's Light*finger*,' she said uncertainly. 'Not Light*bringer*.'

'Is it indeed?' Great-aunt Petronella fixed Sam with a penetrating gaze. 'I remember a time when there were Lightbringers and Flamemakers and all sorts of families whose arts were in the weaving of light. That was before the ban, of course.'

Cordelia would never get used to her great-aunt 'remembering' things that had happened hundreds of years ago. It was particularly strange because she claimed to have forgotten her own age. If Great-aunt Petronella was to be believed, she had lost count in the middle of the last century.

'The ban?' Sam said.

'You mean when Henry the Eighth banned all Making except by the Maker families?' Cordelia asked.

'Yes, the king's ban,' her great-aunt replied. 'There were once hundreds of Maker families. But, fearing that others would use Maker magic to become more powerful than him, King Henry decreed that all but a handful of Makers should stop Making. Those who defied him were imprisoned. Some were executed. It was a terrible time. Families went into hiding, changing their names to disguise who they really were, frightened that the king's men would come to arrest them.

'We helped as many as we could escape to safety through secret passageways under the city. It went on for years, well into Elizabeth the First's reign. Makers of all kinds disappeared: Weather Brewers, Besomers, Dance Spinners, Songtellers – all gone. Some went into hiding, others got away on ships to the New World.'

Cordelia had never heard this part of the story before. She suddenly felt fiercely proud of her great-aunt, helping

Makers to escape the tyranny of a king. If she couldn't fight loudly, at least she'd fought quietly. *If Making is in somebody's blood, it should never be stopped by another human, even if they wear a crown!* Cordelia thought.

'Of course, there are still some Makers in other countries, whose rulers have not suppressed their crafts,' went on Great-aunt Petronella. 'The king's Wigmakers in France, for example, and the Glassmakers in Venice. The Papermakers of China create very special magics, and the Carpetmakers in Persia work wonders with their threads. But in England only the Makers of the Royal Garb are left.'

'But there were so many others!' Cordelia frowned. 'I've never heard of some of them, like the Songtellers, and the Weather Brewers! Why weren't they allowed to continue?'

'Because – just as you say, my dear – there were *so many*. King Henry feared their power might grow beyond his control. He was particularly afraid of magical artefacts being made that might be used against him. Every magical creation the King's Men could find was burnt. Buckleberry Hall was emptied of everything, even the carpets! But some things escaped the flames. Even now an antique chair with unusual properties will occasionally turn up, or an old broomstick with an eccentric personality, made by a Besomer.'

Cordelia felt her eyes become round as coins, and her great-aunt continued:

'King Henry felt he could handle only a handful of Maker families. He decided clothes makers would be most useful to him, so we were the only Makers given permission to continue our craft.'

'Those were the Hatmakers, Bootmakers, Watchmakers . . . Glovemakers and Cloakmakers, right?' Sam ventured.

'Exactly!' Cordelia smiled. She did not add the sixth family – the Canemakers – who had been expelled in disgrace from the Makers' Guildhall thirty years ago. The last Canemaker was currently languishing in prison, awaiting trial for trying to start the very war that Cordelia had stopped.

'The king built the Guildhall for us and made us obey very strict rules: for a hundred years or so, the Makers were only allowed to make clothes for the monarch. Then, during the reign of Charles the Second, we were allowed to open shops. That is, I'm afraid to say, when things began to get a little more *competitive* between the families.'

Cordelia grimaced. To say things were 'competitive' between the Maker families was mild. Aside from an enormous argument two months ago, most Makers hadn't spoken a word to each other in several decades.

'Anybody could be a descendant of an ancient family of magical makers,' Great-aunt Petronella said to Sam. 'You'll occasionally find a clue hidden in the surname. Sometimes it's as simple as a few letters changed.'

Sam stared, speechless, at Great-aunt Petronella.

'So, Sam!' the old lady cried. 'Let us see you *bring some light*: choose a fragment of the refracted sunshine scattered over the floor and start the fire with it.'

She held out a pair of bronze tweezers.

Sam hesitated.

'I don't fink yer right about my name.'

'Lightbringer or Lightfinger, you are more than capable of this task,' Great-aunt Petronella said briskly.

A soft breeze nudged the crystals in the window and Sam's gaze drifted to the diamonds of light, shifting across the floor.

'But ain't it – ain't it breaking the law?' Sam said. 'Even if I *was* a . . . a Lightbringer, it's still *banned*. I'd get chucked in prison fer doing any kinda Making.'

'You're suddenly very law-abiding!' Cordelia teased.

Sam blushed and muttered, 'Don't wanna disgrace the Hatmakers.'

'You'd never disgrace us, Sam,' Cordelia assured her. 'You make everything more sunshiny . . . See, you've already brought light to this house!'

She gave Sam an encouraging nudge, and Sam took the tweezers.

Cautiously, as though she was handling a living thing, Sam picked up a shard of sunlight from the floor. It trembled as she carried it carefully across the room. She laid the bright diamond of light on the stack of wood, paused for a moment, then covered it with the smallest twig.

The piece of sunlight flickered.

Cordelia held her breath.

The fire took. In seconds, the little pile of wood was wreathed in crackling flames.

Great-aunt Petronella's eyes sparkled in the firelight.

Cordelia leaped up. 'You did it, Sam!' she yelped, hugging her friend. 'You *did* it!'

Sam broke into a huge smile.

It felt like the start of something.

They watched in silent wonder as the distilled joy dripped, drop by drop, into the bowl.

With the final drop, Great-aunt Petronella drifted off to sleep, which was usually how their lessons ended.

Cordelia tucked a Lullwool blanket over her great-aunt and Sam carried the Essence of Joy down to the Hatmaking Workshop.

'Jubilations! The joy has arrived!' Uncle Tiberius cried as Cordelia and Sam trooped into the workshop.

While Sam helped Uncle Tiberius squeeze Aurora Bush berries into the Essence of Joy, to make a dye that changed colour like a dawn sky, Cordelia took her hatpin from the special pincushion on the workbench. It was a fine gold pin with an aquamarine on the end of it that glimmered like a drop of living ocean. When her aunt gave it to Cordelia, she said that it was just an ordinary hatpin, but Cordelia was sure she got her most wildly inventive ideas for hats when she twirled it in her hair.

Once it was fixed in place, she began coaxing a piece of Moonbeam into a circle.

'We need more starlight,' Aunt Ariadne announced, emerging through a cloud of steam from her kettles. 'Everyone seems determined to outshine each other at the Harvest Masque.'

The Harvest Masque was a huge party that was held at Vauxhall Pleasure Gardens every September under the full moon. It was the last chance of the summer for everybody to dress up in their most imaginative and outlandish outfits and be admired (or, occasionally, sniggered at) by the whole of London. The Hatmakers had been kept extremely busy creating wild and whimsical headwear for the occasion. Starlight was in great demand for the most dazzling hats.

'We can collect some fresh starlight tonight,' Cordelia suggested. 'Sam could help. I think she'd like to learn more about Light Magic.' She winked at Sam, who beamed.

'Sir Hugo called in yesterday to hear how his headdress is coming along,' Aunt Ariadne told her, stringing Ditty Beads for a Song Bonnet she was creating. The beads warbled as they slid along the string.

Sir Hugo Gushforth was London's most famous actor. Ever since Cordelia had made him a hat to help his terrible stage fright, he had refused to let anybody else make his hats. She had created a Tartan Cap from Bilious Goat tufts for his Macbeth, a wreath of Radiant Bay for his turn as Julius Caesar, and, as *The Daily Slapp* grudgingly reported, 'the largest bicorn this side of the English Channel' for his heroic role in the smash-hit play (written by *and* starring Sir Hugo) *Hero of the High Seas*.

Now Sir Hugo had commissioned Cordelia to create his headdress for the Harvest Masque. He had been chosen to play the leading role of Full Moon at the celebrations. It was a long-held tradition that an actor, dressed as the Full Moon, performed a song and dance to honour the Harvest.

'I shall give the greatest Moon that has ever been seen,' Sir Hugo had confided to Cordelia. 'I hope the princess will be impressed. Perhaps she will even swoon when she sees my glorious Full Moon!'

Sir Hugo was always hoping to make people swoon, especially the princess.

He had given Cordelia a detailed list of everything he wanted on his headdress. Cordelia had spent several days carefully assembling a Titan Grass helmet and painting it with powdered Silverglass. Today, she was planning to shape a supple piece of fresh Moonbeam into a halo, and tomorrow she would decorate it with delicate rays made from the web of a Glamour Spider, threaded with tiny crystals of Selenite.

She set to work. There was lots to do before the shop officially opened for the day.

When the clock of St Auspice's Church chimed a quarter to ten, there was already a queue outside the doors of the Hatmakers' shop. It had been that way throughout the summer. Since Cordelia and her friends had made the Peace Hat that stopped a war between England and France, people from all over the city (and some from even further afield) were desperate to have a hat made by the magical Hatmakers of Wimpole Street.

At two minutes to ten, Aunt Ariadne was ready by the door to greet customers. Uncle Tiberius positioned himself beside the hat-fitting chair. Cordelia climbed on to a stool behind the counter, and Sam stood beside her, ready with a stack of hatboxes.

As the clock chimed the hour, Aunt Ariadne opened the shop door. A horde of eager customers streamed inside.

Soon, Uncle Tiberius was making his first customer comfortable in the hat-fitting chair, Aunt Ariadne was measuring a woman's head with a special instrument that assessed how big-headed she was, and Cordelia was advising a man on the best hat to inspire him with the twirliest dances at the Harvest Masque.

Within minutes, Sam's hatboxing was called upon for the first sale of the day, when Cordelia sold her customer a Dervish-spun Birly Bonnet decorated with Vitus Seeds.

. . . people from all over the city (and some from even further afield) were desperate to have a hat made by the magical Hatmakers of Wimpole Street.

'Thank you, Miss Hatmaker,' he gushed, as Cordelia wrapped the orange bonnet in soft paper and gave it to Sam, who placed it carefully in a chequered hatbox. 'My second cousin on my father's side had an aunt who everyone said was descended from Dance Spinners. She'd cavort across the floor, weaving all sorts of magic. Her dances were especially famed for their peace-making effects.'

'Really?' Cordelia said with a smile.

'Yes, indeed!' the man declared. 'And, between you and me, Miss Hatmaker, it has been said that I dance a particularly pacifying polka.'

All summer long, customers had excitedly shared tales of magical talents in their families. The story of the enchanted Peace Hat that had stopped a war had reignited the interest in magic across the land. Cordelia had seen similar enthusiastic crowds outside the other Makers' shops, though the crowd was always biggest at the Hatmakers'.

Sam finished tying a lemon-yellow ribbon round the hatbox and presented it to the man. He carried it proudly out of the shop, pirouetting several times on his way down the street.

Dozens of customers came through the shop that morning, clamouring for hats of every colour and design. They sold hats off the shelves, resplendent with feathers and frothy with lace, and took orders for more elaborate confections that would be ready for the Harvest Masque in a few days' time.

At some point mid-morning, a young lady wearing an enormous hooped skirt jostled into the shop.

'I want to go to the Harvest Masque as the royal galleon,' she barked at Cordelia, shoving another customer aside. 'You know, from *Hero of the High Seas*.'

Cordelia tried not to roll her eyes as Sam flashed a grin.

Hero of the High Seas was responsible for several strange requests for hats. Sir Hugo's sensational play was a highly fictionalized version of the events that took place on the royal galleon during the peace talks between England and France. In the play, Sir Hugo heroically swung through the rigging, kicking the villainous Lord Witloof into the sea, before throwing himself on to a speeding cannonball, singing a warbly song, and finally kissing the swooning princess. In reality, Cordelia had been the one to swing through the rigging to vanquish Lord Witloof, while Sir Hugo was arrested early in the proceedings with his trousers round his ankles. And, though the French king had tried, nobody had succeeded in kissing the princess. Cordelia didn't mind Sir Hugo taking theatrical liberties with the truth; she had hugely enjoyed cheering his fantastical feats at the gala performance at the Theatre Royal. However, the subsequent requests for bicorns to endow the wearer with supernatural gallantry had become a little tedious.

The customer in the hooped skirts, though, appeared to have a different desire in mind.

'I want to impress Admiral Ransom,' she announced.

'And you think wearing a *ship* on your head will do that?' Cordelia asked delicately.

'Indeed! I aim to dazzle him so thoroughly at the masque that we announce our engagement the following week,' the young lady gushed. 'Just in time to make Archibald jealous and ruin his birthday.'

'Our hats can do many things,' Aunt Ariadne said, passing the counter on her way to help a gentleman with a Jangling Tricorn, 'but we cannot guarantee a proposal of marriage. That would be morally dubious, to say the least.'

As Aunt Ariadne glided away, the customer leaned over the counter to whisper to Cordelia, '*Why* can't you guarantee a proposal of marriage?'

'Our hats are a bit like books,' Cordelia began. 'They contain magic, but it's up to the person reading the book to bring the magic to life. Without the reader, the magic just sits there. Same as a hat. Does that make sense?'

The young lady looked blank.

'It's a bit more subtle than making someone do what you want,' Cordelia tried again. 'You wouldn't want this admiral to be like your puppet, would you?'

'Ooh, that would be perfect! I want a hat that does that!' the young lady said eagerly.

She launched into an enthusiastic description of Admiral Ransom and his very impressive ship, and though Cordelia doubted several elements of the plan to dazzle him, she was very curious to see what the young lady would look like in full sail.

'Will the cannons on my ship be able to fire?' she asked. 'That would really get his attention.'

'I'll look into it,' Cordelia assured her. 'May I take your name?'

'Miss Janet Crust.'

Cordelia smiled. 'Your hat will be ready to set sail on Friday, Miss Crust.'

Satisfied, Miss Crust strutted from the shop.

Cordelia turned to the next customer and then the next, the rest of the morning a blur of orders for Confidence Caps adorned with Toothy Fuchsias, Lofty Bonnets made of Cloud Velvet, and Conversation Top Hats woven with Natterer Bat Whiskers.

Her mind should have been completely concentrating on hats. But whenever it got a chance, it strayed once again to her father's map and its riddle. As she suggested Fabula petals for decorating the brim of a Storytelling Tricorn, her mind drifted to where the spot marked *X* might be; had she overlooked a tavern called the Rose and

Sea, and how on earth could facing the North Wind lead her south?

So it snapped her out of her reverie when her next customer said in a low voice, ‘The North Wind is blowing.’

CHAPTER 4

Standing before Cordelia was a man with a birdlike face. His eyes were bright but anxious, and his whole person seemed rather ruffled.

'Wh-what did you say?' Cordelia stammered.

The man twitched a nightcap on to the counter, then glanced over his shoulder, as though worried he was being watched.

'Tell me,' he said, in a louder voice, 'in your expert opinion, Miss Hatmaker, would this nightcap help a wakeful gentleman fall asleep?'

Cordelia's heart knocked against her ribcage five times faster than usual.

'Yes,' she answered, in a loud voice to match his. 'It's got Sloth Poppy petals in the lining.'

She looked around the shop. Aunt Ariadne and Uncle Tiberius were both busy with fittings. Sam had gone to fetch more ribbons from the workshop. Several customers were examining hats, and none seemed an imminent danger to the man with the nightcap.

'Here, if you look closer, you can see the stitching is finished with Noctus knots,' Cordelia said. She and the man both bent their heads over the cap. It merely looked as though they were inspecting the fine craftsmanship of the nightcap.

'What do you mean, "the North Wind is blowing"?' Cordelia asked in a low voice. 'Is it something to do with –'

'Your father,' the man muttered urgently. 'Is he here?'

Cordelia swallowed, but managed to say, 'My father's ship, the *Jolly Bonnet*, was lost two months ago.'

The man's eyes pierced Cordelia, sharp with meaning. 'You and I both know it would take more than a shipwreck to sink Prospero Hatmaker,' he whispered.

Cordelia felt her chest fill, like a sail fills with wind. This was the first time since her father had gone missing that anybody else had expressed the idea that he might be alive.

'Without him, there is no hope of defeating Witloof!' the man said.

'Witloof? But he's in prison. And he's going to be ex–'

'Give Prospero this message,' the man interrupted. 'If you see him, tell him the North Wind is blowing.'

'What do you –' Cordelia began, but the shop's bell jangled and the man gave a squawk of alarm. He turned and blundered towards the door, knocking a stand of Chiming Tricorns.

'Wait!' Cordelia shouted.

If he knew about the North Wind, could he help her make sense of the map? She charged across the shop, but the tricorns teetered and crashed around her with a noise like a thousand icicles shattering.

'By Medusa's serpents!' Uncle Tiberius cried over the din.

Cordelia emerged from the pile of tricorns to find herself caught in a glare from Aunt Ariadne. She brushed a Wriggling Ribbon off her shoulder and said weakly, 'That man forgot his hat.'

'Ah-ha!' Uncle Tiberius gave a rather forced laugh. 'What an enthusiastic Hatmaker you are, Cordelia!'

He ushered his customer back into the hat-fitting chair.

Cordelia scrambled to her feet and peered out of the window, ignoring the curious gawks of the customers. The street was empty – the birdlike man was nowhere to be seen.

She felt a firm hand close on her shoulder.

'Tidy up this mess,' Aunt Ariadne said. 'Quickly – there is a customer who requires your attention.'

It took all Cordelia's self-control not to tear from the shop and mount a one-person manhunt through London to find the mysterious stranger. Yet, as she placed the tricorns back on their hatstand, she felt lighter than she had in weeks.

He knows my father's alive! Or at least he thinks he is . . .

The waiting customer was a lady, dressed in black from her hat to her boots, with a heavy veil that completely covered her face.

'I would like a hat to help me keep a low profile,' she said, her voice slightly muffled by the veil.

Usually people wanted a hat to make them *more* noticeable, not *less*. But Cordelia had more important things on her mind than this customer's odd request.

Lord Witloof lured the Jolly Bonnet *on to the Rivermouth rocks and claimed to have watched my father drown.*

Cordelia fetched a plain bonnet made from Torpid Straw.

And everyone thought he was dead.

She stopped in the middle of the shop, remembering those dark days when even she had believed she would never see her father again.

But then Father's Quest Pigeon, Agatha, brought back the shell necklace with the portrait of my mother – the one he always wore to remember her by. It must be a sign he's alive.

She added some grey Umbrella Bird feathers to the brim of the bonnet. The customer was silent behind her veil.

And now that strange man came here, wanting to see my father, even though the rest of London believes he's dead, whispering a bit of the riddle I'm trying to solve!

It was extremely puzzling. Cordelia shook her head as she wrapped an Insipid Ribbon round the hat to hold the feathers in place.

And he said my father's the only one who can defeat Witloof. But Witloof's already been defeated . . .

'Here you are: a Low-profile Hat,' Cordelia said, handing it to the lady. 'Put it on and you'll be so unremarkable it'll be very difficult to notice you.'

'Perfect, Miss Hatmaker.'

And why had the stranger seemed . . . afraid?

After lunch, when Aunt Ariadne was upstairs sorting out hat blocks, Uncle Tiberius let Cordelia and Sam out of the kitchen door.

'You deserve an afternoon off,' he rumbled. 'You've both been working so hard. Go and play for a few hours.'

'Thanks, Uncle,' Cordelia said.

He put a copper coin in each of their palms and winked. 'In case you happen to pass Master Ambrosius's Emporium. Don't forget I'm partial to a marzipan fancy.'

Cordelia's mouth began to water. Master Ambrosius made the most delicious sweets in London.

'Mind you stay away from Tyburn,' Uncle Tiberius warned.

Tyburn was where executions happened. And today's event was bound to be frenzied – Lord Witloof was due to mount the scaffold. Surely the birdlike stranger whispering about her father knew that Witloof's wickedness was coming to a very definite end this afternoon?

Sam's happy voice interrupted Cordelia's thoughts: 'We're going to see Goose!'

Cordelia looked up to see Uncle Tiberius frown. Goose was the youngest son of the Hatmakers' oldest rivals: the Bootmakers. Since Cordelia and Goose had danced together two months ago in front of all the Makers, their friendship had been – grudgingly – tolerated by both families. But there was still a lot of muttering and tooth-grinding from Uncle Tiberius if it was mentioned, and Cordelia had not quite worked up the courage to knock on Goose's door yet, in case his mother answered it.

'Bye, Uncle!' Cordelia pulled Sam away down the street before her uncle could change his mind and call them back inside to tidy out the button cupboard.

Although Master Ambrosius's Emporium was not strictly on the way to the Guildhall, Cordelia and Sam *did* happen to pass it.

Then they continued, pockets full of paper-wrapped marzipan fancies, sugar snowflakes, gooey nougat and oozing caramels. They ate their cream cloudbuns as they walked, because stuffing *those* into pockets would not be wise.

It would take more than a shipwreck to sink Prospero Hatmaker.

Cordelia heard the words for the hundredth time in her head. There was somebody else involved in her strange treasure hunt – a birdlike man with anxious eyes. She shivered and glanced sideways at Sam, who was licking cloud fluff off her fingers.

Perhaps it was foolish not to ask her friends for help with the map. Searching London by night these past weeks had been lonely and occasionally dangerous. Sam was savvy and Goose was dependable. Together they had stopped a war, after all . . . But the map felt like a secret between Cordelia and her father, the kind of secret that keeps you close even if you're oceans apart. It was fragile, a spell made of spiderweb she was afraid to break.

Before Cordelia could quite decide whether she should let her friends in on her secret quest, she and Sam arrived at the Guildhall.

This was the ancient magical building where the six original Maker families – Hat, Boot, Glove, Cloak, Watch and Cane – had convened for centuries to work together on fabulous and magical items for the monarchs of England. But when a rift opened between the families thirty years ago, the Guildhall, which had been a place of friendship and collaboration, was abandoned.

Recently, the king and his daughter, Princess Georgina, had reopened the Guildhall, hosting a magnificent party for the Makers, in the hope that the families might settle their differences. Cordelia suspected the party was also an attempt to apologize for the Makers being sent to prison on the orders of Lord Witloof. But if throwing the Makers into prison together hadn't made them friends, throwing them together at a party had not worked either.

Since the party, despite royal encouragement, the five Maker families had stubbornly stayed in their own homes, keeping all their secrets to themselves, and making sneery faces if they saw each other in the street. Only Cordelia, Goose and Sam visited the Guildhall now, meeting there as much as they liked, and discovering the secrets of the building together.

They had inherited a kingdom of grimy riches. There were piles of ribbons that still murmured their magic, and tools of the trades that gleamed when the rust was rubbed off. Drifts of faded feathers covered creaking workbenches. Old bolts of cloth slumped beside cupboards crammed with forgotten treasures. The whole place was full of possibilities, just hidden under a layer of dust.

From the Guildhall's Great Chamber, Cordelia and Sam peered through the doorway into the Bootmaker workshop. Goose was on the floor, sorting through a pile of old boot leathers.

'Hello, Goose!' Cordelia called.

'Look what I found!' he called back, holding up a snarl of tangled bootlaces.

'That's brilliant! Um – what are they?'

'Running Ribbons, I think,' Goose replied. 'They must have been made ages ago. And here – I dug out these old dancing shoes!'

He held up a pair of purple clogs with frayed brocade hanging off them.

'What makes you fink they're for dancin'?' Sam asked.

Cordelia and Sam chuckled as Goose hopped from foot to foot, his knees jerking upwards in turn.

'Well, they were squashed under a heavy pair of boots, but they did a sort of jig when I pulled them free,' Goose said.

'Are you going to try them on?' Cordelia asked.

Goose pulled his boots off and slid his feet into the clogs.

His feet twitched.

'Ha!' Goose laughed.

His left foot gave a little hop as his right knee jerked upwards.

'Blimey!' Sam gasped.

Cordelia and Sam chuckled as Goose hopped from foot to foot, his knees jerking upwards in turn.

'They *feel* like dancing shoes!' he called, as his feet carried him in a figure of eight around the workshop.

'They must be ancient!' Cordelia exclaimed, impressed by Goose's quick steps. 'That's a very old-fashioned dance you're doing!'

Goose whirled, clicking his heels together in mid-air. Slowly, the grin slid off his face.

'Uh – help!' he cried, as his hands began to join in, carving through the air and clapping.

'Just stop dancing!' Cordelia suggested.

'*I can't!*' Goose yelped.

The dance got faster, his arms got wilder, his hops got higher and his face got redder.

'DO SOMETHING!' Goose bawled, rollicking across the workshop.

'Do *what*?' Cordelia said.

Sam bellowed, 'CHARGE!'

They launched themselves at Goose. He landed on his back, arms and legs wriggling wildly.

Sam wrestled a leg and got kneed in the nose. Cordelia seized his other ankle. She felt as though she was fighting a sea serpent as Goose's leg thrashed.

Goose clapped; his hands smacked Cordelia's cheeks.

'*Ouch!*'

'*Sorry!*'

Sam wrenched one clog off. Goose's left leg went limp. She grabbed Goose's other shin, and Cordelia tugged the second clog from his jiggling foot.

Goose's leg and arms fell still. They all lay, panting, on the Bootmaker workshop floor.

'Definitely dancing shoes,' Goose confirmed.

Goose had had enough of the Bootmaker workshop for one day, so they all trooped across the Great Chamber to the Hatmaker workshop.

Cordelia soon unearthed some very old wooden hat blocks; one looked like it was from the time of the Cavaliers. As Goose began polishing it with a stick of beeswax he had brought from home, Cordelia considered telling her friends about her father's map, and about the mysterious man who had come to the shop that morning and had whispered, '*The North Wind is blowing*.'

Perhaps it *was* time to trust Sam and Goose with the secret. Several times she opened her mouth to begin – but, before she could arrange any words in the right order, Sam, who was rummaging among the junk, gave a cry of wonder.

'Blimey!'

She had discovered a very old shard of sunlight lying in a velvet box – light from a long-ago summer, according to the faded label. It crumbled as she picked it up, so she carefully poured the crumbs into an empty bottle.

'Look!' she said, glowing. The bottle, filled with the crumbs of sunlight, shed a pale radiance on her face.

Cordelia smiled. Her great-aunt's story of the lost Lightbringer family was working a subtle kind of magic on Sam.

Sam carried the bottle out into the huge gloom of the Great Chamber. The garlands of flowers decorating the dome, which had been fresh for the Makers' party many weeks ago, were dried and dusty now. But something else was still thriving: a multitude of Dulcet Fireflies. They flitted around, their bulbous tails flickering as they flew. The night of the party, they had glimmered and sparkled over the event. However, nobody had collected them afterwards, so they now lived free in the Guildhall, illuminating the room with their wild light.

Cordelia and Goose watched as Sam whirled the bottle in the dusty air. The fireflies were usually quite shy, but something about the bottled sunlight seemed to make them bolder. Their tails glowed as they gathered around Sam, drawing a bright smear of gold across the gloom. Sam made stars and swirls, using the bottle like a paintbrush, the fireflies following in a molten gold cascade. It was like watching a very independent-minded firework splashing and dazzling across the Great Chamber.

Sam tore up the stairs into the gallery above, the fireflies following her in a triumphant banner of light. Goose and Cordelia ran to the middle of the Great Chamber, clapping and cheering as Sam disappeared along the upper gallery.

'That's pure magic!' Goose whispered.

'Like she's leading a thousand shooting stars!' Cordelia said, awestruck.

'A *Hatmaker*!' a voice mocked behind them.

'And a *Bootmaker*!' a second nasty voice added.

Hatmaker and Bootmaker whipped round. The Bootmaker grabbed the Hatmaker's hand.

Two girls stood in the doorway. They were identical twins, wearing identical yellow dresses and identical spiteful smiles: the Glovemaker girls.

'You're not allowed here,' one spat.

'You're trespassing,' the other added.

'We're not trespassing!' Cordelia objected. 'The Guildhall belongs to every Maker equally. We're allowed to be here as much as you are!'

A pair of boys appeared behind them, with identical tweed suits and identical menacing stares.

'*We* say you're not allowed,' the boys said in unison.

The four Glovemakers lined up in the doorway. Cordelia and Goose gawped at the four pairs of balled fists and four wicked grins between them and the exit. And that was just the fists and grins – the *rest* of the Glovemakers seemed equally threatening. Even their elbows looked like bad business.

Uncle Tiberius always said, 'It's better to talk with words than with fists!'

'Now, listen –' Cordelia began, hoping words would be enough; the Glovemakers' fists looked like they had a lot to say.

'We're not going to *share* the Guildhall,' one of the girls snarled.

'Specially not with a snivelly little Bootmaker,' a boy taunted.

'He's *not* SNIVELLY!' Cordelia shouted, as Goose quietly snivelled beside her.

'Temper, temper, Hatmaker!' the other girl jeered.

The Glovemakers advanced slowly, a wicked glint in all eight of their eyes.

Cordelia backed away, pulling Goose with her.

'D'you have a plan?' he whispered.

'Er . . . no,' Cordelia admitted.

She felt the wall behind her. There was nowhere else to go.

'I think just RUN!'

The Glovemakers lunged for them. Cordelia ducked under eight grabbing arms, dragging Goose with her. They tore around the edge of the Great Chamber.

If they could get to the door – a few steps further –

A flash of acid yellow and a shriek of laughter: the Glovemaker girls had cut them off.

'You can't escape!' they sang gleefully.

Cordelia swerved away.

'Up the stairs!' she cried.

But Goose's hand was yanked from hers.

'*No!*'

The Glovemaker boys had him! They dragged him backwards, thrashing and flapping.

'Let him *go*!' Cordelia charged after them.

She had barely taken a step when her feet left the ground.

'Put me *down*!' she howled, kicking in mid-air, arms pinned to her sides. But the Glovemaker girls just laughed, the little claws on the fingers of their gloves digging into her skin.

The world went sideways, then the great dome of the Guildhall opened up beneath her feet, like a highly decorated crater.

Things only got more confusing as the blood rushed to her head. Goose was being dangled by his ankles too, getting redder-faced by the second.

'*Ooohf!*' Goose squealed, as one of the boys sank a punch in his stomach.

'Stop it!' Cordelia yelled, wriggling. Sweets showered from her pockets, raining on to the floor in a cascade of coloured paper.

'She's full of sweets!'

'Shake her and see if there's any more!'

Cordelia's teeth clacked in her skull. Marzipan fancies and chunks of caramel hit her in the face as they fell.

Things were getting very dark.

Then, in a sudden miracle of blinding light, an avenging angel appeared at the top of the stairs, halo ablaze.

'Let 'em GO!' the angel commanded, descending from on high at an alarming speed.

Cordelia hit the ground. Goose sprawled beside her.

The Glovemakers screamed.

Startled, the fireflies fled to the safety of the dome, so Sam reached the bottom of the bannister without her golden halo.

There was a short pause as all parties assessed one another.

'It's just a *kid*!' a Glovemaker exclaimed.

There was a blur of tweed as the boys pelted for Sam, who darted back up the stairs.

'RUN!' Sam roared. 'I'll be *fine*!'

Cordelia dragged Goose to his feet before the Glovemaker girls could recover their scattered wits. Hatmaker and Bootmaker raced across the Great Chamber. They dived through the velvet curtains, into the dark entrance hall, fumbling to find the exit. Cordelia could hear the Glovemaker girls stomping through the shadows towards them.

There was a sudden flood of sunlight as Goose wrenched open the door. 'Come on!'

They scrambled across the shabby square and down a narrow alley. The Glovemaker girls stormed after them, closing in like thunderclouds.

Up ahead Cordelia spotted a glimpse of Bond Street. She felt hope blaze – Bond Street was teeming with people. It would be easy to shake off the Glovemakers there.

She and Goose burst out of the alley into the surging throng. The crowd was loud and rowdy, but Cordelia didn't care. The mass of jostling bodies swept them to safety, up the street.

'What – what about Sam?' Goose wheezed, looking around for her.

'She'll have escaped out of a window!' Cordelia said. 'Let's go round the back of the Guildhall and find her.'

She tried to shoulder through the bodies packed tight around them, but it was impossible.

'Here he *comes*!'

'The CONDEMNED!'

A black wagon rolled slowly through the middle of the mob. The air soured, curdling into jeers.

Cordelia's stomach dropped.

The wagon loomed above her. A figure sat inside it, dressed in shadow. Cordelia could feel him: he had the dark pull of a planet.

It was the man who had wrecked her family's ship and claimed, with savage joy, that the waves had taken her father.

Witloof.

The crowd was frantic: a beast with thousands of eyes and teeth.

Goose grabbed Cordelia's hand and tried to drag her to safety. But they could not fight their way out: they had been swallowed whole by the mob. It was all they could do to stay on their feet.

There was only one place they could be going – the one place Uncle Tiberius had warned Cordelia to stay away from.

Tyburn.

The name struck like midnight.

The crowd crushed into the square – there was the scaffold, dark against the sky. The people roared when they saw it standing ready. This was better than the theatre, better than cock fights or dice. This was a chance to see a villain vanquished and a life leave a body. Half of London had turned up.

The Hatmakers themselves had received an invitation from the palace to watch this execution as though it was a play. Aunt Ariadne had silently put the scroll in the fire; they would never accept such an invitation. But now Cordelia was there, in over her head and struggling not to panic. Goose was crushed against her, wild-eyed. His hat had been knocked off and his hair looked even stranger than usual.

'I – I don't want to see this,' he wheezed. 'I don't want – to be here.'

'Nor do I!' Cordelia cried. 'But just – stay on your feet! If you fall, you'll be trampled!'

The blast of a trumpet sounded over the crowd. 'All hail His Majesty King George!'

The crowd was fraught and fevered, but the golden promise of a monarch made them turn. Cordelia saw King George and Princess Georgina mounting a dais swathed in velvet. Palace guards stood round them.

The people roared their approval as the king raised his hand in greeting.

'Hold on to me, Goose!' Cordelia yelled. 'Don't let go! *We mustn't get separated!*'

He grasped her so tight she felt his nails dig into her wrist. She was shoved, crushed, she couldn't breathe, but she pushed onwards –

'STAND BACK!'

A sword flashed, inches from her eyes. She had reached the wall of royal guards.

'Miss Hatmaker!' she heard a cry from above her. 'And – is that Master Bootmaker with you?'

The pale face of Princess Georgina peered down at her.

'Your Highness!' Cordelia gasped. 'We – we got caught up –'

The princess was already issuing orders to her guards. Rather than tussle with the crowd, the guards simply lifted the children off the ground, passed them through the air and deposited them at the king's feet.

Cordelia stood up shakily. The curtsey she made to the king nearly folded her legs back underneath her. Goose was in a heap on the floor.

'Ah, so a Hatmaker has come to see the show after all!' the king said.

His Majesty was ruddy-faced and vigorous as ever, but his daughter, Cordelia thought, looked rather wan.

'Oh, Father, don't,' the princess whispered. 'It's too barbaric.'

'Nonsense!' the king cried. 'Witloof's going to get justice done to him, as he deserves, the treacherous beast.'

There was a deafening roar as the wagon disgorged a figure on to the scaffold.

'There he is, the villain!' the king shouted, banging his chair. 'I love this bit!'

The figure of Lord Witloof was pelted with a volley of rotten food.

'He's decided to hang,' the king told Goose conversationally. 'I'd have gone for the chop, personally. It's quicker, though rather old-fashioned. Ah, well. Perhaps he wants to stay all in one piece.'

Goose was looking decidedly unwell.

'Have you recovered from the side effects of the Rage Clothes, Your Highness?' Cordelia asked the princess.

The Rage Clothes, made on the orders of Lord Witloof by his accomplice Miss Canemaker, had briefly turned the princess into a blazing-eyed Fury, who hurled insults like hand grenades.

'If truth be told, Miss Hatmaker,' the princess said, 'I am always expected to be polite and ladylike. It was really rather invigorating being angry.'

Cordelia smiled. 'Yes, feeling angry sometimes is important,' she said. 'As long as it doesn't burn you up from the inside.'

Her Highness shivered.

'If only there was something that *could* warm me from the inside now. Never mind the Rage Clothes – Witloof's glass crown froze my very soul. I feel cold all the time.' The princess pulled her cloak tighter round her shoulders.

Cordelia shuddered, remembering the twisting glass crown that Lord Witloof had forced the princess to wear. It had turned Her Highness into an ice-eyed version of herself, unable to move or speak. Even today, though the afternoon was warm, Cordelia noticed that the princess's lips were pale, and her fingers shook.

'We invited Witloof's sister to the execution, but she hasn't come,' the king announced. 'His only remaining relative. Thought she might like the chance to see him off. I was going to give her this. Here, you can have it instead.'

Goose was determinedly studying his boots, so the king tossed a small object to Cordelia.

It was a glass pocket watch on a golden chain. She recognized it immediately: Lord Witloof had carried it everywhere. Cordelia remembered the moment she had realized, with a sickening belly-twist, that Witloof had trapped a living butterfly inside the case. The butterfly was now nothing but a sad flake of ash behind the glass.

'It doesn't work – there's no wind-up key – but quite the souvenir nevertheless, eh?' His Majesty smiled. 'The pocket watch of a traitor!'

The watch was cold as a lump of ice in Cordelia's hand. 'Thank you,' was all she trusted herself to say, hoping her voice sounded grateful and not full of revulsion.

She looked over the heads of the fitful crowd at Lord Witloof. Gone was the pompous politician he had pretended to be. He was now unmasked: he wore his ugliness plain on his face, for all to see.

A priest with a Bible mounted the scaffold, but Witloof waved him away. The crowd seized up, hissing. This was depraved behaviour: the condemned man would not even make his peace with God!

His Majesty flapped a hand at a steward, who stepped forward. His thin voice rang over the churning undercurrent.

'Lord Whitstable Geraldine Lindsey Graham Witloof, you are hereby condemned for the crime of high treason! Do you have any last words?'

Lord Witloof held up his hand.

'He's going to do a speech.' The king sighed. 'Timewasting!'

The whole of Tyburn fell silent, a sea of people staring up at the figure on the scaffold.

'You will never defeat me, for I have darkness at my command!' Lord Witloof taunted. 'And soon my dark rain will fall upon you all!'

A sudden wind muttered around the square as Lord Witloof approached the noose.

'Dark reign?' the king blustered. 'Poppycock!'

A steady drumbeat began. Cordelia's heart beat triple time. She wanted to bury her head in her hands and cover her ears until it was all over, exactly as Goose was doing. But she found she could not look away.

The executioner stepped forward.

Lord Witloof smiled as a black sack was pulled over his head.

The drums rolled. Then there was a crack like shattering glass.

A storm strong enough to wreck a ship broke over Tyburn. It ripped around the square, tearing hats off heads and knocking people to the ground. A cloud the size of a castle erupted into the air, building itself into a great black tower above the scaffold. Its furious form shuddered with thunder.

'What devilry is this?' Cordelia heard the king cry before his voice was torn away by the wind.

A doom-deep rumble shook the cloud apart: it tumbled down in an avalanche of hailstones.

Chaos broke out below. The wind swept an invisible arm across the square, flattening people as they fled. Rain as thick as whip-tongues lashed the crowd.

'EXECUTIONER! DO YOUR DUTY!' the king roared.

The executioner pulled the lever.

A shard of lightning speared the sky and Lord Witloof disappeared.

*A shard of lightning speared the sky
and Lord Witloof disappeared.*

The noose swung empty above the panicked crowd.

'WHERE DID HE GO?' bellowed the king.

Lord Witloof had vanished.

People scattered like beads from a broken necklace. Ten thousand feet pummelled the ground.

'*Tear the scaffold apart!*' the king brayed. '*Find the villain!*'

But the guards' first duty was to protect the royal family. The king and princess were whirled away to safety, the king still shouting.

The air was curdled with freezing rain. Cordelia and Goose stood abandoned on the dais, the crowd pouring around them like water rushing past a rock.

'Witloof's going to get away!' Cordelia cried.

A bolt of lightning shattered the scaffold, hurling deadly splinters everywhere as she charged down the steps.

'Don't go *towards* it!' Goose yanked her back. 'Let's get out of here!'

Hatmaker and Bootmaker staggered across Tyburn turnpike, heading for the safety of Hyde Park.

They took shelter under an oak tree, its branches thrashing in the gale. Goose fell to his knees. Cordelia collapsed against the trunk.

'Where did he go?' she panted.

Witloof had disappeared like in a conjuror's trick.

Cordelia's hand was numb with cold. She was still holding the pocket watch the king had given her. Her fingers were frozen stiff round it – she had to peel them off the watch one by one.

'Ow!' she cried, dropping the watch on the grass.

'What's wrong?' Goose croaked.

Cordelia's hand was stinging with cold fire. She shook it, blew on it and danced around, yelping. After a very painful minute, her palm stopped prickling as her fingers began to feel warm again. She frowned at the watch, which was lying beside Goose.

'There's something very odd about that watch,' she said.

She picked it up gingerly in her handkerchief. It had left a perfect black circle in the green grass.

As quickly as it had arrived, the storm subsided. The wind dropped to nothing and the bulging rainclouds shrivelled to white scraps and floated away.

'The weather's behaving very strangely,' Cordelia observed, as the sun came out and Hyde Park's birds began, cautiously, to sing.

'Witloof's somewhere out there!' Goose shuddered. 'We should go home.'

Hatmaker and Bootmaker hurried through London. Cordelia was very glad to see the warm glow of Hatmaker House's windows as they scampered down Wimpole Street.

Before they reached it, the kitchen door was thrown open.

'Dilly!' Cook cried. 'Where have you *been*? London's a-rumble with news of Witloof's escape!' She flung her arms round Cordelia and Goose, crushing them to her bosom in a hug that threatened to render them senseless.

'Oh, Dilly! Goose!' Cook sobbed. 'You terrible, wonderful children!'

Aunt Ariadne appeared in the doorway, face alight with relief.

'We were so worried!' she cried. 'Sam was frantic when she got home and you weren't back – she thought you must have got swept up in the mob heading for Tyburn. She and Jones are out looking for you! And – that villain escaped!'

Uncle Tiberius pushed past her.

'I *told* you to stay out of trouble!' he barked, ushering the tangle that was Cordelia, Cook and Goose into the kitchen.

'We *tried*,' Cordelia explained, able to breathe freely once Cook released her. 'But trouble sort of came and swallowed us up!'

Cook busied herself heating milk in a pan on the stove.

'You're not hurt, are you?' Uncle Tiberius growled at Goose.

'I – I don't think so,' Goose said uncertainly.

Uncle Tiberius poked the fire vigorously. Cordelia saw a flash of green handkerchief as he dabbed his eyes.

'You both look like you've been in a washtub!' Aunt Ariadne chided.

Cordelia and Goose were still rather damp.

'One moment the sky was blue,' Cordelia said. 'Next – an enormous storm!'

Aunt Ariadne sat them down beside the kitchen fire, where their clothes steamed gently as they dried.

Goose glanced across the table. There was a jumble of sticks and string lying on it. Cordelia poked them.

'Oh – I was trying to distract myself from worry by making the masts for that Ship Hat,' Uncle Tiberius muttered.

Goose's eyes lit up.

'Can't make head or tail of the blasted thing,' Uncle Tiberius continued. 'Heaven knows how they make real ships!'

The door slammed open and Sam charged into the kitchen.

'Yer all right!' she cried. 'I was afraid somefing bad had happened to ya!'

'I was afraid of the same thing!' Cordelia said. 'But you escaped the Glovemakers?'

Sam grinned. 'Lucky I knew a window I could climb out of.' She winked.

'There's someone in the shop,' Jones announced, stumping into the kitchen in Sam's wake. 'Somebody might want to see to her before she starts kicking up a proper palaver. She's – er – wearing the boots for it.'

Frowning, Aunt Ariadne disappeared into the shop.

Cook added nutmeg and cinnamon to the milk, singing a ditty as she stirred. 'Here we go, my cherubs,' she said to Cordelia and Goose. 'Hot milk to help with the shock.'

'I – I feel a bit shocked an' all,' Sam said.

Cook smiled and poured Sam a mug too.

'LUCAS BOOTMAKER!'

Goose whipped round, eyes wide. His mother stood in the doorway. Aunt Ariadne appeared behind her.

'I've been worried SICK!' Mrs Bootmaker bellowed. '*This* is what comes of running around with a *wretched Hatmaker*!'

'Mother!' Goose objected. 'Don't say that! It's rude!'

He stood up, facing the furious wall of his mother. He had a frothy milk moustache, but it hardly undermined his dignity.

'Cordelia is my friend,' he said nobly. 'As you well know.'

Cordelia watched in fascination as Mrs Bootmaker's eyes bulged out of their sockets. Goose's resolve appeared to melt along with his milk moustache.

'Tread softly, Nigella,' Uncle Tiberius crooned. 'If you *can* in those boots.'

Uncle Tiberius and Mrs Bootmaker saved their choicest insults for one another, and always delivered them in devastatingly polite tones of voice. It was a kind of compliment, if you looked at it upside down and back to front.

'Indeed, Tiberius,' Mrs Bootmaker replied, her voice dripping with poisoned honey. 'I wonder if you've been using too much Quaggy Ribbon in your hats; it appears to have turned your brain into a swamp. So perhaps you should not tread *anywhere*, lest you sink in up to your neck, and that ridiculous hat is all of you that is left.'

The tension between Uncle Tiberius and Nigella Bootmaker stretched so tight Cordelia felt it would be possible to walk the air between them like a tightrope. Nobody moved for several moments. Goose looked like he might never blink again.

'You Hatmakers STAY AWAY from the Bootmakers!' Mrs Bootmaker then bellowed. 'Or you'll get a Blunderbuss Boot in the backside!'

She swooped down on her son. Goose's feet did not appear to touch the floor on his way out of Hatmaker House.

'Blimey,' Sam muttered. 'Poor Goose.'

They listened to the Bootmakers stomping all the way down the mews. Suddenly Uncle Tiberius burst out, 'By Archimedes' bathing cap! The young Bootmaker's made sense of those masts!'

On the kitchen table, the masts of Janet Crust's wooden ship sat in the sugar bowl, perfectly assembled.

After a dinner of warm bread and Butter Mushroom soup, Cordelia allowed herself to be sent to bed early.

She yawned her way upstairs to her bedroom and threw a bundle of pink Lilt twigs into the fireplace. The twigs sang a soft song as they caught light.

Cordelia took out the pocket watch and examined it. It glinted in the rosy firelight, but it was still ice cold even when she held it close to the flames. The ash trapped within it shifted.

She prised open the watch and tipped the flake of ash on to her hand.

'This was a butterfly once,' she murmured. She made out the blackened pattern of a butterfly's wing before the ash turned to shadow on her palm.

Her heart dropped with a sudden pang of sadness. Her fingers were cold so she held them close to the fire. She stared into the flames, thinking about everything that had happened.

First, there was the mysterious man turning up at the shop, whispering about the North Wind. Then London's most notorious traitor escaped from his own execution; that sudden strange storm had seized hold of the sky, allowing him to disappear into thin air.

With a jolt, Cordelia remembered what the man in the shop had said of her father: *Without him, there is no hope of defeating Witloof!*

She pulled the telescope out from under her bed and twisted it. The map slid out from its secret compartment, smooth and blank.

'I have to discover where this leads! It's more urgent than ever!'

The stars weren't out yet. She would have to wait a few hours.

'Why couldn't you have written me a letter explaining things, Father?' she burst out.

There must be a good reason why he had made the place so hard to find.

She just hoped she was clever enough to find it.

Cordelia woke from a dream that the stars were gone: Witloof had stolen them out of the sky.

She tumbled off her bed and ran to the window. The stars *were* gone. It was dawn. She had dozed off and slept right through until morning.

'No!' she groaned. 'A whole night wasted!'

The last star winked as it faded.

'I'm sorry, Father,' she murmured, feeding the blank map back into the telescope. 'I'll go out tonight. I *will* find the place.'

A whole day to wait before she could do anything useful! She knew that a diligent Hatmaker would concentrate on finishing Sir Hugo's hat, but she was too restless for Hatmaking. She turned from the window and walked back across the hearthrug.

If only I had something useful to do!

The glass watch glinted coldly at her feet. Cordelia seized it.

'There's someone who could tell me more about this watch! If I dare pay him a visit . . .'

People would disapprove. It would be frowned upon. In fact, what Cordelia was considering was practically banned . . .

But she did not care if it wasn't allowed. Some things were more important than rules.

For once, Cordelia was down in the kitchen before Sam. Even the other Hatmakers had yet to show their faces.

Cook bustled around, lighting the stove and kneading dough studded with raisins. Jones was full of London's gossip as he carried in a crate of vegetables from the market.

'They say the storm was one of the fiercest in living memory,' he announced, depositing a basket of beans on the table. 'But it only lasted ten minutes. It knocked half the chimney pots off in Berkeley Square, and blew all the petals off Lord Buncle's Whispering Lilies!'

Cordelia helped Jones bring in a basketful of herbs, the pail of milk and a small brick of yellow butter, asking questions all the way from the carriage to the kitchen table.

'Has anyone seen Witloof? Does the king have his guards out looking? Do they think he has a hideout somewhere?'

'The king's redcoats – mind those eggs, Dilly! – tore apart what was left of the scaffold looking for him. But nobody's seen hide nor hair of the villain – I'll take that cabbage.' Jones turned wide eyes to Cordelia. 'But the turnip merchant says he heard a strange wailing on the wind last night.'

If Jones's information was interesting, it was nothing compared to some of the gossip Cordelia heard in the shop that morning.

'There are twice as many guards outside the palace today,' a woman examining a Trifling Tricorn said. 'And I wouldn't be surprised if the king orders Hard-boiled Helmets for them all.'

'The lightning was so strong it made people's wigs stand on end in Piccadilly!' a gentleman claimed as he tried on a Lace Beret.

'I saw the storm from Hyde Park,' announced a young lady buying a bicorn decorated with silver Swash-buckles. 'It looked like a great purple fist crushing Tyburn!'

Cordelia and Sam exchanged astonished glances over a hatbox. Aunt Ariadne appeared to be trying not to roll her eyes.

After lunch, they found Goose lurking in the mews.

'How did ya get away from yer ma?' Sam asked. 'After yesterday, I thought you'd be a prisoner in yer own bedroom till you were old enough to grow a beard!'

'I – er – I caused a diversion,' Goose admitted. 'I threw a spool of Rollick Ribbon into a pile of Bounding Bootlaces, and they all got tangled up and wriggled around the workshop. Mother was so busy chasing them I had the chance to sneak out.'

Cordelia was impressed. 'Brilliant!'

Goose smiled, but the pride in his eyes flickered uncertainly.

'I – I don't want to go to the Guildhall,' he murmured. 'In case . . . in case . . .'

Cordelia rubbed her elbow, which was still bruised from being dropped on the floor by the Glovemakers.

'I actually had somewhere else in mind to go this afternoon,' she said. 'The Watchmaker's.'

Goose's mouth fell open as Sam's clammed up.

'You're not serious?'

Cordelia drew Witloof's glass watch out of her pocket.

'I want to see if he can tell us anything about this.'

The watch spun slowly on its chain.

'I – I gotta go and check the fireflies are all right,' Sam muttered. 'Gonna make sure the Glovemakers aren't using 'em for target practice. D'ya mind?'

Sam had stolen a watch from the Watchmaker a few months ago, and Cordelia wondered if her friend's reluctance to pay him a visit might have more to do with guilt than anything else.

Goose (who didn't know the details of Sam's life of crime) looked as though he was about to argue that there was safety in numbers.

'Don't worry, Sam,' Cordelia said, before Goose could open his mouth. 'We'll be fine. Just be careful in the Guildhall by yourself.'

Cordelia and Goose turned down Tenterten Street as Sam scurried away.

'Is this a good idea?' Goose hesitated. 'Makers don't tend to pay each other friendly visits.'

'Actually, Goose, *you're* the only Maker who's chosen to go into another Maker's house in three decades!' Cordelia pointed out. 'You've been the only one brave enough!'

This had the desired effect. Goose puffed his chest out like a Boor Pigeon and strutted down the street. Cordelia followed, grinning. They only became a little deflated as the tall shape of Watchmaker Lodge loomed above them.

'I've heard he uses *bones* in his watches,' Goose whispered. 'From children's fingers!'

'Really?' Cordelia shuddered.

Goose nodded. 'Mother said.'

They gazed uncertainly at the large circular window at the top of the house, where two long clock hands moved slowly round.

'She might have said that to make you stay away,' Cordelia reasoned.

'Maybe,' Goose said. 'She also told me that Hatmakers – er – that you weave ribbons for your hatbands that steal people's thoughts.'

Cordelia turned to Goose. 'Well, we don't,' she told him. 'That would be very bad magic.'

'I know,' Goose said sheepishly. 'I'm just – I'm just a bit scared.'

Cordelia smiled. 'I am too, but you can't be brave if you don't get scared!'

Before Goose could quite wrap his head round this concept, Cordelia stepped forward and pulled the doorbell.

There was a sound like the thud of a giant's heart somewhere deep inside the building, then a whirring that rattled the windowpanes.

CUCKOO!

A huge yellow bird burst out of a hatch just above their heads, its wings splayed wide.

'AAAAAARGH!' Hatmaker and Bootmaker cried.

As suddenly as it had appeared, the bird folded its wings and retreated into the hatch, and a small person opened the door of Watchmaker Lodge. It was a child, about seven years old, eyes startlingly wise in his young face.

'Hello,' the child said. 'I'm Grasshopper.'

'Hello – Grasshopper,' Cordelia gasped, a little breathless.

Perhaps Grasshopper mistook Cordelia's gasp for a stifled laugh. His round eyes flicked down, but he put his chin in the air.

'It's my nickname,' he explained. 'My real name is Tempus, but Grandfather calls me Grasshopper. He says I'm like the most important part of the watch – the bit that keeps everything ticking over, which is called a grasshopper.'

Cordelia stuck her hand out.

'Pleased to meet you,' she said. 'I'm Cordelia.'

Grasshopper's eyes brightened. He took her hand and shook it energetically. 'Sorry if Bridget gave you a fright. She's always very enthusiastic just after I've wound the house.'

Goose shoved his own hands firmly in his pockets. Cordelia suspected he was making sure no Watchmaker could steal even his littlest finger bone to use in a watch.

This seemed to remind Grasshopper to be suspicious.

'Why are you here?' he asked.

'We'd like to see your grandfather,' Cordelia said. She could feel the watch in her pocket: it was cold against her leg, even through several petticoats.

Grasshopper scrutinized them.

'I'm not s'posed to let strangers in without an appointment,' he said uncertainly.

'We're not strangers, we're Makers!' Cordelia reasoned. 'I'm a Hatmaker, and Goose here is a Bootmaker.'

Grasshopper appeared to think this over.

'All right,' he said. 'Grandfather's Time's Changing Clock has been clanging all morning and he told me we should greet change gladly when it comes.'

Cordelia and Goose followed him down the narrow front hall. Cordelia looked back. Perched over the door was the huge yellow bird. It was wooden! The bird was an enormous, intricately carved piece of clockwork!

'Grandfather's in his workshop,' Grasshopper told them, leading them into the parlour. He pointed upwards.

Cordelia felt as though she was standing at the bottom of a deep well. The ceiling was high above them, lost in the gloom. Two great chains hung down in the middle of the room, made of iron thicker than anchor rope. The chains moved as though a giant at the top of the well was hauling one bucket up and lowering another at the same time.

'How do we get to the workshop?' Cordelia asked. There did not appear to be any stairs.

'Like this.' Grasshopper hopped on to a link of the chain that was travelling upwards. 'Make sure you hold on tight!' he instructed, as he was pulled steadily into the air.

Goose spluttered.

'Come on, Goose,' Cordelia said firmly. 'We've come this far.'

She took hold of a link in the chain. It was so heavy that it hardly swayed as she hopped on.

Her stomach flipped as she felt herself leave solid ground.

There was a sudden lurch and Cordelia clutched the chain tighter, grinning. Goose had scrambled on below her.

They passed the first floor: a wallpapered corridor with three closed doors and huge toothed brass gears turning slowly through the space.

Cordelia thought she could hear Goose muttering, 'Can't be brave if you don't get scared, can't be brave if you don't get scared!'

The next floor had twelve life-sized carved figures on a track, waiting to peep from the windows of the house when the clock struck the hour. The floor above that was covered from wall to wall in pocket watches, like a thousand silver insects scraping and clicking. The next floor contained shelves of jars, all chiming different notes.

Cordelia looked down. Goose clung to the chain, his knuckles white.

'Hop off here!' Grasshopper called from the next floor up.

He came into view, waiting for them on the top floor. Cordelia stepped unsteadily off the chain, but Goose panicked and misjudged it. Cordelia grabbed his arms to stop him sliding over the edge.

'Got scared – was brave,' Goose croaked.

'Well done, Goose!' Cordelia whispered.

'Grandfather's in here,' Grasshopper said softly. 'Wait until I say . . .'

There was only one door on this floor. With a *whoosh* that shivered Cordelia's arm hairs, a brass block as big as a sarcophagus swung down from a gap in the wall, past the door, and up into a gap in the opposite wall.

TICK.

'The pendulum makes sure that anyone who enters the workshop has a healthy respect for the power of time,' Grasshopper told them. 'You've got to treat it wisely.'

The brass block came swinging back again, heavy as a carthorse, slicing past the door and back into the opposite wall.

TOCK.

'Ready?' Grasshopper asked.

Cordelia nodded. Goose squeaked, which Grasshopper took as a 'yes'.

'Go!'

He opened the door. Cordelia stepped – and Goose dived – through.

Somehow, they both arrived in the Watchmaker's workshop in a heap on the floor, which meant the first view Cordelia got was of the ceiling. Ropes and chains were swagged across it, attached to cogs and woven through pulleys in a vast and complicated arrangement.

She sat up. The Watchmaker stood framed in the light of a wide round window. He was stooped with age, as though time itself was measured in the bend of his back.

'A Hatmaker and a Bootmaker,' he said. His voice was quiet and clear. 'I haven't been visited by another Maker for two generations. No wonder my Time's Changing Clock has been whirring today.'

In the great circular window behind him, two enormous watch hands moved almost imperceptibly round. Gears and pulleys above their heads shifted in increments across the ceiling.

'The whole house is a clock!' Cordelia breathed.

'And it all runs like clockwork.' The Watchmaker nodded. 'Grasshopper sees to that.'

Grasshopper pulled Cordelia to her feet, ushering Goose up too.

'But I promise you, not one single piece of the clockwork is made out of a child's finger bone,' the Watchmaker told them seriously.

Goose's mouth fell open. 'Y-you h-heard me?' he stammered. 'All the way downstairs?'

'Grandfather can hear a mouse's heartbeat from across the room,' Grasshopper informed them proudly.

'Anyone who deals in Time needs to be a good listener,' the Watchmaker said. 'You need to be able to hear the rings of trees growing.'

He beckoned them over to his workbench, picking up a tiny pair of tweezers.

'This is a Nick of Time,' he said. Clamped between the tweezers was a hair as fine as a spiderweb. 'It's no more than a Jiffy, really. If you listen carefully, you can hear its sound: like the in-breath before a song.'

Cordelia listened. Very faintly, she thought she heard a tiny inrush of air.

'There! You see, each timepiece – like each piece of Time –

has its own particular tick,' the Watchmaker continued. 'But the watch you've brought me must have stopped, because I can't hear it ticking.'

Cordelia took Witloof's watch from her pocket and laid it on the workbench.

The Watchmaker's face closed like the hands of a clock at midnight.

'I hoped I'd never see this watch again,' he said. 'But Time has a way of returning wicked things to their Makers.'

Witloof's glass watch gleamed innocently on the table.

'It's wicked?' Goose muttered fearfully.

'*You* made it?' Cordelia asked.

The Watchmaker inclined his head. 'I made the clockwork,' he said. 'Lord Witloof brought me the empty glass case. He wanted me to make the clockwork to fit inside it.'

There was something curt about his voice. It was clipped, like the tick of a second hand. He fell quiet, staring down at the silent watch.

Grasshopper edged towards it. 'Strange,' he murmured. 'It doesn't have a winding mechanism.'

'Hop,' the Watchmaker said suddenly, 'please be a good boy and fetch some tea for our guests.'

Grasshopper trotted out of the workshop. As the door closed behind him, the old Watchmaker turned troubled eyes to Cordelia.

'Miss Hatmaker, I have made many a timepiece in my time,' he said. 'I have made sundials and moondials and Styx-water clocks. I have wound watches with threads of Idle Spider silk, made Time-and-Tide Timekeepers for sailors and hourglasses filled with Saharan sand. But I have *never* made a pocket watch that didn't need a winding mechanism.'

He picked up the watch carefully, by its chain. 'Except this one. And it came at a terrible price.'

The pocket watch gleamed, sunlight winking through its glass case, flashing off its fine silver clockwork. Cordelia felt like time was caught between two ticks of a clock hand as the Watchmaker gathered himself to continue.

'Several years ago, when Lord Witloof came to Watchmaker Lodge with the empty glass watchcase, I pointed out the flaw in the design – all clockwork needs a winding mechanism. Even a magical watch must be wound once a day, otherwise it stops.'

The Watchmaker stared at the frozen hands on the glass watch, as though turning them backwards might turn back time.

'Lord Witloof said my job was to make the clockwork, not to ask questions. But Dawn – my clever, kind daughter, Dawn – told him that we would not help with something we both felt was so darkly powerful. The timepieces Dawn made were wondrous things: Starwheels and Chrysalis Clocks, Flowerblooming Bells and Sunrise Chimes. She did not like the icy glass case that set a chill in the air around it, and she told Lord Witloof so. He was angry. He left in a storm, breaking things on his way out, shattering clocks and hurling the pieces at my daughter.

'As she shut the door on him, my Dawn grew suddenly cold,' the Watchmaker whispered. 'Even her two children could not bring warmth back to her.'

A tear fell from his eye and landed on the watch. It froze, frosting over a tiny patch of the glass.

'Witloof came knocking again the next night,' he went on. 'Said he knew what would cure Dawn. Said he would tell me – for a price.'

'If you made the clockwork that he wanted,' Cordelia said.

'Indeed.' The Watchmaker slid a knife between the leaves of the watchcase, opening the lid. 'And in the course of fitting the clockwork I discovered its secret.'

He turned abruptly and walked to the window. For a moment, Cordelia thought that he was simply staring out, remembering. Then she saw something flutter in the light: a moth. The Watchmaker caught it by a wing. Returning to the table, he laid the struggling moth in the open chamber of the watch.

'No!' Cordelia cried.

But the Watchmaker snapped the lid down over it before it could fly away.

'Let it out!' Goose demanded.

The old man held up a hand for silence.

Tick. Tick. Tick. Tick.

The glass watch was working once again. The moth twitched within it.

'It uses the life force of the creature trapped inside it,' the Watchmaker told them. 'It leeches life from the creature to turn the hands.'

The silver hand sliced ten precise seconds round the face of the watch before Cordelia could bear it no longer.

She snatched up the watch, its coldness burning her fingers, and prised it open.

The moth fluttered clumsily on to the table and lay, antennae quivering, on its side. The Watchmaker looked down at it.

'Desperate to save Dawn, I made the clockwork and took it to Lord Witloof at the palace. I begged him to fulfil his part of the bargain. He told me that my daughter had been cut by his Leechglass knife as she chased him out of Watchmaker Lodge.'

'What's *Leechglass*?' Goose asked.

'Leechglass is ice-cold, no matter how warm the day, and it sucks the life from whatever it touches, like a leech sucking blood. It was invented by the Glassmakers of Venice, though the secret method of making it was lost centuries ago.'

The Watchmaker indicated the glass watch. 'This Leechglass watchcase must be very old. It's a dangerous thing to wear every day, so close to the chest. It will leech the humanity right out of a heart, over time.'

Cordelia and Goose stepped back from the workbench.

'Witloof told me that somebody wounded by Leechglass would freeze up and eventually perish, unless they drank the Essence of Magic.'

'The Essence of Magic?' Cordelia repeated. She had never heard of such a thing.

'Leechglass steals life, and only the Essence of Magic has the power to restore it. They are absolute opposites. I begged him to tell me where I could find the Essence of Magic, but he just smiled. "I said I knew *what* would save your daughter, not *where* to find the cure." Those were his precise words. I realized I had been tricked: he didn't have the cure after all.

'His last threat before calling the palace guards to throw me out was to say that if I spoke to anyone of what had happened, he would sneak shards of Leechglass into my grandchildren's playthings. That they would suffer the same fate as my daughter . . .

'I returned home distraught, to find my daughter's time had run out. My darling Dawn never rose again.'

Cordelia felt her heart throb with sorrow.

'I kept quiet,' the Watchmaker croaked. 'Because I could not risk losing my grandchildren too.'

The workshop door opened, and Grasshopper loped into the room, carrying an enormous tea tray laden with cups and plates and biscuits.

'Hop, you wonderful boy!' The Watchmaker smiled at his grandson, the sadness in his eyes evaporating. 'What a feast!'

Grasshopper put the tray down on a table by the window. As Hatmaker, Bootmaker and Watchmakers were making themselves comfortable around the tea table, a mouse streaked across the floor, straight towards Goose.

'*Argh!*' Goose yelped, dancing on the spot as the mouse shot under his feet.

'Tick!' the Watchmaker shouted. 'TICK!'

Cordelia jumped up in alarm. The Watchmaker was suddenly as loud and discombobulating as a clock gone wrong.

A laugh pealed in the hall.

'*Tickory!*'

A small figure raced into the room and threw itself into the old man's arms.

The Watchmaker broke into a chuckle. 'This is Tickory, my younger grandson.'

Tickory appeared to be trying to hide his entire small self inside his grandfather's jacket.

'He's not usually shy,' the Watchmaker told them, 'but we haven't had visitors since . . . for a long time.'

'Hello, Tickory,' Cordelia ventured.

Bright eyes flashed at her from behind a flap of jacket.

'Sorry about the mouse,' Grasshopper said to Goose. 'It's only clockwork.'

The Watchmaker's jacket giggled as Grasshopper poured the tea and offered everyone currant-and-thyme biscuits.

'So,' the Watchmaker said, giving Cordelia and Goose a meaningful look, 'we have learned something very important this afternoon – which is, of course, that Watchmakers don't use children's finger bones in our clockwork.'

Goose looked sheepish. Grasshopper offered him a sugar lump.

'But there is something even more important that I want you to understand before you leave today,' the Watchmaker said. 'At present, the Makers are scattered like the pieces of a broken clock – and, like a broken clock, they cannot work as they should. You see, a clock only works when all its pieces are put together properly. Only then might we have a chance of defeating Witloof. Only people united in their power to create can stop a man with such a destructive soul.'

'You mean – Makers should try and work together?' Cordelia said.

Goose made a doubtful face.

The Watchmaker nodded. 'Yes. If I hadn't been too afraid to ask for help in my darkest hour . . .'

He cast a sorrowful glance at Grasshopper and Tickory, who stared curiously back at their grandfather.

'The most important thing, I venture, is this,' the Watchmaker concluded. 'Now, more than ever, Makers need to make peace with one another.'

'Even with the Glovemakers?' Goose asked ruefully.

'Even with the Glovemakers,' the Watchmaker said firmly.

GONG.

A deep sound – the kind that makes your heart jolt and your belly shiver – rang through the room.

'Ah, the Time's Changing Clock has made up its mind,' the Watchmaker said with a smile.

As the *gong* faded away, it left a ripple behind, the way speaking a new idea out loud can change the world.

'Have another biscuit,' the Watchmaker suggested. 'I always find a biscuit helps me chew things over.'

'Thank you, Mr Watchmaker,' Cordelia said, taking a biscuit.

'Please, let's have no Misters among friends. Call me Tyde.'

'All right, then – Tyde. Please call me Cordelia.'

'And you can call me Goose,' Goose added.

'I'm Hop,' Grasshopper said.

'And I'm Tick!' the Watchmaker's jacket piped up.

Cordelia had been trying to thread Selenite beads on to Glamour Spider silk all evening. Every time she got several beads on the thread, she would lose concentration and her mind would wander.

That glass crown the princess wore must have been made of Leechglass too . . .

The thread in her hands shrivelled and turned brown, and the Selenite beads went rolling across the floor like tiny moons coming adrift from a planet.

Cordelia sighed. 'Not *again*!'

Glamour Spider silk was very delicate. If a Hatmaker thought ugly thoughts while working with it, the silk shrivelled up instantly. When her mind drifted to Witloof or Leechglass or the purple bruise of the storm above Tyburn, the silk withered away.

'Oh dear, Dilly,' her aunt murmured as Cordelia retrieved the beads.

Sam helped. She had been followed home from the Guildhall by a dozen Dulcet Fireflies, which flittered around her head, blinking gold. One of them buzzed under a table to show her where a bead had gone.

Cordelia smiled as Sam handed it back. She was about to try threading the beads again, but put the silk down quickly when her mind conjured up the image of the butterfly turned to ash.

'Aunt, do you know anything about Leechglass?' Cordelia asked.

Aunt Ariadne looked up in surprise. She was in the middle of stitching tendrils of twilight on to a magnificent Gladsome Rose headdress for the Duke of Devonshire, but she laid it aside hastily.

'Leechglass?' she repeated. 'Where did you hear about that?'

'In a book.'

Cordelia did not think it wise to admit to visiting the Watchmaker. She also did not want to mention Witloof's watch, which was now safely locked in the Watchmaker's Menacing Cabinet. All Makers had a Menacing Cabinet, in which they kept the most evil and dangerous magical ingredients safely under lock and key.

'Leechglass was first made by alchemists in medieval times,' Aunt Ariadne told her. 'They were trying to turn lead into gold, as alchemists were obsessed with doing back then.

They never succeeded in making gold, but in one sinister experiment they created some strange, cold glass. They called it Leechglass, because it sucked the life out of anything living.'

'Are people *allowed* to make it? It sounds Menacing.'

'The secret has been lost, thank goodness, so nobody *can* make it any more,' Aunt Ariadne told her. 'Any antique Leechglass objects that are found should be kept under lock and key. I'm not sure how it was made, but a great deal of magic was destroyed to create just a tiny amount of Leechglass. It is most Menacing.'

'I'm really glad the secret was lost,' Cordelia said.

She thought of Witloof's ice-cold watch, stealing the magic from a butterfly to turn its silver hands. She decided not to risk working with the Glamour Spider silk any more that evening; her thoughts were whirling too much to settle reliably on something good.

Instead, she watched Sam turning herself into a playground for her fireflies, looping her fingers for them to dart through, and sending them swirling around her hands. Watching the golden lights nip and whizz round Sam, and the delight kindled in Sam's eyes, warmed Cordelia's heart again.

The Watchmaker had said that the Makers needed to be brought back together again, to unite against Witloof. But that seemed much too large a task for the youngest Hatmaker to attempt, even if her friends could be convinced to help.

She looked outside. The stars were coming out.

There was only one thing she could do.

That man who came into the shop yesterday said my father's the only one with a hope of defeating Witloof. So I've got to find the place on the map tonight.

Cordelia waited until midnight, after she'd heard Aunt Ariadne set the star bowl on the roof and everyone in Hatmaker House had gone to bed.

It was a clear night and the stars twinkled above the city. The buildings were dark cliffs against the sky. London was quiet. Lord Witloof's disappearance had cast a sudden chill across the city, making its residents retreat inside.

'It gives me more freedom to explore,' Cordelia said, trying to find her best bravery, though her voice sounded small in the large dark.

She padded down a side street, heading for the Thames, so intent on her mission that she did not notice the figure slipping through the shadows behind her.

When she reached the Strand, she stopped. Beyond the embankment, the water muttered against the riverbank. There was a knot of redcoats outside an alehouse, but otherwise the street was deserted.

Cordelia unfurled the map. It lit her face with a pale silver glow as the ink shone in the starlight.

'All right,' she said, trying to sound businesslike. '*At the sign of the Rose and Sea . . .*'

She peered at the map. Its lines seemed fainter than usual. Was the ink fading?

'It *can't* be . . .'

At this time of night the stars should be at their brightest. The sky was cloudless, but the stars seemed dimmer somehow, less sparkly.

Strange.

Cordelia squinted at the map again. It grew fainter. Something was going horribly wrong with it. Or going wrong with the stars themselves. She desperately held the paper up to the failing starlight.

'No – wait!' she gasped as the silver lines vanished.

The sky was dark from horizon to horizon.

She tasted bitterness in the wind. Black fog curled round the treetops, creeping closer, closing in.

A shadow loomed behind her.

'*Caught ya!*'

'AAARH!'

Cordelia whirled round, heart pounding jungle drums in her chest.

'I *told* ya it ain't safe at night!'

It was Sam, her face a vivid mix of anger and relief.

'Why are you following me?' Cordelia demanded, the words coming out crosser than she meant them to.

'I'm tryin' ta make sure ya don't get hurt!' Sam scowled. 'Yer like *family*, Cor! I'd never forgive meself if somefing happened to ya.'

'*Like* family?' Cordelia repeated. 'Sam, we *are* family!'

Sam glared at Cordelia. 'If we're family, Cor, ya gotta trust me. That's what sisters do. *Trust* each other.' Her face was blazing with the kind of fierceness it's impossible to argue with.

'You're right,' Cordelia admitted.

'What's all this business of risking yer neck every night?' Sam demanded.

Cordelia unclenched her hand and smoothed out the map. Ready or not, it was time to share the secret.

A flake of black ash landed on the pale paper.

'What's that?'

The girls turned their faces upwards.

Ash was falling from the sky, silent as black snow. A speck landed on Cordelia's forehead. Despair blossomed like a dark flower where it touched her skin.

'Let's get outta here!' Sam yelped, grabbing Cordelia's hand. 'C'mon – I know somewhere not too far!'

She dragged Cordelia along the Strand. The ash came down thickly, in a veil too dense to see through. They drew up the hoods of their cloaks and ran.

Sam only stopped when they reached an old building propped beside the Thames, between the new stones of

Blackfriars Bridge and the warehouses of Fleet Street. The place looked like it had been very proud and tall at some point in its history, but over time it had slumped into bad posture and forgotten to wash its face. A statue glared down from the roof, its mouth open in a stone scream.

'Is this a den of iniquity?' Cordelia asked. Although Cordelia had no idea what it meant, she had heard Cook and her washerwoman friend from across the street whisper in scandalized voices about *dens of iniquity*, and she was rather keen to see one first-hand.

'It sorta is,' Sam said. 'It's a tavern: the Compass and Main.'

The night air was tar-thick and tasted burnt.

Sam pushed Cordelia through the door.

It was a relief to be out of the streets, swirling with fragments of darkness like pieces come loose from a nightmare.

Cordelia's face was smeared with shadows from the ash. Gloom seeped into her skin. Yet as the golden lamplight danced over her, she felt the shadows evaporate. It was like taking off a heavy cloak. She blinked at Sam, whose frown was slowly lifting.

'That was *horrible*,' Cordelia croaked.

Sam nodded in bleak agreement. 'Somefing must be on fire.'

'Must be.'

'Let's get somefing to drink.'

The Compass and Main was surprisingly busy for one o'clock in the morning. Its dozen customers looked like heroes and villains from theatrical melodramas, all drinking and playing cards. Flickering lamps shed pools of light across the worn velvet benches.

Sam and Cordelia sidled up to an old wooden bar at the back of the tavern. Sam ordered ale from a gruff woman, whose grunts she seemed to be fluent in, then they sat down at a table beside a merrily crackling fire.

Outside, ash was falling steadily in a dark veil.

'We can't get home till it stops,' Sam murmured. 'Hope it doesn't go on all night.'

'What *is* it?' Cordelia stared at the darkness clotting against the windows. 'A building burning, d'you think?'

But Sam was not to be distracted by the strange ash storm. 'Cor,' she said seriously, putting down her tankard. 'You said we're family, and family don't hide things.'

Sam's solemn, trustful stare pierced Cordelia to the heart. It was time to let Sam into the secret. After all, the Watchmaker had said it was foolish to try to do things alone.

'You have to promise not to breathe a word to *anyone* at home,' Cordelia said. 'I don't want them hoping – hoping this means something if it turns out to be nothing.'

Sam nodded. 'I promise.'

Cordelia took a deep breath and unfurled the map.

'It's a map that can only be read by starlight,' she explained in a low voice. 'The stars are blotted out, so the ink disappeared.'

Sam raised her eyebrows. 'What's it a map *of*?'

Cordelia shook her head. 'I don't know. I've been trying to find out for weeks now.'

Sam held out her hand. Cordelia gave her the blank map.

'My father sent it to me from his sinking ship, but I don't know why,' she said quietly as Sam inspected it.

'D'ya think it's a treasure map?' Sam asked, holding it an inch from her eyes, trying to see the invisible ink.

'Aren't *all* maps treasure maps, one way or another?' Cordelia said. 'Just depends on the treasure you're looking for.'

Sam stared at the paper thoughtfully. 'You don't have to do this alone. I'll help.'

Cordelia was filled with a rush of gratitude.

'D'you know anywhere called the Rose and Sea?' she asked. 'Or if there's a secret river somewhere in London?'

Sam chewed her lip, thinking.

'There's a riddle,' Cordelia explained, and she recited it to Sam.

'At the sign of the Rose and Sea
Runs the Fast River secret beneath.
Face the North Wind and follow him south,
There you'll find the hidden mouth.'

'The Rose 'n' Sea? And a *secret* river?' Sam frowned. 'You sure it's in London?'

'Right next to the Thames. That's the only bit I'm sure about.'

Cordelia studied Sam's creased forehead, hoping it would smooth out in a sudden moment of inspiration. But it only got wrinklier and more confused until Sam finally shook her head.

'If I could just solve one bit of it!' Cordelia exclaimed. 'And now that horrible ash has stopped the stars shining, so the whole night's wasted!'

'Fings never make sense when ya haven't had enough sleep,' Sam said wisely.

'But there's no *time* to sleep!' Cordelia jumped up. 'I'm sure the map will tell me where my father is! Witloof's escaped and Father's the only one with a hope of defeating him!'

Sam caught Cordelia's arm. 'Sit down!' she hissed. 'Don't make a scene. Nuffin' good comes of stirring it up in a place like this.'

But it was too late. The hubbub in the Compass and Main bubbled away into silence.

'Witloof!' a sailor barked from across the room. 'He's a devil! Said he had *darkness at his command*, didn't he?'

'This black ash is his doing!' a lady with a moustache added. 'It's the *dark rain* he promised from the scaffold!'

The chilling words Witloof had shouted came back to Cordelia.

Soon my dark rain will fall upon you all!

'He's a viper!' another sailor claimed. 'He *slithered* outta the noose!'

'Naw, he's a goblin wearing a man's skin!'

'Goblins ent real, you collywobble! He's a *werewolf*.'

'Ent the full moon fer three days, pudding head!'

Several sailors broke into a scuffle and the card table fell over.

'See what happens?' Sam muttered to Cordelia.

A one-legged soldier got unsteadily to his foot. 'I saw him flying into the sky above Tyburn, trailing the storm behind him like a cape of darkness!' he bellowed.

'Pipe down, Jenkins,' a sailor scoffed. 'We all know ya like a drop or two of Mrs Strange's Peculiar Liquor.'

'So what if I do? I saw what I saw!'

The soldier removed his wooden limb and hit the sailor over the head with it.

Sam sighed. 'Whenever Jenkins takes his leg off, it's a sign fings are gonna get rowdy. Come on!'

They made their way across the room, dodging the scuffle but getting stuck in a fisticuffs between two women arguing over the nature of dark rain.

A gargantuan boom of thunder exploded overhead.

The fight stopped in its tracks.

Cordelia and Sam ran to the door and flung it open.

They watched as a storm came down in a great wall of water.

'Mercury and Pyrefire!'

Cordelia poked her nose out from under her quilt.

'Aunt Ariadne?' she called.

She rolled out of bed, shuffled across the floor, still wrapped in her blanket, and peeked from her trapdoor into the corridor below.

'Are you all right, Aunt?' she asked.

'The starlight's murky!'

Aunt Ariadne was holding the silver Starbowl. The starlight that had been gathered in it last night was dirty, its lustre dulled.

'It looks like soot!' Aunt Ariadne frowned.

Cordelia glanced up at her window. Through a crack in the curtains, she could see that the sky was bright blue. The storm last night had cleared in time for morning.

'What could have done it?' Aunt Ariadne fretted. 'Our chimneys weren't alight!'

Cordelia bit her lip. It must have been that strange ash that had tarnished the starlight. But she could not tell her aunt this, because it would require a very awkward explanation about how she could possibly know.

Aunt Ariadne sighed. 'I'll have to pour it away and start again.'

'Wait!' Cordelia called down, an idea brewing. 'Shall I take it to Great-aunt P and see if we can filter out the dirt? It might make an interesting lesson this morning.'

Her aunt smiled, passing the Starbowl to her niece. 'You're very helpful, Cordelia Hatmaker.'

Cordelia blushed.

She dug under her bed and dragged out the hatbox in which she kept her most treasured possessions. She sorted through it, carefully laying aside her Elysian Eagle feather and her Ceylon nutmeg. She eased her Venetian song-bottle out from under a very battered copy of *The Mythmaker* – her father's favourite book, which he had given her the day he left on his last voyage.

The song-bottle was pale green, with a sparkling topaz stopper. Her father had brought it back from Venice last year. The memory returned vividly, carried on the music, as she pulled the stopper out.

'This was made by the Glassmakers,' he had told her, presenting her with the delicate vessel. 'They know glass like the rest of us know breathing – instinctively.'

He described how he had watched the great Glassmaker Grimaldi turning molten glass into glowing orbs, breathing songs into the shapes he made. The glass held music, just as seashells hold the sound of the sea in their whorls.

'This one contains a seagoing song,' her father had said, unstoppering the bottle and holding it to her ear.

Music streamed from the empty bottle into the air.

'Whatever you keep in the bottle will be suffused by the music,' he had murmured. 'So be careful: if you keep cordial in here for a long time before drinking it, it might give you a major-minor yearning to go seafaring.'

'But I *already* have a yearning to go seafaring, Father!' she'd declared. 'When can I come with you on a voyage?'

'One day, my little Hatmaker. There are so many wonders to see in the world. Some wonders you have no inkling of yet, but some are right outside your front door. Let's start with those and work up to a sea voyage.'

Cordelia had taken the bottle like it was a delicate bird's egg and held it solemnly in her hands as the sweet ache of the music faded from the room.

Now she carefully scooped a handful of the grimy starlight out of the Starbowl and trickled it into the bottle. She felt flashes of darkness mixed with the tingle of the stars, but soon she had enough in the bottle so that it radiated a pale light.

She knelt in the corner of her room, pulled a small knot of wood out of a floorboard and whistled into the hole.

Seven seconds later, Sam was perched on her windowsill. Cordelia beckoned her to the floor and pulled the quilt over them both.

'Look!'

Cordelia held up the map. The bottled starlight was just strong enough to reveal the ink glimmering faintly on the page.

'Do you recognize any of these streets?' Cordelia asked.

Sam's finger traced the eight roads converging in the circle. 'I never seen anyfing like this in London. The old city's too higgledy-piggledy for these straight roads.'

'Even *one* street name would be helpful.'

'Maybe they ain't streets.'

'They *must* be. Maps are always of things like streets and paths,' Cordelia said. 'Or stars, or oceans.'

Sam grinned. 'Ain't a map of the ocean just a big blob of blue?'

'There's all *sorts* of things in a map of the ocean!' Cordelia began enthusiastically. 'Sea monsters and strange tides and underwater mountains and lost islands and fret winds that take you to places you never knew existed until you get there, and shores you can't find unless you know which currents to ride.'

Sam's eyes glowed with wonder.

This talk of different types of maps had set Cordelia's mind awash with new possibilities. 'Maybe I've been thinking about this too logically,' she said. 'If they're *not* roads – what could they be?'

'Canals?' Sam suggested.

'Hmmm . . . except it's mostly dead ends and loops. Only these eight roads *go* anywhere. The rest of them are trapped in this sort of slightly jumbled stack. Surrounded by a long lane with a sharp angle in it.'

Sam pointed at the words inscribed around the edge of the paper. 'This is the riddle?'

'Yes, see – *the Rose and Sea . . . Face the North Wind . . .*'

'That's 'im, isn't it? The North Wind?' Sam indicated the gurning face of the North Wind wedged in the crook of the road.

'Yes – and it says that somehow you've got to *face* him and *follow* him at the same time . . . Oh, it's useless! I've run out of ideas!'

Cordelia threw off the blanket in frustration. Her thoughts, like her hair, were disordered.

'Right,' Sam said in her most businesslike tone. 'The only fings we know is that there's a place near the Thames called the *Rose and Sea* and there's a secret river that's fast but it don't 'ave a name. Come on – let's take another look.'

Sam dragged the blanket over their heads again.

The line *Runs the Fast River secret beneath* shimmered under her finger.

Sam frowned in concentration. Although she could not read many words yet, she was getting good at recognizing letters.

'Big *F* – little *a* – little *s* . . . little . . .'

'Little *t*,' Cordelia prompted.

'Yeah, little *t*, tha's right,' Sam agreed. 'Big *R* – little *i* – little *v* . . .'

Cordelia's spirit began to quiver, like one of Cook's puddings, with excitement.

'Sam! That's it! It's not the fast river,' she said. 'It's the Fast River.'

'What's the difference?'

'Capitalization!'

Cordelia pointed to the letters again.

'Ah, yes. Big *F*,' said Sam. 'Not a little *f*.' She moved her finger along the line of the word. 'And big *R*, not little *r* . . .'

'*Capital letters*,' Cordelia whispered.

'What's that mean, then?'

They shucked the blanket once more and blinked at each other in the daylight.

'I think it means it's a *name*.'

'Fast River? I dunno a river called Fast River.'

Cordelia was on her feet and down the ladder in a heartbeat.

Uncle Tiberius was in the Hatmaking Workshop, decorating a curling Ardourwood branch with a spangle of cut-out Sunbeams.

Cordelia burst into the workshop, already talking: 'Uncle, d'you know if there's a Fast River anywhere in London? I mean, a river named Fast? Capital *F*.'

Uncle Tiberius winced as he pricked his thumb on a sharp point of sunlight.

'Morning, Cordelia,' he muttered, sucking the bead of blood off his thumb.

'Morning,' Cordelia panted. 'Uncle, have you –'

'Yes, Fast River, Dilly. I'm thinking.'

Cordelia hopped from foot to foot as her uncle contemplatively picked up another shape of Sunbeam and threaded it on to a silver Mesmeric Thread.

'There are several small rivers that flow into the Thames,' he said eventually. 'Tributaries.'

Cordelia felt her hope bubble up.

'There's the Tyburn, and the Wandle, and the Effra,' he went on. 'But they're all just streams, really, and quite slow. There isn't a river called the Fast River, as far as I know.'

Cordelia's hope ebbed away again.

She was at the door when her uncle added, 'There's the Fleet, of course, but that's underground.'

'*WHAT?*' Cordelia yelled.

Uncle Tiberius jumped and got a splinter from the Ardourwood branch.

'Cor*delia*!' he shouted. 'No shouting in the workshop!'

'Sorry, Uncle.' Cordelia lowered her voice to a whisper as bright as a shard of sunlight. 'But you're saying there's an *underground* river in London?'

'Yes. The Fleet!' Uncle Tiberius suddenly looked slightly manic. He held up his thumb with the splinter in it. 'Better get this out, Dilly darling, before it makes me hot-headed!'

Wood from the Ardourwood Tree could turn even the meekest person into a tearaway if it wasn't properly paired with something to soothe the soul. A splinter would cause an antic disposition if left untreated.

Cordelia found the pair of tweezers kept for such emergencies. She had to grab her uncle's hand and hold it steady before gently pulling the splinter out.

'That's better,' he rumbled, sucking his thumb for the second time that morning as the mania receded from his eyes.

'Isn't "fleet" an old-fashioned word for "fast"?' Cordelia asked, her mind whirring.

'I don't know about that, Dilly. I do know it's the reason Fleet Street is called Fleet Street.'

'*Fleet Street!*' Cordelia yelped, completely forgetting to whisper. 'Is that where the river's hidden?'

Sam peered in through the workshop door. Cordelia beamed at her.

'Yes, there's supposed to be a place where you can hear it under the road,' Uncle Tiberius said. 'Why all this interest in a river?'

But Cordelia was already out of the door and rushing down the stairs, Sam sliding down the bannister after her.

At the bottom of the stairs, they held a conference in urgent whispers.

'I need to go to Fleet Street *now*, to see if I can see anything that might give me a clue,' Cordelia said. 'But Cook's in the kitchen and Aunt Ariadne's in the shop, and we're *meant* to be doing lessons . . .'

'You need a diversion.'

Cordelia admired how quickly Sam caught her meaning.

'Nothing too messy – we don't want to create any stress that'll disrupt the hats being made,' Cordelia warned. 'The last thing we need is an angry aunt on our hands. Cook's been beating the carpets even more violently than usual this morning. I think that horrible ash storm got to everyone.'

However, before they could hatch a plan, there was a knock at the back door that proved to be a huge diversion all of its own.

'Oh, my royal jellies!' Cook shrieked. 'You're back! I never did think we'd see you again!'

In the middle of the kitchen stood Jack Fortescue, the cabin boy from the Hatmakers' sunken ship.

'JACK!' Cordelia cried. 'I thought Miss Starebottom sent you to Jamaica, nailed in a crate!'

'I *was* sent to Jamaica –' Jack smiled ruefully – 'but I only got halfway there.'

He was thinner than he had been when Cordelia had last seen him, lying in a makeshift sickbay at Wapping Docks. Cook began to rectify that immediately. She hustled him into a chair and poured him a tankard of Honeymilk tea.

'By Lazarus's hat!' Aunt Ariadne and Uncle Tiberius were in the doorway, staring as though Jack was a ghost.

Cordelia threw herself down beside Jack. 'D'you know where my –'

'Dilly, give the boy some room!' Cook commanded, placing a plate of jiggly scrambled eggs on the table. 'Eggs for strength. Eat up, Jack.'

Nobody argued with Cook when she was being imperious about food. Jack wolfed down his eggs as the Hatmakers gathered round him. Sam sidled into the room, eyeing Jack curiously.

Cordelia didn't even wait for him to swallow the last forkful.

'What happened? How did you survive?'

Jack looked down at his empty plate. 'I don't know where to start,' he croaked.

Cordelia felt her heart crack.

She wrapped her arms round his thin shoulders. Aunt, Uncle and Cook raised a chorus of objection.

'Cordelia!'

'He needs space!'

'Be gentle!'

But she squeezed him tight.

Far from crushing Jack, the hug seemed to give him strength. Cordelia felt his trembling quieten.

'Start at the beginning,' she said softly. 'With the *Jolly Bonnet*.'

He took a deep breath.

'We were bringing the Athenian Owl feather back for the king's hat,' he began. 'It was smooth sailing and clear skies all the way across the Channel. As night fell, we sighted the

Rivermouth lighthouse, shining to guide us past the rocks. We were all glad to be nearing home. But then . . .'

His hands fluttered as though flailing through water. Cordelia caught them and held them tight.

'I've got you,' she said steadily.

'There was something wrong with the lighthouse,' he continued. 'But we didn't realize *what* until it was far too late.'

'It was Witloof,' Cordelia told him. 'With a lantern on the cliff. Luring the ship on to the rocks.'

'*Lord Witloof?*' he gasped, eyes wide.

'Now he's more widely known as "the escaped traitor" Witloof,' Cordelia said grimly.

Jack shuddered. He seemed to turn inwards again.

'We realized we'd been tricked when we spotted the rocks almost under our prow . . . Captain Hatmaker called orders to turn the ship, then the storm struck out of an empty sky. One moment it was starry; the next, thunderclouds erupted above us. A great spear of lightning shattered the mast. There was a shriek, like a monstrous bird wheeling on the wind . . .' His eyes blazed with some dreadful memory. 'Captain Hatmaker . . .'

Cordelia's stomach swooped like a plummeting seabird.

'He was at the ship's helm, wrestling against the might of the storm. The rain was coming down so hard I could hardly see. He yelled to me: "Get this to Cordelia!" The wind was shrieking, so I couldn't hear properly. I think he shouted,

"Tell her – *look to the stars*!" But before I could take it from his outstretched hand –'

Jack's hands clenched round Cordelia's, trying to grab for something out of his reach.

'He was snatched off the deck – and – and ripped into the sky.'

In a lightning flash, Cordelia saw the ship, caught between storm and sea. And her father torn upwards into a roaring sky.

'H-how?' she croaked. 'By *what*?'

'The wind,' Jack muttered. 'The wind had wings and claws.'

Aunt Ariadne shook her head. 'You need rest, Jack,' she said gently.

'You've been sea-struck.' Uncle Tiberius patted him on the back.

'And half-starved, by the look of you,' Cook added.

'Wait! He isn't finished!' Cordelia insisted.

She could see the shipwreck in Jack's eyes. It needed to be told.

Jack flashed her a grateful look and went on. 'The telescope landed on the deck at my feet. I grabbed it and tucked it inside my shirt. Then the world went sideways. The wind hurled the ship against the rocks . . .'

Jack dragged his eyes to meet Cordelia's, as though struggling against a powerful undertow.

'The *Jolly Bonnet* was my home,' he whispered. 'She broke apart around me. There was water – water everywhere – and dark deep beneath. And rolling and churning and crushing. Then stillness. Stillness like being on land, or maybe stillness like being dead, I couldn't tell which.

'Then there was a dry blanket – the smell of cooking . . . Sometimes, a concerned face watching. Later there was shouting. I was slung like a sack over someone's shoulder. I came to my senses in a wooden shed, one eye peering at me.'

Cordelia remembered finding Jack in a reeking boatshed in Wapping Docks, watched over by a decaying sailor with an eyepatch.

'The man forced me to drink something bitter from a medicine bottle, and I fell back into that terrible dark at the bottom of the ocean . . . Then there was you.'

Jack blinked at Cordelia. 'I couldn't tell if you were a dream or real. But I had to do as Captain Hatmaker asked. The telescope was still tucked inside my shirt. I – I gave it to you, didn't I?'

Cordelia squeezed his hands. 'You did,' she assured him. 'Thank you.'

Jack's hands unclenched, releasing the long-held promise.

'Why all this fuss over a telescope?' Uncle Tiberius blustered. 'In the midst of a shipwreck!'

Cordelia's eyes flicked to Sam, listening intently from her perch on top of the cupboard. Only the two of them knew about the map. Even Jack, who had carried the telescope through a shipwreck, did not know the true reason he had done so.

'I don't know,' Cordelia said to Uncle Tiberius. It was only half a lie. She didn't know where the map led, after all.

'Next time I woke,' Jack went on, 'my head was pounding and I was half-dying of thirst. I was trapped in a wooden box. I thought it was a coffin – thought I'd been buried alive.

'I yelled and kicked as hard as I could till someone forced the box open. I'd been nailed inside a crate marked CARGO and put in the hold of a ship bound for Jamaica. The sailors thought I was a stowaway. I swore I wasn't. "How could I have nailed *myself* into the crate?" I said. They threatened to throw me overboard anyway, but I begged to be allowed to earn my passage instead.

'They put me to work, all right – scrubbing decks. The ship's cook said there wasn't rations enough for an extra body on board, so he only gave me old biscuit. More weevil than biscuit, really.'

'We've no weevils in *our* biscuits!' Cook announced fiercely, rolling up her sleeves. 'You'll see – I'll set to work proving it right away!'

She began shovelling flour into her biggest mixing bowl as Jack went on with his story.

'When we stopped for supplies in Bermuda, I slipped away and sneaked aboard a sugar ship bound for London. This time I *was* a stowaway. I managed to stay hidden for the whole journey, with the rats among the sugar sacks. We docked at Wapping this morning and . . . here I am.'

Jack sat back, looking at the Hatmakers. 'I thought – I *hoped* – p'rhaps Captain Prospero would be back . . .'

Aunt Ariadne shook her head. 'You were the only survivor, Jack,' she said quietly. 'Everyone else drowned.'

'You can't drown in the sky!' Cordelia argued.

'*Cordelia*,' her aunt warned.

Cordelia had seen the quiet disbelief in her aunt and uncle's faces as Jack talked of the wind taking her father.

'He isn't sea-struck!' Cordelia insisted, jumping up. 'That's what he *saw*! My father was – was snatched into the sky. He didn't drown. I *told* you!'

Even as she said it, she realized how unlikely it sounded.

'Dilly! We've all had a shock. Sit down and –'

But Cordelia wasn't listening. She whirled round to Jack. 'Does the "Rose and Sea" mean anything to you?'

Bewildered, the boy shook his head.

But at least she knew where the Fast River might be found: Fleet Street. She had to get there as soon as she could. The map – the very map that Jack had unwittingly given her – crinkled in her pocket.

'I'm going for a walk!' she announced.

'Not now, Cordelia!' her aunt objected.

'But I –' Cordelia began, backing towards the door.

At that very moment, Sam toppled from the top of the cupboard, upsetting Cook's mixing bowl as she fell. There was a cloudburst of flour. Eggs went everywhere.

Cook gave a screech of outrage.

By the time the flour had settled, Cordelia was gone.

Chapter 16

Snatched off the deck and ripped into the sky.

Cordelia marched so fast it was like she was trying to escape the thoughts swirling around in her mind.

'There was a shriek in the wind!' she burst out, to the great alarm of a passing fop, who flapped his handkerchief like a surrender flag. 'What bird *shrieks*?'

According to Jack Fortescue, she should be searching the skies for her missing father. And those last desperate words he had yelled to Jack: *Tell her – look to the stars!*

The same phrase was written on the back of the map. Was it a clue to read the invisible map by starlight? Or did it have some deeper meaning Cordelia had not fathomed?

By the time she reached Fleet Street, she still had not made any sense of it.

Fleet Street was straight and narrow, crammed with people and carriages. The tall buildings rising on either side housed big inky presses that printed most of London's books and newspapers.

Cordelia dodged round a boy selling copies of *The City Cogitator*, who blasted her ears with: 'ST JAMES'S PARK A BLACKENED RUIN!'

From what Cordelia could see, selling newspapers mostly seemed to involve a lot of shouting and shoving. She set off down Fleet Street, into a squall of broadsheets. For several moments, the world was black and white and entirely made of paper.

'TREES BURNED TO ASH NEAR THE PALACE!'

'WITLOOF'S DARK RAIN COMES DOWN ON LONDON!'

None of the yelling paper sellers was as excellent at their job as Sam had been, Cordelia felt.

'GHOST TREES APPEAR OVERNIGHT!'

Uncle Tiberius had said there was a place where the River Fleet could be heard rushing under the paving stones. Surely that would be the place the riddle referred to, where the Fast River runs *secret beneath*. Perhaps there she would find the Rose and Sea?

But the street was enormously noisy, full of the clamour of voices shouting news, wagons clattering down the road, and the deep shunt of printing presses, the heartbeat beneath it all. Cordelia didn't have a hope of hearing the murmur of a secret river.

She even tried listening with her feet, as her father had taught her to do, feeling for the shudder of running water trembling through her soles. But the constant trundle of the carts shook any chance of that.

Then she felt a whisper on the back of her neck.

It was the wind, blowing through a cleft in the buildings.

She turned and the wind grazed her cheek.

There was a narrow alley across the street, with a sign hanging there. It was round, but its edges were fluted – like petals.

Cordelia dived across the road.

She was hampered by a lad determined to sell her a copy of *The Weekly Bluff*.

'REWARD FOR WITLOOF INFORMATION!' he bellowed, three inches from her face. 'TWENTY GOLD PIECES! ALL GOOD INFORMATION TO MRS TEMPEST AT THE SARGASSO!'

She stepped into the alleyway. The noise of Fleet Street faded.

She took another two steps. The feel in her feet was different.

Another step. She felt her blood rushing faster.

Glimmering at the end of the dark alley, a muddy swathe of water drifted innocently past: the Thames. But there was a pulse in the soles of her feet that did not match the slow shrug of the river. This was urgent – fast. *Fleet*.

Crr-eeeak.

Cordelia looked up at the shabby wooden sign hanging above her, creaking in the slight breeze. It wasn't a rose. It was a compass.

She was standing outside the den of iniquity that she and Sam had visited the night before: the Compass and Main Tavern.

Last night she had barely seen the building in the midst of the swirling ash. In daylight, she saw that there was a painting on its front, faded with age. It showed a compass: eight lines converging in a circle, like the spokes of a wagon wheel.

'A *compass rose* . . .' she murmured.

Painted below it were sweeping lines that must be –

'The sea! "Main" is an old word for "sea". The Compass and Main *is* the Rose and Sea!'

The world seemed to turn sideways as Cordelia realized: the map wasn't a bird's-eye view – it was a diagram of the side of this building! The jumble of dead ends and lines on the map were actually the old Tudor beams. The circus of eight roads was the painting of the compass!

She stood in the street, amazed. After all her nights of starlit searching, she had found the place in the middle of the day!

'In fact, I haven't quite found it yet. I've got to *face the North Wind and follow him south*,' she muttered. '*There you'll find the hidden mouth*. Lucky I know the riddle by heart.'

She looked along the rooftops for a weathervane, to find the North Wind.

A stone statue gurned in the angle of the roof. She had spotted it last night, but it had been too dark to see its wide eyes and curly beard. The statue looked very much like he was blowing hard on people's heads . . .

'*He's* the North Wind!' Cordelia cried.

The statue was gazing not down at the pavement but out towards the river.

'Does the riddle mean follow his *eyes* south?'

She darted across the road to look out at the river.

The Thames was a wide, slow thoroughfare. Tiny skiffs, large barges, and some creaky vessels that Cordelia was surprised could even float all shared the waterway.

'But where's the *hidden mouth*?' she wondered.

She turned to the North Wind. He looked directly at her from his crook in the roof. A fresh wind lifted her hair.

'It's close! I can *feel* it.'

She turned back to the river again, leaning over the balustrade. A large clump of green weeds grew out of the wall below, obscuring her view. But, beneath the weeds, an eddy in the brown water was swirling up mud from the riverbed.

'It's the mouth of the Fleet!' Cordelia gasped. 'The *hidden mouth*!'

The eyes of the North Wind watched her as she climbed on to the balustrade. Her stomach lurched. One wrong move would mean a long drop into the river, which contained what looked (and smelled) like some rather unsavoury flotsam.

There were carved notches forming a precarious ladder down the sheer river wall. She wiggled round, clutching the stone columns of the balustrade. Her foot found the first notch.

Soon, she was halfway down, the river sloshing below and the sky spiralling above. She couldn't look at either without feeling dizzy, so she looked at the stones right in front of her nose. Her hands were unhelpfully slick with sweat.

The next foothold gave way under her.

Her fingers lost their slippery grip.

For a moment, she was poised between the wall and the river. Then she fell, grabbing at the weeds as she went.

'*Aaaaaargh!*'

She slid through a confusion of ivy, was swallowed, somehow, into the stone wall and landed moments later in a gloomy tunnel.

Water swirled and bounded around her knees.

'The Fleet!' she cried.

Behind her, an iron grating shunted back into place with a decisive *THUNK*. The Fleet gushed through the grating out into the Thames, its mouth hidden by a curtain of weeds.

And Cordelia was trapped in a tunnel that stretched away into absolute blackness.

'Can't be brave if you don't get scared!'

She set off into the dark.

The tunnel entrance shrank to the size of a silver coin behind her. Cordelia waded onwards, failing to be fearless but succeeding in being brave.

The river lapped at her ribcage. It hissed past, whispering things that sounded like threats or warnings.

'I'm going on!' she told it fiercely.

The river surged around her chest.

'I've *got* to find my father!'

A wave slapped her face.

'NO!' she spluttered. 'I won't go back!'

The river was a wild thing, and she was up to her neck in it. But the cobweb thread connecting Cordelia to her father pulled her on, strong as an anchor rope.

A silver rectangle gleamed ahead. Cordelia thrashed towards it.

'*INTRUDER!*' came a shriek from above.

A great fist of river smashed over her head.

'*Aaaargh!*' she screamed.

Her scream turned to bubbles as the water forced her under.

Cordelia gripped a crevice in the rocky wall, pushing her face towards the light. She spat out a mouthful of river.

'Miss Hatmaker!'

Everything was awash with silver. After the pitch-dark of the tunnel, the dazzle hurt her eyes.

An agitated face loomed above her. It was the birdlike stranger who had come into the hat shop!

'How on *earth* did you get in here?' he cried.

Cordelia opened her mouth to answer, but the river sloshed over her head.

'Fleet!' the man said in a warning voice, as though commanding a stubborn dog. 'Down!'

The river dropped to Cordelia's waist, leaving her gasping.

'How did you get past the river?' the man asked. 'No man may pass the Fleet's waters without permission!'

'I'm not a man,' Cordelia pointed out, wiping water from her eyes.

Through a silvery blur, she saw shelves taller than treetops reaching up towards a rocky ceiling.

'Ah, yes, I suppose that's true,' he muttered. 'Not a man. *There's* a flaw in the defences.'

Cordelia staggered up a set of rocky steps. She collapsed at the top and began shivering violently – mostly from cold, but also a little from indignation.

'This is irregular, *most* irregular,' the man said, fretting.

Cordelia scrambled to her feet. 'What's not regular?'

'To have a child in the library!' His face was vividly perplexed. 'On top of everything else!'

'The *library*?' Cordelia repeated.

If this was a library, it was like none she had ever seen. No library had a river running through the middle of it, dancing along a channel cut into the rock floor. At the far end, a great wall of silver rippled. A waterfall! Its endless cascade of star-speckled water created a column of light that illuminated the whole room.

A hundred stone pillars soared up to the ceiling, wooden shelves suspended between them. But the shelves didn't hold books. Upon them were thousands of different objects. Cordelia could see stones, scrolls, shards of crystal, bottles and bellows and scraps of cloth, wind chimes and tapestries, collections of feathers, dried flowers, jagged slabs of tree bark, and small piles of earth.

'What is this a library *of*?' Cordelia asked.

The man turned startled eyes to her.

'This cannot do, even for Prospero Hatmaker's child!' he cried. 'You have seen too much already!'

'What? No!' Cordelia objected as the man hustled her down the steps back towards the river. 'Please!'

If this was a library,
it was like none she had ever seen.

She had been searching for this place for so long. She couldn't get thrown out now she'd found it. The truth about her father must be mere inches from her fingers!

'My father wanted me to find this place!' she insisted.

But the man was forcing her down the steps, back into the agitated water.

'As librarian, it is my duty to protect the library! Fleet!' the man commanded. 'Return this person to the Thames and do *not* allow her back here.'

'*No!*' Cordelia protested. 'He sent me a map!'

What was it that was written on the back of the starlight map? She desperately tried to remember . . .

The Fleet gathered itself around her knees, sloshing intently, and began to pull –

'He told me to *look to the stars*!' Cordelia cried desperately.

The librarian's face dropped, as if he had let go of an armful of Wizenwood. His eyes went wide.

'Well, Miss Hatmaker,' he said, 'that changes everything.'

Before the Fleet could pull Cordelia off her feet and drag her away down the tunnel, the librarian was hauling her back up the steps. A little eddy clung doggedly to her leg.

'Fleet!' the librarian scolded. 'This is no time for games!'

The river unwrapped itself from around Cordelia's ankle and slopped indignantly back down the steps.

'Miss Hatmaker, please follow me.'

The man led Cordelia down the length of the library. She squelched along behind him, too busy taking in the strange treasure trove to worry that she was soaked from head to toe.

This was the place her father wanted her to find. *A library.* But this library did not appear to contain any books.

They passed shelves stacked with silver spyglasses labelled **Atmospheric Phenomena**, and luminous jewel-coloured bottles labelled **Magical Bodies of Water – Lakes, Rivers,**

Puddles, etc. Scrolls in bottles were labelled Enchanted Islands and Peninsulas. A collection of twigs and leaves had the label Mystical Trees. On the shelves above, the branches were bigger: Enchanted Forests. Cordelia saw the inscriptions Arden, Wildwood and Underearth beside different branches.

They passed a round table that appeared to be a single slice of tree trunk twelve feet wide, and hurried across a stone bridge over the river, to the other side of the room.

The waterfall fell in a jumble of sound and light, its starry water rushing down from a hole in the sparkling quartz ceiling. The librarian led her to a messy desk that stood against the solid rock wall. He rummaged through the clutter, pushing aside stacks of scrolls, scattering a flurry of goose-feather quills, and pulled out an empty glass bottle, sealed with red wax.

'What's this?' Cordelia asked.

Her father's personal seal had been pressed into the wax. It was the pattern of his favourite constellation, Ursa Minor, made with the end of his Fleetwood hatpin.

The librarian looked at her seriously.

'You are Prospero's nominated successor. He has given you his pass phrase: *Look to the stars*. This means you are to take his place.'

'*What* place?' Cordelia asked. 'Do you know where he is?'

But the librarian was rummaging around his desk again. He produced a letter opener.

'Open the bottle,' he instructed.

Mystified, Cordelia took the letter opener and cut away the sealing wax. The cork was firmly stuck, so she used her teeth to pull it.

'Careful!' the librarian warned.

With a *pop* the cork came out. Cordelia staggered backwards. Suddenly – miraculously – her father's voice flowed from the bottle, as clear and close and wonderful as if he was standing right beside her.

'*I, Prospero Hatmaker* –'

'Father!' she cried joyfully.

'Hush,' the librarian said, stopping the flow of words by placing his thumb over the mouth of the bottle. 'These words will only spill out once before they are gone.'

Cordelia's cheeks were wet, but she nodded.

The librarian removed his thumb and Prospero Hatmaker's voice continued.

'*. . . name my daughter, Cordelia Hatmaker, as my successor in the Secret Society of Mapmakers. She is now Keeper of the Westerly Map.*

'*Dilly, dearest, there isn't much room in this bottle, so I will explain what I can and let Peregrine tell you the rest. Peregrine cares about the library above all else. You can trust him.*

'*I cannot speak freely in case this message falls into the wrong hands but I have given you the Westerly part of Merlin's Map. Keep it safe and secret: that is now your duty as a Mapmaker.*

'*You are the magic you seek, littlest Hatmaker. Remember the seven little gifts your mother gave you, and the story of the Little Bear who helped Guinevere when she was lost? We're never really lost when we can see the stars in front of our eyes.*

'*And as you take my place as Mapmaker, remember that . . .*'

The words dried up.

Cordelia tipped the bottle upside down and the last few drops of Prospero's voice trickled out.

'*I love you, littlest Hatmaker.*'

Cordelia clutched the empty bottle, listening for any scrap of her father's voice still lingering in the air.

There was silence, except for the rush of the waterfall.

'You're a Mapmaker now, Miss Hatmaker.' The librarian looked as surprised as she felt.

Cordelia shook her head slowly.

'But I thought . . .' she murmured. She had thought she would find her father – or at least a clue to his whereabouts – when she discovered the place on the map.

She plunged her hand into her pocket, feeling for the familiar crinkle of the starlight map – the map she had carried through so many hopeful nights. She pulled a handful of pulp from her pocket: water had turned the precious map to mush. But it did not matter: she had reached the end of the trail and her father was not here. Instead, she'd found a baffling message in a bottle and a flustered librarian, blinking owlishly at her from behind his desk.

'Where is he?' she demanded, shaking the message bottle upside down, as though answers might fall out. 'Where is my father?'

'I don't know!' the librarian cried. 'That's why I came looking for him at the shop.'

Cordelia remembered his frightened eyes, his whisper across the hatshop counter –

'What did you mean when you said, *The North Wind is blowing*?'

The librarian flapped some papers in an agitated way.

'It is a distress signal of sorts,' he admitted. 'To assemble the Mapmakers in times of crisis. If a Mapmaker receives the message "*The North Wind is blowing*", they must come to the library at once, because something has gone dreadfully wrong.'

Cordelia stared at the librarian.

'What has gone dreadfully wrong?' she asked.

The librarian looked gravely back at her.

'Dozens of maps have been stolen.'

'*Stolen!* By whom?' But deep in her belly Cordelia already knew. 'Witloof,' she whispered.

The librarian's stricken face confirmed it.

'He is going to destroy all the magical places hidden in the maps, one by one,' he said, shredding a scrap of paper anxiously. 'He has already begun. Last night . . .'

With a shudder like a shadow falling, Cordelia remembered the black ash swirling through the night sky. She knew now:

it had been the remnants of ruined magic, falling like petals of despair to kiss misery on to her skin.

'But . . . you said without my father there's no hope of defeating Witloof,' she faltered.

The librarian's expression became solemn.

'Miss Hatmaker, you have just taken your father's place as Mapmaker. Now the hope of stopping Witloof falls to you.'

Cordelia was momentarily struck dumb. When she found her voice, it came out rather smaller than she meant it to, more mouselike than lionesque.

'Stopping Witloof? *Me?* Stopping him from what?'

'Goodness! I'm doing everything backwards today, I must apologize!' the librarian exclaimed. 'Let me start at the beginning. I haven't even introduced myself properly – I am the Peregrine of whom your father spoke – Peregrine Crane.'

He made a little bow.

Determined to show Peregrine that she was strong and capable and brave, Cordelia stuck out her hand.

'Unconventional!' he declared, shaking it. 'But then Prospero is unconventional. There is no rule to say that a child cannot be a Mapmaker . . . It's just never happened before.'

Cordelia stared at the towering shelves holding thousands of objects.

'So I'm a – a Mapmaker now?' she murmured. 'And this is a library of maps?'

'Yes, it is,' Peregrine confirmed. 'And yes – you are.'

Cordelia shivered.

'My dear, you are drenched!' he cried. 'I am ever so sorry. I should have done this the moment you arrived.' He took a fire-bright feather from a sconce on the wall. It was alive with a kind of flame. 'A tailfeather given by the Firebird,' Peregrine said, sweeping it over Cordelia's sodden clothes. A gentle heat spread through her, right to the tips of her fingers.

'The *Firebird*!' she gasped, as her clothes emitted clouds of steam. 'I thought it was a myth!'

'Not at all,' Peregrine assured her, dusting her shoes with the feather. 'If you wish to seek the Firebird, there's a map in this library that will show you the way.'

Cordelia's feet stopped squelching in her boots. She was now perfectly warm and dry from head to toe.

'A Firebird feather never creates actual flames, so I keep it here for making tea and drying Mapmakers after they wade up the Fleet,' Peregrine said. 'As in any library, real fire could be devastating. These maps are made of bark, and moss and leaves and branches, and delicate stones and shells that would shatter in a fire, not to mention the water maps that would evaporate. "No fire" is the first of the three rules.'

He replaced the feather carefully in its sconce.

'Rule number two: no taking maps without permission. The last Mapmaker who took a map from the library without permission was expelled the moment his deceit was discovered.'

Cordelia nodded.

'And the final rule: no revealing the secret of the Mapmakers – no telling *anybody*, on pain of instant expulsion! If you bring a flame, steal a map or whisper a word of the Mapmakers, you will be expelled at once!'

The Fleet sloshed warningly.

Cordelia frowned to show how seriously he could take her. 'I won't bring a flame, nor steal a map nor whisper a word of the Mapmakers to anybody. I promise.'

She was promising her father most of all. He had sent her here – not to find him but to take his place as Mapmaker. She wished he had given her an explanation about where he had gone, but the starlight map and the message in the now-empty bottle would have to be enough. It was clear he needed her to do something even more important than finding him. She would not let him down.

'How am I meant to stop Witloof?' she asked, jutting out her chin, glad her voice sounded strong and daring again.

Peregrine's stern expression softened.

'There is much I must explain to you, Miss Hatmaker. Have a seat. I'll make some tea.'

Cordelia could not sit still. She paced around the library, questions racing through her mind, as Peregrine stirred tea leaves into a copper kettle. She examined a Honig Blossom that led to the Runnymead Meadows, wiggled a piece of Windknot Moss that would guide a person through Ben Nevis's Befuddling Fog, and inspected a twisting twig that showed the way into the Obscure Forest of Boscobel.

With a jolt, Cordelia realized that Mapmaking was, in fact, highly illegal. The Mapmakers had continued their work for centuries, in defiance of the king's ban.

'Did the Mapmakers become a secret society when Henry the Eighth was king?' Cordelia asked Peregrine as he set out teacups.

'We've been secret since long before then,' he replied, pouring the tea. 'We went underground – quite literally – in the Dark Ages.'

The tea was hot and strong and sparkled with Fleetwater stars from the shimmering waterfall. Peregrine dug out a box of ginger biscuits. Cordelia perched on the round table and Peregrine sat at his desk, dunking a biscuit in his tea.

'First, there is a bit of history it's important you understand,'

Peregrine began. 'Over a thousand years ago, a magician named Merlin saw humans abusing the magic of the natural world. Armies felled enchanted forests to build forts, diverted sacred rivers to make moats and dug out fairy hills to find iron for weapons. So much magic was destroyed that the skies were blackened with shadow ash – and this moment in history became known as the Starless Days. To protect the remaining magical places from harm, Merlin drew a veil around them. He made maps to show the ways into the hidden places, so they wouldn't be lost forever. The maps were kept secret: only those whom Merlin trusted were allowed to use them.

'King Arthur appointed knights to help Merlin, and thus the Secret Society of Mapmakers was begun. Although the legends tell that these knights slayed dragons and killed trolls and routed giants, their true purpose was quite different: if the knights heard rumours that a magical beast was about to be attacked by a violent mob, they would seek it out, pretending they were going to slay it. In truth, they sought the creature out to save it. That way, the knights rescued thousands of magical creatures and stopped many magical places from being destroyed.'

Peregrine smiled at Cordelia over the rim of his teacup.

Her brain buzzed like a swarm of Bombination Bees. *Dragons? Trolls? Giants?*

'I've never seen a giant!' she said. 'Or a troll! Or a *dragon*!'

Peregrine chuckled. 'Well, of course you haven't; the Mapmakers did an excellent job of hiding them! Now, of all the magical places that Merlin concealed, the most important was an ancient tree – the Elixir Oak – whose roots went so deep they reached the source of magic itself.

'Every king, emperor and warlord wanted to find this tree. If you imagine the whole land as a human body, then the Elixir Oak was its heart. Its sap ran with the Essence of Magic. It was said that drinking an acorncup of its dew would restore a man to life, even at the brink of death.

'Like a heart, this tree pumped magic around the entire land. Merlin knew that, if it fell into the hands of a greedy leader, its power would be used to destroy rather than to create. So he hid the Elixir Oak behind a wall of enchantment, and protected it with a circle of standing stones, which we now call Stonehenge. He created a hidden doorway, fashioned a key to open it and made a map to show how to find it.

'Merlin gave the key to Queen Guinevere, a lady of the utmost integrity. But he still didn't feel the tree was well enough protected, so he divided the map into four pieces and gave them to his four most trusted Mapmakers to keep safe. All four parts of the map must be assembled to show the way to the secret doorway.'

Peregrine fixed his gaze on Cordelia. She knew, vaguely, that she must look rather strange. Her mouth was open, her eyes were wide, and her eyebrows were as high up her forehead as they could possibly go. But she was so full of amazement that she could not make her face behave normally.

'You are now the keeper of one quarter of that map,' Peregrine told her.

Cordelia made an effort to appear a capable Mapmaker. She pressed her lips together and dragged her eyebrows down into an earnest frown.

'Uhm – the Westerly quarter,' she said, remembering her father's words.

Peregrine nodded. 'We must assemble Merlin's Map as a matter of urgency, Miss Hatmaker! We need to get to the Elixir Oak before Witloof destroys any more magical places!'

Cordelia continued to frown. 'But how – how did Witloof even know about the maps? I thought the Mapmakers were a very secret society.'

Peregrine looked grave. 'Witloof *was* a Mapmaker. It was he who was expelled for taking a map without permission. Years ago, he stole a Hagstone that showed the way to Bleak Isle. Since he took it, nobody's been able to find their way back there. And that was only the beginning of his wickedness.'

Peregrine swept his arm towards a set of empty shelves.

'Three nights ago, the maps to every hidden magical place in London, except one, were stolen. And I know it was Witloof!'

'Three nights ago?' Cordelia said. 'That was the night *before* his execution!'

'Yes – so how did he manage it from his prison cell?' Peregrine fretted.

'He's ordered people to steal for him before,' Cordelia said, remembering how Sam had been forced to break into Makers' houses to steal Menacing ingredients for Witloof.

'I arrived in the morning to find maps missing and this note.' Peregrine brandished a ripped bit of paper.

I WILL DESTROY EVERY PRECIOUS MAGICAL PLACE

The writing had evil intent in its scrawled form. Unable to look at it a moment longer, Peregrine crushed the note and hurled it to the floor. He jabbed a finger at a tapestry hanging on a pillar. It was a map of the land, made from faded green moss. Glinting all over it were tiny stars picked out in gold thread.

'Everywhere you see a star on this tapestry, you will find a corresponding map in the library,' Peregrine said. 'Every star represents a magical place, hidden from plain sight.'

The whole land was sparkling with hidden magic. Even across London itself, dozens of gold stars were sprinkled.

'All these places are at his mercy. He's destroyed one already.'

Cordelia was shocked. 'Destroyed? How?'

'Did you hear about the burnt trees in St James's Park?'

'The paper boys on Fleet Street were yelling something . . .' Cordelia said.

'Yesterday, hidden in a quiet corner of St James's Park was an ancient orchard of Golden Apple trees. You could only find it if you had the Golden Malus Map to guide you. Today, it is nothing more than a field of blackened stumps, exposed for all the world to see. When Witloof destroyed the orchard, he also destroyed the enchantment keeping it hidden. Only someone truly evil could cause that kind of destruction.'

Cordelia remembered the bleakness the ash had caused: like a thousand burnt butterflies had been emptied out of Witloof's Leechglass watch at once. It had been the burnt wreckage of a magical orchard raining down on London.

'He hates the Makers and he hates magic too,' she said grimly. 'He said from the scaffold that his *dark rain* would fall on us all. He's doing this to terrorize everyone. We've got to stop him!'

'Yes, we must,' Peregrine agreed. 'We must do anything we can to stop him.'

He stared at the tapestry glinting with magic, his jaw clenched.

'Go home and fetch the Westerly Map!' he instructed her. 'I will send a message to the other Mapmakers and we will assemble Merlin's Map here this midnight and use it to stop Witloof right away!'

It hit Cordelia all of a sudden.

'I – I don't have the piece of Merlin's Map,' she faltered. 'I don't even know what it looks like!'

'Merlin's Map was not a piece of paper that he cut into four pieces. He divided it into the four elements: earth, air, fire and water. The Westerly Map is a crystal vial of water, in the shape of a raindrop. Smaller than my thumb,' Peregrine explained. 'I am keeper of the Northerly portion. The keepers of the Southerly and Easterly parts (whose identities, of course, must be kept secret) have them hidden safe. But they are ready to assemble the moment the librarian gives the word. It has been that way for thirteen hundred years.'

Cordelia had never seen a crystal vial like the one Peregrine was describing, let alone been given it by her father. Thirteen centuries of tradition towered like a mountain above her.

'I don't have it,' she whispered.

Peregrine blinked. 'But Prospero said in his message that he gave it to you.'

'Perhaps it's hidden in Hatmaker House,' Cordelia said, dragging her heart hopewards. She could think of dozens of places where her father could have concealed a small crystal vial.

'I'm a Mapmaker now,' she went on. 'That's why my father sent me here: to become a Mapmaker and help protect the magic. So that's what I'm going to do.'

Even as she spoke, Cordelia felt her heart clench with regret. The starlight map had not led her to her father. And, with no more clues about where he might be, and an urgent task at hand, she knew she must set aside her search for him. But she was so full of determination to do her duty as a Mapmaker she could feel all the iron in her blood.

'I'll go home and find it right away,' she said. 'But there's still one thing I don't understand . . . Can you *only* find a place with the map in your hand? You know where these magical places all are, so can't we sneak into one and catch Witloof?'

Peregrine smiled ruefully.

'Miss Hatmaker, I admire your courage,' he murmured, 'but you have a lot to learn about how Mapmaker maps work, and alas we have precious little time to spare. Rather than me *telling* you how the maps work, let me *show* you. As it happens, I can do so on your way home.'

He pulled a grey chrysalis out of his jacket.

'This is the only map to a magical place in London that Witloof – or his thieving minion – did not manage to steal, because I was using it at the time,' Peregrine said. 'It's the map to my home.'

As Cordelia watched, the chrysalis unfurled in the palm of his hand and a rainbow Flos Moth flapped into the air.

Out on the Thames, the air was fresh and generous after the underground library.

Peregrine steered his Fleetwood coracle across the path of a barge, and they bobbed in the frothy wake of a tea clipper. The Flos Moth Map flitted just ahead of them.

They followed it under Blackfriars Bridge and a little way downriver, to where the water turned in eddies, drawing mud spirals in the shallows around the reeds. To anybody watching, it would have looked like a dried leaf blowing in the wind.

'Every map has its own unique key,' Peregrine explained. 'The key is always something found in nature – a birdcall, a certain kind of light, the span of a hand, sometimes a song.'

'What's the key to Merlin's Map?' Cordelia asked.

'*That* key is shrouded in mystery,' Peregrine said. 'The legend goes that it was eventually passed from Queen

Guinevere to her daughter, and she passed it on to her child, and so on. And somehow it got lost down the generations. At some point it was picked up by someone unknowingly: the legend insists that the one who keeps the key will never see it, even though it is right before their eyes.'

'But if we don't know who has the key, how will we get through the doorway to the Elixir Oak, even when we have all four pieces of the map?' Cordelia asked.

Peregrine didn't answer; he was focused on jiggling the oars back and forth, making the boat spin.

'See these spirals –' he peered down at the eddies of mud under the boat's prow – 'there's a certain one that we have to follow. Watch the map –'

The moth map appeared to be doing a very complicated dance.

Cordelia's stomach swirled as the boat turned a full circle and plunged into a thick stand of bullrushes. Reeds slashed sword-like leaves across her face.

'Now for the key!' Peregrine called. 'This key is a whistled tune. Listen carefully.'

His whistle made Cordelia think of Zon birds greeting the day.

The reeds parted to reveal a small lagoon. The sweet musk of Quag Blossoms sang above the rich odour of the river mud. Marshfire Orchids quivered, like candle flames, on slender stems. Behind them, the reeds formed a dense green wall, silencing the outside world. Sunlight reached fingers in, turning the lagoon into a pool of molten gold.

Peregrine held out his hand. The moth map fluttered on to it, folding itself back into a chrysalis. He tucked it carefully into his pocket.

They floated towards a bar of silver sand that emerged between the reeds. Peregrine jumped out of the boat and pulled it ashore. Cordelia clambered out.

They had slipped through some happening of magic to a place entirely hidden from the outside world. They were on a small island, lush and green.

Flos Moths fluttered on the warm air, their wings shimmering in the light.

'Welcome to my home,' Peregrine said, sighing happily.

The Flos Moths left trails of fragrance as they looped around Cordelia. The island was about the width and length of a frigate – but where a mast would be on a ship, an Ardourwood Tree grew.

Cordelia saw a hammock swagged in its branches, and a tidy kitchen arranged at the base of the tree trunk, with Gripe Vines holding the pots and pans above a small stove. There was a comfortable-looking armchair half-sunk in the flower-starred grass nearby, and a bookshelf made of Wizenwood branches, woven with Night-light Vines, whose blooms would brighten like strings of lights when it got dark.

'It is a haven!' Peregrine pronounced. 'Almost a heaven, in fact.'

A moth skimmed down and landed on Cordelia's hand. Close up, she saw that its wings were bright as flower petals.

'Sir Francis Drake hid here for several days after accidentally offending Queen Elizabeth,' Peregrine told her, pointing at some letters carved into the tree trunk.

F ♥ E

'He only came out after she promised not to execute him. This has always been a place of refuge. You see, unless you are using the correct map, it is impossible to find your way into a magical place. So, once you're concealed inside, you are entirely safe from discovery.'

'Witloof must definitely be using the maps he stole to hide in,' Cordelia said.

'Highly likely,' Peregrine agreed.

Gentler than a kiss, the moth on Cordelia's hand took flight. It left a tiny dazzle of happiness on her skin.

The hats the Hatmakers made were like small pieces of rainbow fashioned into headwear. But following a Mapmaker's map into a hidden magical place was like stepping into the rainbow itself: everything looked different.

'This particular place has been concealed for almost four hundred years,' Peregrine told her. 'We must protect these places with our whole hearts and souls, because it is magic like this that *feeds* our hearts and souls.'

As if in answer, or in thanks, a moth landed on Peregrine's forehead.

Looking at the librarian, who wore the kind of rapturous expression usually found painted on saints' faces in churches, Cordelia smiled.

Hatmaker House was especially quiet because Jack was asleep. He lay in a cot in the kitchen, where Cook could keep an eye on him and give him fresh Honeymilk tea at a moment's notice.

Jack was wearing the Hatmakers' most luxurious and special nightcap, made of the velvet found on the undersides of Sloth Poppies, woven with lullaby-spun threads. Usually, it could only be afforded by dukes; today, it adorned the head of a cabin boy. Cordelia sneaked in through the back door, past Cook and into the hall.

She heard her aunt and uncle busy with customers in the shop as she crept upstairs.

The first thing Cordelia did was pull her father's telescope from her box of treasures and take it apart. But the crystal vial had not been cleverly concealed inside it: aside from the compartment where the map had been hidden, the telescope had no more secrets to reveal.

'Perhaps he left it somewhere for me to find,' she muttered, peering under her wardrobe, to find nothing but a forgotten hair ribbon and a loitering Somnus spider.

When she had investigated every hiding place she knew of in her own room, Cordelia moved on to other nooks and crannies in Hatmaker House.

Quietly, she searched among the Timor Ferns, in the cupboard of Invisibility Buttons, behind the books on Secrecy, and among the Angelus Shell chimes. She looked in the Quest Pigeons' aviary, and inside the chimney pots on the roof. But she did not find the crystal vial.

She crept into Sam's bedroom. Sam had so few worldly possessions that the room was still almost exactly as Cordelia's father had left it.

Prospero Hatmaker did not keep a very tidy wardrobe. (Cordelia had definitely inherited that habit from him.) She flung aside jackets strung with shells, tossed out tattered pantaloons, and carefully removed a greatcoat made entirely of porcupine quills.

She pulled a blue dress, shedding seed pearls, from the bottom of the wardrobe.

The dress was frayed at the cuffs and patched with splashes of red fabric, stitched with spider web. The hem was ragged, caked with dried mud. This dress had been worn by a swashbuckling kind of woman.

Mother.

Cordelia instinctively reached for her necklace, before remembering it was still hidden under her pillow.

There was a faint sweetness about the dress. It smelled like flowers from a hundred summers ago.

Cordelia buried her face in the fabric. She stood for a long time, breathing the scent in. Was this what her mother had smelled like? Why had her father kept the dress? Why was it causing an ache in her chest?

'This isn't helping,' she muttered into the silken folds.

Draping the dress like a cape round her shoulders, she plunged back into the wardrobe. All that remained was a sheaf of papers. Cordelia riffled through them.

There was a newspaper cutting from over eleven years ago, some old letters, a few pages from a ship's log and – her heart thumped – a map!

Cordelia held it up to the light. It did not appear to be magical: it was a sea chart of the North Atlantic Ocean. It was definitely not the tiny crystal bottle she was looking for, but still – a map.

Then she noticed something unusual about it. The sea chart itself was printed, but somebody had drawn snaking lines across the page. There was a dotted line with a dashed line shadowing it, zigzagging across the Atlantic. The point where the dotted and dashed lines met was circled. A date, *18th February*, was written beside it – Cordelia recognized her father's handwriting. Next to the line of dashes was the word *Harpy*. And beside the dotted line was written: *Jaunty Bicorn*.

'That was our ship!' Cordelia gasped. 'The *Jaunty Bicorn*. The ship I was born on.'

It was also the ship that her mother had died on.

And Cordelia realized with a jolt – like lightning hitting a mast – that 18th February, eleven and a half years ago, was the date of the storm that had sunk the ship. The date her mother had died saving her from the raging waves.

The dotted line signifying the passage of the *Jaunty Bicorn* came to an end in the circle.

'That must be where it sank,' Cordelia murmured.

But why did her father have a map tracing the course of the doomed ship? And what was *Harpy*? Cordelia had a fleeting image of a monstrous winged woman, savage with talons and fury. She shuddered.

'Did ya find it?'

Cordelia dropped the sea chart.

It was Sam, with her halo of Dulcet Fireflies, in the doorway.

Cordelia stared at her blankly.

'That place on the map?' Sam prompted. 'Was it where you thought? Near the Fast River?'

'Uh – no,' Cordelia said. 'No, I – I didn't find it.'

The lie was hard to speak – it felt too big to fit convincingly in the words.

But Peregrine had said she would be expelled from the Society of Mapmakers if she broke the rule of secrecy. She couldn't risk that happening, not when it had been her father's wish that she would help protect the magic.

'It – uh – it wasn't there,' Cordelia finished lamely. 'There was nothing.'

'Yer hiding something from me again, Cor,' Sam said.

'I'm not!'

'Whatcha looking for in here, then?' Sam asked.

'Nothing!' Cordelia cried.

She glanced guiltily around at the mess she had made. Clothes were strewn across the room. She'd emptied the wardrobe, even checked for hidden panels in the bed, and a false bottom in the bedside table.

Mostly to avoid Sam's eyes, Cordelia hurriedly shuffled the papers back into a stack and bundled her father's clothes and her mother's dress into the wardrobe, taking care not to be poked by the prickly greatcoat. She went to put back the stack of books her father kept on the bedside table, but Sam dived in front of her and, hands and books colliding, knocked an oil lamp over. Coins spilled out of the bottom, rolling over the floor.

Cordelia stared as Sam scrabbled to gather them up, the fireflies darting excitedly around.

'Where did those come from?'

'Nowhere – they're mine!' Sam cried, sweeping the coins into a small pile of copper and silver. She straightened up, cupping her paltry treasure in her hands, and stared, defiant, at Cordelia.

'So we've both got a secret, then,' Cordelia said tersely. 'I won't ask about yours if you don't ask about mine.'

Sam nodded. The coins clinked in her hands.

Cordelia slipped away to search elsewhere, while Sam carefully stashed her secret hoard back in the base of the lamp.

'Did my father give you anything else to give to me?' Cordelia asked Jack, in what she considered to be a casual voice, over dinner.

Jack shook his head. 'Just the telescope.'

'Not even a small crystal bottle?' Cordelia pressed.

Jack's mouth twisted in commiseration.

'Captain Hatmaker kept anything important locked in the trunk in his cabin,' he told her. 'But it all went down with the ship. Everything went wrong so fast there wasn't a chance for him to get to the cabin before the storm struck.'

Cordelia remembered her father's cabin on the *Jolly Bonnet*. It had been full of maps, unfurled on every surface. He must have been mapping magical places all around the world. It made sense that he had kept the Westerly Map among all his mapmaking equipment.

She tried not to show her disappointment, even as she felt her hope hit the bottom of the ocean.

What if Father had meant to hand Jack the crystal vial? But the storm took them by surprise and he didn't have time . . .

'A small crystal bottle?' said Uncle Tiberius. 'Whatever for?'

'Is it for Sir Hugo's headdress?' Aunt Ariadne asked. 'That reminds me: we all need to think about our own costumes for the Harvest Masque. It's only a few days away.'

'Are you coming to the masque?' Sam asked Jack.

Jack shook his head. 'Actually, I'm going to go and live with my big sis. She doesn't know I'm alive yet – I've got to go and break the news!'

'She'll be overjoyed to have you back,' Uncle Tiberius rumbled.

Jack looked momentarily seasick.

'Don't know if I'll ever be ready to go back on the ocean,' he admitted. 'Even though I miss it all the time . . . p'rhaps I'll get used to life as a landlubber.'

'Nettles for mettle!' Cook announced, setting a bowl of extremely green nettle soup in front of Jack.

He regarded the soup with uncertainty. It appeared to look back at him with a vaguely threatening expression.

'Not sure why Cook's feeding me enough for a voyage to the Cape of Good Hope,' he muttered to Cordelia as Cook stepped back to the stove. 'My sister only lives in Wandsworth.'

Cordelia was glad when the soup Cook put in front of her was tomato.

Jack was only allowed to set out for his sister's house after he had eaten two bowls of nettle soup and three helpings of bread-and-butter pudding. Before he left, Cordelia added one last thing to the basket Cook had packed for him: her precious Venetian song-bottle that sang a sea shanty. She poured out the grimy starlight, filled the bottle with Cook's redcurrant cordial, and tied a Courage Ribbon round it.

'Drink this in a few weeks,' she told Jack, 'if you still miss the sea.'

Cordelia searched for the Westerly Map until she couldn't keep her eyes open that night. The next morning, she got up early to hunt among the tiny vials and glass bottles of liquid light in the Alchemy Parlour.

Out of the wide parlour window, she saw black ash floating through the morning sky. Witloof had destroyed another magical place!

'No!' she moaned softly, watching as rain chased the black ash down through the sky.

She applied herself to her search with extra determination. She also used considerable stealth, as Great-aunt Petronella was still asleep beside her lilac fire.

She found bottles labelled **Sunlight**, **Moonlight**, **Dawnlight** and **Twilight**. But there was no small crystal vial the size of her thumb, shaped like a raindrop. Cordelia replaced the bottles quietly, careful not to wake her snoozing great-aunt.

Next, she crept to the Library and scribbled a note to Peregrine:

Still searching!
I'll send word as soon as I find it! CH

Having secured the note to Gertrude's leg and sent the Quest Pigeon out across London with instructions on how to find Peregrine, Cordelia continued her search, fighting the feeling that it was all in vain.

'I think the Westerly Map is at the bottom of the sea,' she told Agatha, who cooed in a consoling kind of way.

Nevertheless, watched by the curious Quest Pigeons, Cordelia looked behind all the books in the Library. She pulled out an old tome on Greek myths. After peering behind it (and seeing no glint of crystal hidden there) she found herself leafing through it. She turned to the page on Harpies.

> A rapacious monster with a woman's head and body, and a bird's wings and claws. Feathers and talon-clippings are considered *very Menacing* and should *never* be used

on garments, where they will provoke unrestrained fury and choler. As an interesting side note: feeble or despotic men may be particularly frightened of Harpies. They may call a woman a Harpy if threatened by her wits or power.

There was a hideous picture beside this paragraph, of a woman writhing mid-air, claws like knives in gnarled hands, carried on monstrous, muscular wings.

Cordelia imagined those dark wings sweeping across the sea in pursuit of a ship . . .

'There you are!' It was her aunt at the door, looking very businesslike.

'Harpies live on a faraway island, don't they?' Cordelia asked quickly. 'They wouldn't come to England?'

'Harpies?' Aunt Ariadne frowned. 'Nobody's seen one for centuries, Dilly. Most people think they never existed at all. Just a myth. Come along, Sir Hugo is here to collect his hat.'

'Already!' Cordelia gasped.

She scampered out of the Library.

It was only later on that the thought occurred to her: *If nobody had seen a Harpy for centuries, where did the feathers on the princess's Rage Hat come from?*

Cordelia was tired of having to wipe her hand every time Sir Hugo kissed it, so she stuck her hands in her pockets as she entered the shop.

'Ah! The Creatrix of Headwear!' Sir Hugo declared. When he saw her hands weren't available, he swept his very wide bicorn from his head and sank into an elaborate bow.

'Hello, Sir Hugo.' Cordelia bowed back. 'How's your Moon coming along?'

Sir Hugo flapped his lashes bashfully. 'Like the great skyward orb, it is still a little lacking. But, happily, both my own Moon and the heavenly counterpart still have two days to ripen into our full glory.'

Aunt Ariadne's forehead crinkled in confusion.

'Sir Hugo means it's going to be two days until the real moon is full,' Cordelia translated for her aunt. 'And, by then, he'll be ready for his performance as the Moon at the Harvest Masque.'

'Exactly so!' the actor cried. 'And I have come to collect the headdress that will help me dazzle all who gaze upon my moonish face.'

'I have a few final touches to add to it, Sir Hugo,' Cordelia said, trying to ignore her aunt's disapproving glare. (She could almost hear the admonishment: *A Hatmaker should always have the hat ready for the customer!*) 'I won't be long – just a few minutes in the workshop!'

'I shall accompany you!' Sir Hugo declared. 'I shall serenade your fingers as they work.'

'Do you have to?' Cordelia asked.

He did. He bounded upstairs behind Cordelia, giving her an intricate description of his Moon ballet as they went.

'And then a *pas de bourrée* – that's French – and I finish with a *grand jeté*!'

'What does that mean?'

'A big jump,' he told her.

In the workshop, Cordelia got out a wooden box from under a table, in which she had been growing a small cluster of Luminant Mushrooms in chocolate-dark earth. The mushrooms glowed like coins, creating their own light. She fixed several on to the headdress with silver wire, where they would float like planets orbiting Sir Hugo's head.

The actor sang his 'Moonsome Moonsong' to her as she worked.

'Perhaps the princess would consider a duet?' He stopped mid-melody, then he thought better of the idea. 'Nay, nay, she would be more impressed if she watched me do a solo.'

'Much more impressed,' Cordelia agreed, sprinkling a final dazzle of Zenith Nectar over her creation. 'It's ready, Sir Hugo.'

She presented the actor with the headdress. His eyes glowed and his voice was a cascade of raptures. It took several ecstatic *oohs* and *aahs* before he could form actual words.

'By Titan's trousers! I shall be the heavenliest body at the Harvest Masque!' he finally cried. 'The princess will be overawed – indeed, she will be Moonstruck!'

'Try to keep the headdress in the dark as much as possible – it will be glowiest that way when you appear for your dance,' Cordelia advised, closing it in a hatbox and securing it with a ribbon. 'Sunshine fades moonlight, so don't let it get in the sun.'

After doing several (what she guessed were) *grands jetés*, Sir Hugo jumped down the stairs and danced his way out of Hatmaker House, leaving Cordelia alone in the workshop.

In the silence left behind by the actor, she gazed at the magical ingredients collected there. There were many precious treasures gathered from nature that helped people to connect with the magic inside themselves.

She looked at the Rollicking Roses that encouraged people to dance, and the Zingen Cactus Spines, which inspired people to sing. She considered the Cordial Blossoms, whose sweetness helped the buds of friendship to bloom, and the Benignus Crystals, which kindled hearts to kindness.

Her father had collected so many of these treasures on his travels. Now Cordelia truly understood where many of these things came from – they were from secret magical places, hidden by enchanted maps. Her father must have spent half his travels gathering ingredients, and the other half carefully protecting those places. That was why he had been away so much of her childhood: he had the very important responsibility of keeping magical places safe from harm.

Now it was her responsibility.

But if Witloof got his way, soon there would be no magical places left, and no more magical ingredients for the Makers.

'I've got to stop Witloof somehow!' she said. 'And if the piece of the map is at the bottom of the ocean, I'll have to find another way to stop him!'

An Angelus Shell chimed in agreement.

Shortly after Sir Hugo's departure, Cordelia and Sam found themselves being ushered out of Hatmaker House.

'You've earned the day off,' Aunt Ariadne said kindly from the doorstep. 'Tiberius and I still have a lot of hats to finish before tomorrow.'

'But I could –' Cordelia began.

'You worked so hard on Sir Hugo's headdress, Cordelia. And, Sam, you've been doing wonderfully with your reading and writing.' Aunt Ariadne pressed silver coins into their palms. 'There's enough money to hire a rowing boat in the park or see the tumblers at Marylebone Gardens.'

But Cordelia did not want to hire a rowing boat or see tumblers. She wanted to stay inside and keep looking – no matter how hopelessly – for the lost piece of Merlin's Map, while simultaneously devising an alternative plan in case the map was nowhere to be found.

Before she could invent an excuse convincing enough, Aunt Ariadne had shut the door.

Cordelia considered climbing in through the window, but she didn't think it would be an easy thing to explain – breaking into her own home to search for something that was probably at the bottom of the sea.

'Where are your fireflies?' she asked Sam. 'Shouldn't we go back inside and check on them?'

'Nah – they're nocturnal. They're sleeping under my bed, won't wake up till twilight.'

'Oh.'

Cordelia had been determined to ignore the slightly awkward feeling lingering between them since she had discovered the coins hidden in Sam's lamp . . . Sam seemed determined to ignore it too. They wandered along, heading for Bulstrode Street, where Goose lived. Sam whistled and scuffed her boots as they went.

If I can't find my part of the map to Merlin's magic, I'll have to use my own magic to stop Witloof, Cordelia decided silently. *Luckily, it's currently made of absolute determination and unstoppable resolve.*

She could feel the magic in her belly. Today, it felt as though it was made of a tiger's roar.

A paperboy on the corner yelled, 'WITLOOF INFORMATION REWARD NOW FIFTY GOLD PIECES!'

'*Fifty?*' Sam's eyes lit up. 'Blimey!'

What had Cordelia heard a paperboy yelling yesterday on Fleet Street? Mrs Tempest at the Sargasso Chocolate House was the person to report any sightings to . . .

'How about a nice cup of chocolate?' Cordelia suggested.

The Sargasso Chocolate House had high ceilings, powder-blue walls and a crowd of glamorous customers.

The Sargasso Chocolate House had high ceilings, powder-blue walls and a crowd of glamorous customers. The very air was sugared: it was sweet to breathe.

A doorman in a pink silk suit and white powdered wig peered down at Cordelia, Sam and Goose (whom the girls had collected on their way).

'Would you like a table?' the doorman enquired. 'Or are you here to waste Mrs Tempest's time with silly rumours about Witloof's whereabouts?'

'Has anyone been here with information?' Cordelia asked eagerly.

The doorman raised one haughty eyebrow.

'Everyone – that is to say, the entire population of London – has been at the Sargasso today with *information*.' He cast a scornful glance at the window, where a bunch of ne'er-do-wells had their noses pressed against the glass. Cordelia recognized several of them from the Compass and Main. Jenkins tapped on the window with his wooden leg.

'They all insist they're owed a reward,' the doorman said. 'They're refusing to leave, and dirtying the windows with their grubby noses. So, if you're here to claim you saw Lord Witloof dancing a jig at Hyde Park Corner –'

'We'd like a table, *if* you please,' Goose interrupted loftily.

The doorman sniffed but signalled to a waiter.

'Please follow me.'

The waiter led them past ladies with tiny straw hats perched on very tall wigs, and foppish gentlemen wearing heavy make-up (the warmth of the room making the rouge melt down their cheeks).

People do rather strange things in order to be fashionable, Cordelia thought, squinting at a wig that was listing to one side like the Leaning Tower of Pisa.

Behind a marble-topped counter, a pink-cheeked woman wearing an excessively frilly mob cap was stirring copper pots full of thick, dark chocolate.

'That must be Mrs Tempest,' Cordelia whispered.

Sam and Goose goggled at the chocolate pots.

'Ahem.' The waiter indicated a table.

They sat down. The smell of chocolate was liquid and delicious all around them.

'Cordelia, why are we here?' Goose asked soberly, fixing her with a searching look. 'It's not really just for hot chocolate.'

His voice was so serious it drew her eyes back to him like a compass needle is drawn towards north.

'What d'you mean, Goose?'

'It's about your father, isn't it?' Goose continued. 'You're desperate to find Witloof because he sank your father's ship.'

'Finding Witloof won't bring back yer pa,' Sam added quietly. 'No matter how hard ya wish it would.'

Cordelia could not quite meet her friends' eyes. She wished she could tell them the truth – that Witloof was threatening the magical places her father had protected.

She could not tell them about the Mapmakers: she could not risk getting expelled. But perhaps she could tell them *something*. If not the whole truth, then at least a piece of it.

'It *is* about my father,' she began. 'But it's also about so much more. Witloof is destroying the magic our families have been Making with for centuries! That's what caused those horrible ash storms and the dark rain – and it will fall again if we don't stop him!'

Cordelia swept an arm round at the customers, laughing and chattering at the other tables.

'I can see so many of our hats on these heads! And they're wearing your boots, Goose, and I bet they have Cloakmaker capes and Watchmaker watches and even Glovemaker gloves, all woven with magic that makes their lives brighter.'

Goose nodded.

'Magic brings joy – but it goes deeper than that, deeper than clothes. It goes right to our souls. It's what we're made of. If Witloof harms magic, and we stand by and do nothing, it's like – like we're in a tree and he's chopping it down!'

She could look her friends in the eye now because she wasn't hiding the very heart of the truth from them. This was it.

'We need to stop Witloof before he destroys all the magic he can get his hands on.'

'Three hot chocolates?' The waiter loomed, holding a steaming jug above them.

He placed three delicate china cups on the table and poured the hot chocolate from an impressive height before stalking away.

The children stared at each other. Cordelia could see her own determination reflected in her friends' faces.

'I understand,' Goose said solemnly. 'And I'll do everything I can to help – even if it's scary.'

Cordelia grinned.

It was a relief to tell her friends at least part of the truth.

'We're in this together.' Sam raised her cup. 'To stopping Witloof!'

They sipped. The chocolate was delicious: molten and smooth. Cordelia imagined it might be what her great-aunt's Vesuvian lava would taste like if mixed with cocoa.

'So, what's the plan?' Sam asked.

Cordelia glanced over at Mrs Tempest.

'I'm going to pay my compliments to the chocolate maker,' she said, sliding off her chair. 'See if she's heard anything about where Witloof is.'

'We'll keep a lookout here,' Goose said with a serious nod.

Cordelia wove through the room. She sidled up to the wide marble counter where Mrs Tempest worked. The chocolatey odour was opulent up close, almost overpowering.

Mrs Tempest was dressed as a sort of shepherdess, with milk-white flounces, lemon-yellow bows and creamy lace all over. Though she wore a confection of a dress, her face was a sour thundercloud, her hair afrizz with irritation.

'Good afternoon,' Cordelia began politely.

Mrs Tempest looked up. It was more of a glare, really, but Cordelia smiled a determined smile back at her.

'What is it this time?' Mrs Tempest snapped, hurling a handful of powdered nutmeg into one of her chocolate pots. 'Saw Lord Witloof in a mermaid's tail crossing the river in a seashell, did you? Or was he riding a white horse past Westminster Abbey? Or posing as a waxwork in the window of Mrs Salmon's Freakish Emporium? The tall tales I've heard today!'

Cordelia was impressed by the wild imaginations of her fellow Londoners.

'I'm actually here to –' she began.

'You're not getting your hands on those fifty gold pieces!' Mrs Tempest snapped, stirring a pot. The contents bubbled sulkily. 'My chocolate's been soured today; I've been so pestered by wretches telling me preposterous stories.'

Cordelia privately thought that preposterous stories are often the best kind, but she didn't share this perspective with Mrs Tempest. Instead, she said, 'Mrs Tempest, may I have a look at your hat? I'm a Hatmaker, you see. I'm planning a costume for the Harvest Masque, and your hat is just the right shape.'

Tutting, Mrs Tempest swept the mob cap off her head. Cordelia caught it.

'Oh!' she exclaimed. 'What an exemplary bonnet!'

Mrs Tempest rolled her eyes and turned away to pound cocoa pods.

Cordelia pulled a ribbon from her own hair. It was a Convivial Ribbon with a Cordial Blossom sewn on to it, which she liked to wear because it sounded so similar to her own name.

This should work!

Mrs Tempest was busy with her pestle and mortar, sending puffs of cocoa dust into the air. She did not see the Hatmaker quickly weave a new ribbon round the mob cap and tie it in a Friendship Knot.

'Thank you,' Cordelia said, holding the newly beribboned cap out to Mrs Tempest. 'That was very helpful.'

Mrs Tempest scowled, slapping the cap back on her head.

The Hatmaker watched the chocolate maker's face change. The hard line of her mouth softened and the crease between her eyebrows disappeared.

Cordelia felt a bit guilty. She knew Aunt Ariadne would be deeply disapproving if she ever discovered that Cordelia had altered Mrs Tempest's hat without telling her.

However, when Mrs Tempest looked up at her, there was a friendly expression on her face, and Cordelia completely forgot all feelings of guilt.

Mrs Tempest dipped a ladle into a pot of bubbling hot chocolate. 'Here, sugar puff, tell me if you think this needs any more spice.'

Cordelia sipped the chocolate.

It was delicious.

'It's *delicious*,' she confirmed.

Mrs Tempest sprinkled a tiny pinch of salt into the pot and dipped the ladle again. 'Now try that.'

Cordelia sipped again. She felt her eyes widen.

'Even *more* delicious!' she declared. 'Your hot chocolate really is magic.'

Mrs Tempest's lips twitched in a tiny smile.

'That's what they whisper,' she said, winking at Cordelia.

Cordelia wondered if Mrs Tempest secretly mixed her chocolate with magic, the way she suspected Cook did with her culinary creations. Perhaps that was why the Sargasso was renowned as the best chocolate house in the city . . . Though this was a most intriguing thought, Cordelia was determined to stay focused on what she was there to discover.

'It must be very – very *vexing* – to have people coming up and telling you silly rumours while you're trying to work,' she said conversationally. 'But have you heard any you think might be true?'

Mrs Tempest stared at the far corner of the room.

'None that *I* think are true,' she said. 'But perhaps *she* will.'

'She?' Cordelia repeated, following her gaze to an empty table in the corner.

'Aye.' Mrs Tempest pointed. 'She's been watching and waiting all day.'

Cordelia realized there was somebody sitting at the table. If Mrs Tempest had not pointed, Cordelia would never have noticed her, even though she was quite a contrast to the other customers in the chocolate house.

The lady was dressed from head to toe in black. Amid the sea of pastel silk worn by the rest of the patrons, she was as conspicuous as a fly sitting on a lemon meringue pie.

'She's the one offering the reward money for information about Witloof's whereabouts. She promised me there'd only be a few people coming by. Little did she realize what a hullabaloo there'd be about it all!' Mrs Tempest said cheerfully. 'But if you offer gold for a good story, you're bound to get a tall tale.'

'I think I'll go and talk to her,' Cordelia said. 'To see if any of the tales are . . . short enough to be believed.'

'You come back and see me soon!' Mrs Tempest twinkled, the Cordial Blossom jiggling on her cap.

Cordelia set her sights on the table in the corner and crossed the parlour. She had to narrow her eyes and not blink too much; it was rather like trying to spy the lady through a blurry telescope.

When she got closer, she realized why.

It was the lady who had come into the shop a couple of days ago, wanting a Low-profile Hat. She was wearing the hat, which was why Cordelia hadn't noticed her at first. Even though it was proving rather inconvenient now (as she had to approach the table while squinting out of the corner of her eye), Cordelia was impressed by the power of the hat she had made.

'Hello,' she said.

The lady sat perfectly still.

'That hat makes you difficult to see, but not completely invisible,' Cordelia told her politely.

The lady sighed. 'I suppose you *did* say that when you sold it to me,' she conceded. 'What on earth did you do to Gail?'

'Gail?' Cordelia repeated. 'Oh – you mean Mrs Tempest!'

'Usually, she's frostier than the winter wind. That's why I chose her – I thought she'd winnow the truth from the rumours. But you've melted her somehow.' The woman sounded grudgingly impressed.

Cordelia glanced at the chocolate maker, who was dancing as she stirred her pots of chocolate. A waiter lingering nearby looked alarmed by this sudden change of behaviour, not to mention the pirouettes.

'Why are you offering fifty gold pieces for information about Witloof?'

The lady tilted her head but didn't answer. So, despite the fact that Aunt Ariadne would have been horrified by her lack of manners, Cordelia sat down at the table without being invited.

'Let's just say you *did* offer gold,' she continued. 'Have you heard any good information about where he might be?'

'He sank your family's ship,' the lady said. 'You want revenge.'

For a moment, Cordelia's voice was caught somewhere between her heart and her throat.

'Actually, it's – it's much more important than revenge,' she spluttered, trying to recover some composure. 'I'm trying to stop him doing something terrible.'

'Then we have something in common.'

Cordelia frowned. Politeness was a lost cause now, so, in a final act of uncouthness, she put her elbows on the table.

'Who are you?' she demanded.

'My name is Win Fairweather,' the lady said.

'What are you hiding, Win Fairweather?'

'We all have something to hide, Cordelia Hatmaker.'

'*I* don't.'

'What about that new ribbon on Mrs Tempest's hat?'

Cordelia felt her ears get hot.

'I want to find Witloof, and you do too,' she said. 'I thought we could help each other. He needs to be stopped before he does more damage.'

'I agree. And how –' Win broke off, staring out of the window.

Cordelia turned to see black ash floating down through the sky outside, like pieces of a bad dream come loose from a nightmare.

'The dark rain!' she cried. 'Not again!'

She turned back to the table to find that Win Fairweather was gone. She had taken advantage of Cordelia's momentary distraction.

'*Wait!*' Cordelia shouted, jumping up.

Half the Sargasso looked round.

A waiter carrying a heavily laden tray was jostled, and Cordelia caught a glimpse of black-clad elbows pushing past him. Girls in sherbet-coloured dresses were shunted sideways and splashed.

'Win! Wait!'

Cordelia darted towards the door but got snarled up in a mob of furious girls, who seemed to think it was her fault that their dresses were suddenly covered in steaming hot chocolate.

'It wasn't me!' Cordelia gasped, dodging around them and out into the street. Nowhere could she see Win Fairweather. She cursed her own excellent Hatmaking.

A stinging piece of ash landed on her hand. Another touched her forehead and she drew her hood up.

Goose and Sam tumbled out of the chocolate house's door.

'Cor, what's happened?'

They huddled under the Sargasso's glass awning as the ash spiralled through the sky, dimming the daylight with its dark veil.

'It's Witloof's doing, isn't it?' Goose shuddered.

Cordelia nodded grimly. Another magical place was being destroyed. That made three.

'Did you see the lady in black?' she asked, flinching as another speck of ash stung her skin.

Sam wrinkled her nose. 'Glanced her.'

'She's the one offering a reward for information about Witloof!'

'*I* got Witloof information,' an indignant voice piped up. 'But I ain't allowed inside!'

It was Jenkins, the soldier from the Compass and Main.

'How come they said they want Witloof information, but, when push comes to shove, you get pushed aside, then shoved out the door?' the old soldier complained. 'Ain't nobody taught 'em any manners?'

BOOM!

A storm broke like a Thundergoose egg above their heads.

Rain hissed down. Cordelia felt the smear of ash trickle down her cheek.

'I've just thought!' Goose grabbed her arm. 'There *is* someone who might know where Witloof's hiding, if we're brave enough to go . . .'

The Tower had been built to survive siege and warfare: its walls were solid stone, house-thick and storeys-tall. The black teeth of a portcullis were bared above the barred gates.

'How do we get inside?' Cordelia wondered.

The Tower was impenetrable without an army and several hundred cannons.

'That bit's easy,' Goose said. 'We just have to pay the entrance fee.'

'Entrance fee?' Cordelia spluttered. 'It's not the British Museum!'

'I know,' Goose agreed. 'But, for some reason, people seem to enjoy scaring themselves silly by looking at the prisoners.'

'Looks like we get tickets over there.' Sam pointed at a knot of people clustered at the massive wooden gate.

A small door opened in the huge gate and a man wearing the black-and-red livery of the Tower guards poked his head out.

'Next tour starting now!' he announced.

Cordelia, Sam and Goose joined the group. A dozen people jostled in front of them.

'Thruppence for the three of you,' the guard told them at the door.

Goose (rather regretfully) dropped three pennies into his hand and the children shuffled into the dark gatehouse.

'Welcome –' the guard smiled a trollish smile – 'to the Tower of London! There are dangerous and depraved villains locked up in the Tower. You must not stray from my side!'

Cordelia, Sam and Goose followed the tour into the chilly inner courtyard of the Tower. The last time they had been here, it was to rescue the Makers and the king, who were at the Tower on a much less voluntary basis than the tourists were today.

Cordelia glanced around the stone-faced buildings. The windows seemed to be watching with narrowed eyes.

'Where d'you think she'll be?' she muttered.

Goose pointed up at the tallest, grimmest tower. 'Traitors' Tower.'

The guard was now busy giving the tourists an enthusiastic re-enactment of an execution on a chopping block. Nobody was looking their way.

'*Go!*' Sam hissed.

They scurried across the courtyard. A raven cawed above them – it sounded like a warning – as they slipped into the shadow of Traitors' Tower, unseen.

It was dark and dripping inside. The wind – Cordelia hoped it was only wind – wailed along the empty passageways. Ranks of locked doors led away down a gloomy corridor. It smelled of wet rock and ancient misery.

'How do we find her?' Sam murmured.

'I don't know,' Cordelia admitted, taking a few tentative steps down the passage. 'She could be behind any of these doors.'

The wind seemed to be sobbing quietly now.

Cordelia began to whistle a sweet-bitter tune.

Goose joined in. Sam added her voice too.

After a chorus, they stopped and listened.

The lilting song came back to them faintly, from down the dark hall.

'This way!' Cordelia said.

They followed the thread of song onwards. It led them along the corridor, through an archway and up a stone spiral staircase, twisting up and up. Cordelia glanced out of a slit window. They were as high as birds fly.

Finally they reached a door. Cordelia tried to ignore the fear gnarling her stomach.

Goose seemed to be feeling something similar. He caught Cordelia by the arm. 'Is this a bit like walking into a bear's den?'

'This was your idea, Goose,' she said steadily, hoping he couldn't sense how fast her heart was beating. 'And it's a good idea – it's the best chance we've got to find out where Witloof is.'

'Keep yer voices down,' Sam murmured.

Goose nodded curtly.

Cordelia pushed open the door.

They were at the very top of the tower, in a cramped space that contained only two cells. The first cell had nothing but a straw mattress and a bucket imprisoned behind the iron bars.

But there was a person hunched in the corner of the second cell.

The face that looked back at Cordelia was paler and thinner than the one she remembered. Then the woman frowned. That frown was very familiar.

'Miss Starebottom?' Cordelia murmured, creeping closer.

'That's *not* my name!'

With a furious fling of limbs, the woman hurled herself against the bars. Cordelia stumbled backwards. The last time she had seen her governess, Miss Starebottom had tried to run her through with a swordstick, and been dragged away with hate in her eyes, swearing revenge.

Those eyes seemed different now, dimmed in the gloomy prison.

'I mean . . . Delilah Canemaker,' Cordelia said shakily.

The name, spoken aloud, caused some kind of magic in Delilah's eyes. It was a flint-and-tinder kind of magic: it lit something.

'That's *me*,' the ex-governess whispered. 'I'm a *Maker*.'

She had once been neat and prim, with tidy hair and a tame expression. Now her hair was unkempt and her face was made of scraps and wishes scrunched up around sharp eyes.

'You want to know where Lord Witloof is, don't you?' Delilah asked. 'The guards have already come and asked me that question. They used threats and . . . iron things.'

She shied away, clutching her arms round herself. The wind wailed like it was hurting.

'I'll tell you what I told them,' she hissed. 'Witloof was finished with me on that ship. He needed me to make the Rage Clothes. Once I'd made them, he had no use for me any more. That's how he treats people – he uses them up and throws them away.'

'So, you *don't* know where he is?' Goose asked.

He was standing with Sam out of sight, near the door, as though he was worried his ex-governess was a Gorgon and therefore dangerous to look at directly.

'Is that Lucas Bootmaker?'

'Yes, it's me,' Goose answered stoutly, not moving.

'Scared of me, Lucas?' Delilah pressed herself into the corner of her cell to get a look at Goose. 'I wasn't a very nice governess.'

'Not *nice*? You tried to get our families executed for treason!' Goose cried. 'And you made us do a *lot* of algebra.'

'Keep yer voices down!' Sam hissed, glancing at the door.

'For trying to kill the Makers – I'm sorry,' Delilah murmured. 'And the algebra was unforgivable. But I *did* give you sweets,' she added in a pleading kind of voice.

Cordelia watched Delilah Canemaker's face. It was like watching clouds change in the sky.

'We'll forgive you for everything,' Cordelia told her, 'if you tell us where Witloof is. We want to stop him.'

Suddenly the woman was gripping her prison bars.

'I don't know where Witloof is,' she said. 'But I *do* know his deepest fear.'

Cordelia found herself drawn forward. 'He's got a *fear*?'

'He fears the Makers.'

'Why?'

'Because Makers have the power to create. Witloof only has the power to destroy. The power to create is infinitely greater. The Makers have the means to undo Witloof's power,' Delilah continued earnestly. 'That's why he was determined to destroy you all.'

The Watchmaker's words echoed in Cordelia's mind: *A clock only works when all its pieces are put together properly . . .*

Delilah jerked an arm through the bars.

Cordelia flinched. But Delilah was only holding out a tiny twist of straw.

'This is a cane I made. It's got some hope woven in it,' she whispered. 'You can have it.'

It was twisted like a barley stick and knotted neatly at both ends: a tiny, beautiful work of handmade magic.

'Don't you need it more than we do?' Cordelia asked.

'If you're hoping to defeat Witloof, you'll need it most,' Delilah replied.

Cordelia took the tiny straw cane.

'We should go, Cordelia.' Goose was scowling, pulling at her shoulder. 'She's a liar. She's probably tricking us right now.'

But Cordelia was remembering the story Uncle Tiberius had told her – how Delilah Canemaker had only been a little girl when her father had committed terrible treason; she had been plucked from her comfortable life and left to starve in a workhouse.

'You were only a child,' Cordelia said.

That child, who had been left alone in the world thirty years before, was plainly visible today: in the shadow-quick way Delilah's frowns changed to smiles, hope chasing fear across her face. Canemaker beckoned Hatmaker closer.

'I told the guards something else, but they didn't believe me,' she whispered. 'The night before Witloof's execution, I heard him whispering to someone outside his window.'

She jerked her head at the empty cell. There was a narrow window where the wind came whistling through.

'It's a hundred feet in the air!' Goose scoffed. 'Unless he was talking to one of the ravens, there's no way that's possible!'

'It's true! I heard him!' Delilah insisted. 'You Bootmakers, always so solid, with your two boots on the ground.'

In his indignation, Goose seemed to forget his fear. He stepped forward.

'Who *was* it, then?' he asked. 'This mysterious person whispering outside the window?'

'I couldn't see who it was – it was dark!' Delilah shot back.

'Shhh!' Sam hissed. 'Someone's coming!'

Footsteps tromping steadily upwards echoed on the stairs.

'And the very top of Traitors' Tower is where we keep our most notorious prisoner!' a voice boomed. The guard and his tour party were approaching.

Delilah's face quickened with fear. '*You must leave!*' she hissed.

'A diabolical villainess!' The guard's voice, bouncing off the bare walls, was getting closer. 'Conspired with Lord Witloof to commit high treason!'

'*Go!*'

There was only one way out – down the stairs. But the guard and his group were marching upwards.

'It's too late!'

'*Hide!*' Delilah urged.

Cordelia, Goose and Sam did a sort of desperate silent dance around the space, but there was nowhere to go.

'Behind the door! And slip away when they're through!' whispered Delilah.

Sam yanked Cordelia and Goose behind the door. The guard was almost upon them.

They flattened themselves against the wall, pulling the heavy door right up to their toes. Cordelia had to turn her face sideways to stop her nose being squashed.

She saw the guard's broad back.

'Have a good look,' he brayed, rattling the bars with his cudgel. 'She's a vile one! Tried to blame her treacherous actions on an old stick that once belonged to her father!'

Cordelia could just see Delilah's eyes, wide and frightened, as a dozen people peered in at her. For a moment, those frightened eyes locked with Cordelia's and flashed bright with a spark of defiance.

'*GO!*' Delilah cried.

The guard thought the prisoner was shrieking at him, but Cordelia knew the instruction was meant for her.

Delilah flew at the guard, seized his arm through the bars and sank her teeth into his hand.

There was uproar.

The chaos gave Cordelia, Goose and Sam the chance to dart out from behind the door and pelt away down the stairs.

Several streets away from the Tower, Cordelia turned to stare back at the grey slab jutting into the sky. Only two months ago, Witloof and Miss Canemaker had plotted that all the Makers would end up inside that grim prison . . . But today Miss Canemaker had helped Cordelia, willingly. Could somebody change that quickly?

'How *could* there've been somebody whispering to him outside his window?' Cordelia muttered.

'She must've bin lying,' Sam said, squinting at Traitors' Tower. 'No way anyone could climb that.'

Cordelia turned to look at her friend, who was assessing the tower with a professional eye. She remembered watching in astonishment as Sam scaled the Guildhall tower, quick as a spider. Sam had been working for Witloof at the time.

With a horrible, cold plunge, Cordelia was visited by suspicion. Her mind's eye conjured the secret pile of coins hidden inside the oil lamp, and Sam hurriedly gathering them in her hands.

'She must still be working for him!' Goose's voice cut across Cordelia's spiralling thoughts. 'You can't seriously trust her.'

Cordelia felt breathless for a second, from the icy shock of suspicion.

'Who?' she asked, not allowing herself to look at Sam.

'Miss Canemaker, of course!' Goose burst out. 'Who else?'

Cordelia turned her face into the wind blowing from the Thames. She felt ashamed.

Sam was desperate back then, she told herself sternly. Her brother had been taken away from her. She had no choice! *She's not still working for Witloof. She's changed. She's family.*

But who else could have climbed up that Tower to plot with Witloof the night before his escape? And what about the maps that had been stolen from the library – when Witloof was still in prison? The Fleet had let Cordelia past because she was not a man. Nor was Sam.

'Cor?' Sam's eyebrows were bunched together in concern. 'You all right?'

Cordelia touched the straw cane in her pocket. She could feel the strands of fragile hope twisted into it.

'I was just thinking . . .'

She pushed her suspicions firmly away, as if she were pushing an Insidious Ink Squid back into the deep sea.

'Miss – Miss *Canemaker* told me Witloof's biggest fear is the Makers' power to create,' she said.

'Nonsense!' Goose spluttered.

'But the Watchmaker said it too, didn't he?' Cordelia cried. 'He said we're like the pieces of a broken clock!'

'So you think we should try and put the clock back together?' Goose demanded. 'Even if bits of the clock keep hitting other bits of it on purpose?'

'I think we should start by going into the Guildhall and trying to make friends with the Glovemakers,' Cordelia announced. She did not add out loud, *Because I don't have the Westerly Map but I've got to stop Witloof somehow.*

'I agree with Cor,' Sam said, taking Cordelia's hand. 'What've we got to lose?'

'Aside from life and limb?' Goose muttered.

Cordelia squeezed Sam's hand, feeling a lot of gratitude and a little bit of guilt.

'We'll be walking right into the Glovemakers' clutches!' Goose groaned.

'*We?*' Cordelia asked, not daring to hope.

'Of course "we"!' Goose said stoutly (and slightly resentfully). 'You don't think I'd let you go in there alone, do you? No matter how bad an idea I think it is!'

Cordelia grinned.

'Goose, have I ever told you you're the best Bootmaker I've ever met?'

Goose couldn't help himself: he blushed.

Goose insisted that they couldn't 'just go barging into the Guildhall like a bunch of Headless Gobble Hogs'.

'If we're going to charge headlong into this,' he said, 'we should at least think about what we need to do.'

So Hatmaker, Bootmaker and Lightfinger marched back to Hatmaker House, determined to come up with a plan.

Uncle Tiberius appeared to be waiting for them in the kitchen doorway.

'Ah! Young master Bootmaker!' he called down the mews. 'Might I have a word?'

Goose stopped. 'What does he want?' he asked Cordelia out of the corner of his mouth.

'I honestly don't know.'

Uncle Tiberius's lips were peeled back in what Cordelia suspected was meant to be a friendly smile.

'It's all right, Goose – we'll protect ya if he tries to take yer eyebrows for one of his hats,' Sam said.

'*What?*'

'She's joking,' Cordelia said, compelling an unwilling Goose down the mews.

Uncle Tiberius's smile was rather alarming up close.

'Ah – Lucas! Hello, hello.'

Cordelia thought her uncle might do better in winning over Goose if he stopped smiling so hard. She could see all his teeth.

'Hello,' Goose said.

Uncle Tiberius clapped his hands together, making Goose jump. 'Come in! Come in!' he boomed.

It took the combined efforts of Cordelia and Sam to push Goose through the door.

In the kitchen, Cordelia spied the reason for Uncle Tiberius's strange behaviour: on the table stood the half-finished miniature ship for Janet Crust's hat. The masts were still in the sugar bowl, where Goose had assembled them a few days ago. Beside it lay a carved hull, a small heap of handkerchiefs made of Pomp Cotton and a muddle of Fustian String.

Uncle Tiberius bobbed next to it.

'I – er – I've been having a bit of trouble with the masts. Can't get 'em to stay up. I'm not sure which sail goes where . . . and the rigging got me in a bit of a tangle.'

Goose sat down at the table.

'This is the main mast,' he said, wiggling the longest stick. 'And this rigging goes like this, but you've got to put the sail –' he picked up a handkerchief from the pile – 'on *this* side of the mast, otherwise the ship would be going backwards.'

Uncle Tiberius leaned down to see what Goose was doing. Sam peered from the top of the cupboard.

'There you are, Cordelia!' Aunt Ariadne appeared in the doorway. 'I need your help with a Happiness Hat.'

Goose looked up. 'Don't leave me!' he squeaked.

But Aunt Ariadne bustled Cordelia away to the workshop.

Cordelia pinned a frond of Gaudian Fern to the yellow hatband of the Happiness Hat, and her aunt tucked tinkling Jesterbell Flowers into the brim.

'Are you all right, Dilly darling?' Aunt Ariadne asked carefully. 'After everything Jack told us?'

Cordelia frowned as she picked out an orange thread.

'He said my father got taken into the sky,' she said, twisting the thread between her fingers. 'Which is very mysterious indeed.'

'Oh, Dilly! You're going to run away again, aren't you?' her aunt burst out. 'To go looking for your father!'

Cordelia snatched the Happiness Hat out of Aunt Ariadne's hands before the fern wilted from the sorrow. She seized a pink Merrybird feather from the wall and tickled her aunt under the chin with it.

'Don't cry, Auntie!' she implored, coaxing a smile back on to her aunt's face with the feather.

'After losing Prospero, I just couldn't bear to lose you too,' Aunt Ariadne sniffed.

'I have several very important things to do in London that my father would much rather I do instead of searching for him,' Cordelia reassured her. 'For example – is there any way you can think of to make the Makers become friends again?'

Her aunt smiled weakly. 'That's a lovely thought, Dilly dear. But the one thing Makers can never do is *make* people do what we want. So we can *persuade*, but we can never *make* anyone become friends, even though the Makers' enmity is very silly. Now, run along while I put this in a hatbox.'

Cordelia stood in the doorway, chewing her lip and thinking. If only it *was* possible to make the Makers become friends . . .

Above her, a beam creaked. A shiver of flowers cascaded through the air and settled on her head. Cordial Blossoms. Hatmaker House always had the answer.

She rushed downstairs, trailing blossoms in a frothy wake behind her.

'I've got an idea!' she cried, tumbling into the kitchen.

Goose and Uncle Tiberius had their heads together at the table, poring over the model ship. They had fitted the masts and rigging into the hull and the sails were up. Sam watched, munching an apple. Cook cast rather resentful glances over the entire scene, perhaps because the shipbuilders were using several of her wooden spoons, not to mention her butter dish, to prop up the vessel.

'Hang on, Dilly,' Uncle Tiberius murmured. 'Just doing a tricky little bit of –'

He held the corner of a tiny sail as Goose secured it to a crossbeam.

'The mainsail is raised!' Goose announced.

'By St George's helmet!' Uncle Tiberius cried. 'It's splendid!'

He seized the ship and held it aloft like a victorious Kraken might hold a galleon in its tentacles.

'We could float her on Cook's soup!' he boomed.

'Don't you dare,' Cook warned.

Uncle Tiberius wheeled away from the soup pot, sweeping Goose into one of his crushing bear hugs.

'I could never have done it without you, young Boot – Boot . . . maker.' The last word seemed to get a little scrunched in his throat.

He released Goose, scratched his head and stared at the Bootmaker as though he had asked him to solve algebra problems in fluent Welsh.

'Just got to make a set of tiny cannons!' he announced. 'Must get on.'

He bowed formally and disappeared off to the workshop.

Cordelia turned to the Bootmaker with a wicked grin. 'Oh, Goose – you've become a Hatmaker!'

Goose's face fell.

'Never tell my mother!' he whispered.

Cordelia pulled Goose and Sam into the Hatmakers' shop, which had closed for the night. In the half-dark of the unlit shop, they held a whispered conference.

'I've got an idea to make the Glovemakers be our friends,' Cordelia began, putting on a Gravitas Hat to honour the seriousness of the planning. 'We can ask the Watchmaker kids to help. All we've got to do is get –'

'The Cloakmakers!' Goose gasped.

'Yes!' Cordelia was encouraged by Goose's positive attitude. 'Well, getting the Cloakmakers is actually the second part of the plan, but –'

'No, I mean: look – the Cloakmakers!' Goose pointed out of the window.

Four people were approaching Hatmaker House from across the street. Their upright bearing and haughty expressions were decidedly Cloakmakerish, not to mention the beautiful capes that flowed around them, glimmering in the dusklight.

Cordelia opened the front door just as the most senior Cloakmaker raised his fist to knock. (She had taken the Gravitas Hat off, so she didn't appear too serious, and replaced it with a Felicity Bonnet.)

'Good evening!' she said brightly.

The Cloakmaker stepped back, as if such friendliness was somehow uncivilized. Cordelia smiled at him, hoping her smile looked more natural than Uncle Tiberius's earlier attempt.

The Cloakmaker looked down his nose at her. 'I'm here to speak to the grown-ups,' he drawled.

'Come in!' Cordelia said, beaming.

He raised one suspicious eyebrow. Cordelia arced her arm in a welcoming gesture and ushered them inside.

Goose and Sam watched from the safety of the stairs as the four Cloakmakers stalked into the hall with their noses in the air.

Behind Mr Cloakmaker came Mrs Cloakmaker, followed by their son, Master Cloakmaker. Cordelia wondered if the Cloakmakers knew that when they tilted their heads back, it gave everyone an excellent view up their nostrils. The only nostrils she could *not* see up belonged to the youngest Cloakmaker, who was a little smaller than Cordelia.

The hallway hissed with satin as Cordelia squeezed past the Cloakmakers to call up the stairs.

'Aunt! Uncle! We've got . . . guests!'

Mrs Cloakmaker flinched. Her cloak rustled in a shushing kind of way.

Cordelia noticed the youngest Cloakmaker studying the grandfather clock. Just a couple of months ago, Cordelia had learned that there was an identical clock in each of the Makers' houses. Before the rift between the Makers, the clocks had been used to call everyone together at the Guildhall. Cordelia supposed that the youngest Cloakmaker didn't know this and was surprised to see such a familiar thing in the hallway of a sworn enemy.

Aunt Ariadne came down the stairs, carrying a sheaf of Nodgrass.

'Oh!' She stopped, shocked. The Nodgrass kept nodding gently in her arms as she and the Cloakmakers observed each other.

Uncle Tiberius loomed behind her, like approaching thunder.

'*Cloakmakers!*' he rumbled. 'What d'you want?'

'Your hats are causing havoc with our cloaks!' Mr Cloakmaker snapped. 'We want to make an Elegance Cloak for Lord Buncle to wear to the masque, but he tells us you have made him some sort of ridiculous bicorn with Mystique feathers on it, that will clash with the Tremulous Elver tentacles we want to put on his cloak. Elver tentacles and Mystique feathers together will create too much panache for one outfit – he won't be able to stand upright!'

'This is why the Guildhall was built,' Cordelia began. 'So that all the Makers could work together –'

'I suggest you make a different cloak, *Clodworthy*,' Uncle Tiberius snapped.

Cordelia had to admire her uncle's inventiveness: *Clodworthy* was a new achievement in insulting names.

'I knew you'd say that, *Tiberius*,' the Cloakmaker snapped back. 'I refuse to change the cloak – *you* can change the hat!'

Cordelia realized Clodworthy must be Mr Cloakmaker's first name.

'Will nobody buy your cloaks unless they're brighter than a baboon's backside?' Uncle Tiberius enquired.

'Out*rage*ous!' Mrs Cloakmaker's utterance cut the conversation dead.

'Your cloak really is beautiful,' Cordelia murmured to the youngest Cloakmaker in the silence.

The girl's eyes swivelled to Cordelia in surprise.

'Charity, don't talk to her!' her brother barked.

Charity Cloakmaker sniffed, twitching the hem of her cloak away from Cordelia.

'We have only one thing to say to you, Hatmakers,' Mr Cloakmaker announced icily. 'Your ludicrous hats are causing us Cloakmakers all kinds of ridiculous bother, and we hope a great Croakstone falls on your heads!'

In a dazzling flurry, the Cloakmakers stormed from the house, leaving a crackle of fury behind, as though someone had opened a jar of Lightning Strife.

SLAM!

Uncle Tiberius said, '*Well!*'

He paused, filling his lungs with enough air to blow a ship across the Atlantic, and said '*Well!*' again.

Cordelia, Goose and Sam crept back into the shop.

'So?' Goose said. 'Still think we can make the Makers all be friends?'

Cordelia put the Felicity Bonnet back on its shelf.

'I didn't say it would be easy,' she admitted. 'But I *have* got an idea . . . Aunt Ariadne would probably call it "morally dubious", but it might just work.'

The next morning, Cordelia threw open the door and sauntered into the Guildhall.

Goose strutted beside her.

Both were acting a lot more confident than they felt.

'Just think of Sir Hugo on stage!' Cordelia told Goose. 'Plant your legs wide and yell your lines.'

They stepped into the Great Chamber.

It was a dreadful mess.

The Glovemakers had raided all the Makers' workshops. Torn cloaks were strewn across the floor, with hat blocks, boots and bits of watches scattered among them.

The Glovemakers appeared to have devised some kind of jousting tournament, using ancient mannequins dressed in velvet cloaks and Cavalier hats, boasting Glovemaker gloves on the hands and Bootmaker boots stuck on the end of the legs.

Some of the mannequins looked primed to fight – gloves and boots ready to punch and kick – but others had already been crashed together. Arms and legs lay scattered, separated from the bodies they belonged to, and left on the battlefield.

'I hope this doesn't happen to us,' Cordelia muttered, stepping over some headless wooden remains.

There was a murmur of voices coming from one of the workshops.

Goose planted his legs far apart. Before Cordelia could tell him there was still time to back out, he yelled, 'PRITHEE, GLOVEMAKERS! WE WANT TO TALK!'

'*Prithee?*' Cordelia whispered.

'You said be like Sir Hugo!' Goose hissed back. 'He's always saying *prithee*.'

The Glovemakers emerged from a workshop, arms full of canes.

Hatmaker and Bootmaker stood confidently in the Great Chamber.

'Here to try and claim the Guildhall?' a Glovemaker snarled.

'You can't have it,' taunted his twin. 'It's ours now.'

'We came to have peace talks,' Cordelia announced. 'We want to stop being enemies and work together instead. Why don't we share the Guildhall, the way it's meant to be shared?'

For a moment, there was stunned silence. Then the sticks clattered to the floor as the Glovemakers fell about laughing. They screeched and hooted like Raving Owls.

'Work *together*!'

'With *you*!'

'That'll *never* happen!'

Cordelia and Goose stood their ground. The Glovemakers prowled forward, spite in their eyes.

'Why would we want to *work* with a horrible Hatmaker?' one of the girls sneered.

'And a disgusting Bootmaker!'

Cordelia inched backwards. She had to pull Goose with her: his legs were planted as though he was ready to face down a charging bull.

'If you refuse to talk nicely,' Cordelia warned, backing away three precise inches, 'we'll have to do it the other way.'

'What *other way*?' demanded the Glovemaker boys, taking a menacing step forward.

Cordelia smiled. 'The morally dubious way.'

'NOW!' Goose yelled.

Two Fond Bonnets fell through the air, trailing Affinity Ribbons.

One landed plumb on the head of a Glovemaker boy.

The second bounced off the intended head and flopped to the floor.

There was a moment of stunned silence. Then –

'ATTACK!' a Glovemaker girl screamed.

Chaos erupted.

One girl lunged for Goose, the other for Cordelia.

A pair of nightcaps sailed down from the balcony but missed the heads they were meant for.

'Oh *no*!' Cordelia yelped.

Sam came running down the stairs to help, then went running back up them as a Glovemaker boy with a swordstick pounded after her.

His brother – wearing the Fond Bonnet – tottered forward, arms outstretched.

'Hello, Hatmaker!' he cried joyously. 'I'm Bernard!'

'Hello, Bernard!' Cordelia called, swerving round his sister and hurtling away across the chamber. 'I'm Cordelia!'

Goose, with a Glovemaker hot on his heels, hurled a roll of Ravel Ribbon behind him as he fled. It twisted through the air like a sea snake and wound itself round his pursuer.

'Argh! You blasted Bootmaker!' she shrieked, grappling with the ribbon.

The tail end snapped back through the air, twirling itself round Goose's wrist, attaching him firmly to his enemy.

Two Glovemakers closed in on Cordelia – one friend, one foe. She dodged a hug – Bernard's arms closed over nothing – and rolled away across the floor, narrowly escaping the violent alternative.

'This isn't going to plan!' Cordelia cried.

'You don't say!' Goose hollered in dismay.

He thrashed at his end of the ribbon, trying to get free. The Glovemaker at the other end had her arms firmly clamped to her sides, but she snapped at him like a shark trying to take bites of a seal. Goose was helpless, and Cordelia did not have time to help.

She'd had a bit of a desperate idea. She dodged round a mannequin and dived into the Bootmaker workshop, a Glovemaker right behind her. She dashed along the workbenches, searching for –

'There!'

She grabbed the dancing clogs, throwing herself under a table.

Her pursuer's feet stopped beside her. 'Trapped!' the Glovemaker crowed gleefully.

But Cordelia yanked an ankle, jamming a clog on to the foot. The Glovemaker stamped and staggered. Cordelia managed to force the second clog on to the other foot and the stamps turned rhythmic.

Cordelia darted out from under the table. The Glovemaker swung a slap at her, but her other hand caught it in a clap.

'Listen – we really want to have peace talks!' Cordelia tried for a reasonable tone.

'*Never!*' The Glovemaker lunged.

But the lunge turned into a tarantella and whirled her away around the workshop. Cordelia fled.

As she ran back into the Great Chamber, a shower of dust rained down on her. She looked up. To her horror, she saw Sam high above, edging out along the plaster wall moulding to escape a Glovemaker boy's glinting swordstick.

Sam clung to a plaster garland, but it was old and crumbling. It came away under her hands, falling in a shower of dust.

'I'll get you!' The Glovemaker boy jabbed at Sam.

Sam clambered further along the crumbling ledge.

'*Careful!*' Cordelia cried.

SMACK!

A dizzying blow struck Cordelia on the back of the head. She turned woozily to see the dancing Glovemaker, now performing a Highland fling, skipping backwards away from her.

'Listen!' Cordelia pleaded. 'We just want to talk!'

But the Glovemaker skipped forward, evil intent written all over her face.

'DO A POLKA!' Cordelia yelled. 'With *grands jetés*!'

The Glovemaker's face puckered with fury as her feet obeyed the request. She leaped off across the Great Chamber.

'*Friends!*' came a joyous cry.

Cordelia's arms were suddenly clamped to her sides, as Bernard crushed her in a hug.

'Let go of me!' she grunted. 'Friends – don't – crush – each – other!'

She wriggled helplessly in the arms of the one Glovemaker who wasn't trying to harm them, while Goose struggled to wrench his wrist from the ribbon tying him to his deadly enemy.

A huge chunk of plasterwork fell – a Tudor rose the size of Cordelia's head. It crashed to the floor of the Great Chamber, and Sam only just managed to cling with her fingertips to the old stone wall beneath.

The Glovemaker began a violent Russian squat dance, kicking her way across the floor to visit vengeance on Cordelia.

'What do we *do*?' The breath was being squeezed from Cordelia's body. It was as though she had made friends with a python.

The plan had gone dreadfully wrong.

Salvation came in the nick of time.

The dancing Glovemaker suddenly folded to the floor, yawning. A dark purple nightcap had appeared on her head.

And then Goose's Glovemaker, who'd just had a Fond Bonnet crammed on to her head, enveloped him in a fierce hug – which was a slight improvement on the biting.

Cordelia glimpsed a movement on the stairs. She tried to twist round to see, but she couldn't move in Bernard's tight grip.

Seconds later, Sam's assailant was draped over the balcony, the fury in his eyes growing milder and milder: a nightcap had been slipped on to his head.

'Hey!' a voice piped up beside Cordelia. 'Let her go!'

Small fingers plucked at Bernard's hands.

The Glovemaker's arms loosened. Air rushed into Cordelia's lungs and she turned, with a sigh of relief, to see Tickory Watchmaker staring up at her solemnly.

'We've come for the peace talks,' Tickory announced.

'But things seem to have got a bit out of hand,' Hop Watchmaker said, from the stairs, as he surveyed the now-snoring Glovemaker.

Sam grinned. 'You're a little late!'

'Watchmakers are actually always exactly on time,' Hop told her politely. 'It's just that some people think we're late and some people think we're early. Grandfather says time is relative.'

Cordelia could not dispute this claim. The Watchmakers had saved them from the iron fists of the Glovemakers – their timing was impeccable.

She looked up at Sam, still clinging to the crumbling moulding. 'You all right?'

Sam hitched herself on to the safety of the windowsill.

'Yeah!' she called down. 'But look – there's somefing funny here on the wall! Some lines and gold bits.'

Sam kicked away a few loose lumps of plaster.

There were words, picked out in gold, carved into the dark-grey stone beneath the plaster.

MAKERS, UNITE!

The inscription shone like an order from an ancient god.

'A – little – help – here!' Goose's muffled voice came from the armpit of his erstwhile enemy, who was now crushing him in a hug of ardent friendship.

A few minutes later, the united forces of Hatmaker, Bootmaker and Watchmakers had arranged the Glovemakers in a line. They flopped them on to chairs and (just to be safe) tied them up with some old cloaks.

'It's the only way with bullies,' Sam declared, eyeing the Glovemakers from the safety of the windowsill. 'Gotta stop 'em, otherwise they'll rule yer world.'

The dancing Glovemaker kicked in her sleep, so they eased the clogs off her feet.

'I'm Violet,' her sister announced happily as Goose wrapped the cloak securely around her. 'That's my twin, Vera, sleeping like a lazybones. I like your hair! Does your mother cut it with a bowl? I could do mine the same and we'd be matching!'

'This isn't really ethical, is it?' Goose muttered, pulling Cordelia aside.

'Ethical?'

'I mean: it isn't *good* – it isn't *right*, is it?'

'It's not ideally how I'd like to make friends,' Cordelia admitted. 'And I'm pretty sure we're breaking at least half the Makers' rules . . .'

But she glanced up at the shining gold words they'd just discovered carved into the wall – words that had been hidden for hundreds of years.

MAKERS, UNITE!

'Look at that, Goose. It's a sign, don't you think? The Guildhall *wants* us to work together,' she said.

Goose looked doubtful. 'I'm not sure even *that* will persuade the Glovemakers.'

They turned back to the group. Bernard giggled as Hop and Tick wrapped a cloak round him.

'This is fun,' he said. 'Is it a game?'

'Yes,' Cordelia told him, making sure the cloak was tied securely. 'It's a game where we all have to be nice to each other.'

Once they were secured, everybody stood observing the captive Glovemakers. Two were snoozing soundly under their nightcaps, while the other two smiled beneath their Fond Bonnets.

'What do we do now?' Tick asked.

'We can't talk to them when they're asleep,' Cordelia pointed out.

'Though I do prefer them this way,' Goose added.

Like a chef removing a silver dome, Hop took off the two nightcaps.

Vera and her brother opened their eyes woozily.

'Glovemakers! We need to have peace talks!' Cordelia announced.

Two Glovemakers scowled sleepily back at her. The other two seemed eager.

'What a good idea!' Violet piped up.

'That sounds fun!' Bernard added, the Cully Gull feather on his Fond Bonnet quivering. 'What do you think, Buster?'

Buster Glovemaker's yawn showed all his teeth.

'Let's take your Fond Bonnets off, for the sake of fairness,' Goose suggested gallantly.

He removed Violet's bonnet. Violet immediately tried to bite his hand.

'You beastly Bootmaker!' She juddered her chair towards Goose, who jumped back.

Buster and Vera Glovemaker were no longer sleepy – they were angry. They wriggled and struggled.

'Let me go!'

'Untie this thing!'

Bernard shook his head when Cordelia went to take his bonnet off.

'I like it!' he insisted. 'It makes my brain feel all chocolatey and nice.'

'That's because it's a Fond Bonnet,' she told him.

The other three Glovemakers spluttered indignantly.

'A *Fond* Bonnet!'

'How *dare* you put one of your filthy hats on him!'

'You've poisoned his mind!'

'LISTEN!' Cordelia shouted over them. 'We need to stop *fighting*! Even if we have different ideas about how things should be done. Even if all the grown-up Makers refuse to talk to each other; even if they hate each other – we need to be kinder and wiser and braver than them! We need to make the effort to see things from each other's point of view, and not be mean or hateful. We can do it – I know we can!'

'*Friends forever!*' Bernard cried happily.

The other three Glovemakers looked mutinous.

'Hatmakers make hats that steal your thoughts!'

'Bootmakers run off with people's souls!'

'Watchmakers use children's finger bones in their watches!'

'That's not true!' Tick objected.

'I thought that about the Watchmakers too,' Goose confessed. 'But we visited their workshop and they're actually amazing. I think we need to forget some of the things grown-ups have told us and start finding things out for ourselves.'

'Exactly!' Cordelia shot Goose a proud look, even as three of the four Glovemakers spluttered rudely.

She pointed at the crests over the doors of the Makers' workshops. Each crest had seven stars etched round its edge.

'There's a star for each Maker family on all our crests. And the seventh star symbolizes how we're brightest and strongest when we're working together.'

'The Guildhall *wants* us to work together,' Hop added, pointing to the words MAKERS, UNITE! shining above them. 'Look!'

Violet Glovemaker growled at Cordelia, 'As soon as you untie me, I will crush your head with one of your own hat blocks.'

'And I'll pin you to the wall with one of the swordsticks I found,' said Buster as he glared at the Watchmakers.

'I'll jam those clogs so hard on to your feet you'll be dancing till your feet fall off,' Vera promised Goose darkly.

'Oh, don't be such spoilsports!' Bernard cajoled his siblings.

Cordelia, Hop, Tick and Goose retreated so far that they found their backs against the wall of the Great Chamber. Sam shifted uncomfortably on the windowsill above them.

'I don't think these peace talks are going to work,' Cordelia admitted ruefully, observing the Glovemakers' gnashing teeth. 'We can't force them to wear Fond Bonnets forever . . .'

'So what do we do now?' Hop was trembling.

'We can't leave them like this!' Goose pointed out. 'We'll have to untie them some time or they'll starve, and then we'll be murderers!'

But if they were freed, the Glovemakers would fulfil their violent promises with terrible relish.

'Tell you what,' Bernard said, smiling. 'Untie me first, and I'll give you a head start before I untie *them* – in the name of friendship! Ten seconds!'

Cordelia, Goose, Sam and the Watchmakers eventually agreed. And, as soon as they'd freed Bernard, they fled without hesitation.

'That was a disaster!' Goose gasped, as they tumbled out of the Guildhall into the shabby square.

'And here's another one!' Cordelia wailed.

Thick veils of shadow ash were falling through the air, like malicious whispers.

Hop and Tick scampered away, arms covering their faces, while Goose stumbled back to Bootmaker Mansion through the dark-falling veil. Cordelia and Sam hurried to Hatmaker House, tired and bruised and wincing every time a speck of ash landed on their skin.

Another magical place being destroyed! Cordelia despaired, tearing upstairs. Her heart broke as she wondered what magical site it might be this time.

She hurled herself on to her father's bed and crushed her face into the pillow.

'I'm *failing* as a Mapmaker! I don't know what else to *do*!'

'Cor?'

She felt a small hand on her shoulder. It was Sam.

'Sorry.' Cordelia sniffed, sitting up. 'I'm in your room. Sorry.'

Sam shook her head. 'That's all right, Cor. Stay.'

Cordelia wiped a smudge of shadow from her face. Wretchedness bubbled inside her, and the Insidious Ink Squid of suspicion that she had pushed into the depths yesterday surged back to the surface, uncurling its tentacles.

'If you're still working for Witloof, please just tell me where he is!' Cordelia burst out. 'I've *got* to stop him somehow!'

Sam looked horrified. 'Why – why would ya think I'm working for him?'

'That money, hidden in the lamp!' Cordelia cried. 'Where did you get it, if it wasn't from Witloof? It was you he was talking to outside the window of the Tower, wasn't it? Did you steal for him again?'

Sam backed away, shaking her head.

'You really fink I'd work for that monster outta choice? To make *money*?' she whispered. 'Cor, how could ya say that? How could ya *think* that?'

Cordelia felt the ash still clinging to her skin. She wanted so much to believe Sam, but the shadows shrouding her made it hard to think anything good.

'You promise you're not working for Witloof?' she croaked.

'I promise – *honest*!' Sam cried. 'I *stole* that money, Cor,' she added in a small, miserable voice. 'Before I knew ya. Back when I was a pickpocket.'

She crouched on the floor in a sad little ball.

'I hid the money in the tower of the Guildhall ages ago. When I went back to check on the fireflies the other day, I fetched it. Didn't want the Glovemakers to find it. Cos I . . . I'm . . .'

Sam looked around the room, as though taking in a place she would miss very much.

'I'm saving up to try 'n' get to my brother. I'm gonna try 'n' get a passage on a ship and get him back. I miss him so much it hurts, like there's somefing stuck in my chest that's stopping me breathin' right.'

Cordelia knew that feeling exactly – she missed her father so much the grief had taken up space in the squeeze of her heart. It lived there like a creature, breathing air meant for her.

'I'd do nearly *anyfing* to get Len back – but I wouldn't work for Witloof again, *ever*!' Sam said fiercely. 'I didn't tell ya about my plan cos I thought ya'd think I . . . I didn't wanna be yer sister.'

Cordelia bounded across the room and crushed Sam in a hug so ferocious it rivalled the hugs of even the grizzliest bears.

'Oh, Sam! We'll *always* be sisters, no matter what!' she whispered. 'And we'll get Len back somehow. I promise.'

Sam's face was smeared with shadows, but the light in her eyes grew stronger. She reached under the bed and pulled out a soft cocoon. A dozen Dulcet Fireflies flitted out, dancing around the room to greet the evening.

The soft glimmer of their light gently brushed away Cordelia's and Sam's sadness. The children sat in silence a long time as their hearts gradually grew lighter, though outside the ash still rained steadily from the sky.

'Len loves lights and flames and all sorts,' Sam said eventually. 'He'd love to hear about the Lightbringers. He used to tell me stories, using the moonlight to make shadow puppets, cos we couldn't afford candles. I miss his stories.'

Cordelia missed the stories her father used to tell her too. They would snuggle up on the very bed she and Sam were sitting on now, and he would open *The Mythmaker* and read the tales aloud, the world transformed in the flickering firelight.

'I'll tell you a story, Sam,' she said.

'Really?' Sam looked hopeful. Her fireflies buzzed around her head.

'Get comfy.' Cordelia smiled. 'I'll be right back.'

Cordelia dashed upstairs and retrieved her father's old book from the hatbox under her bed. When she returned, she found Sam curled up on a blanket, her eyes eager and the fireflies settled like stars in her hair.

Cordelia settled next to her on the bed.

'*Once upon a time*,' Cordelia began, opening the old book at her favourite story, '*a young queen called Guinevere got lost in the forest near Camelot*.'

Guinevere had wandered in the forest all day, following a stream and picking the wild strawberries that grew on the mossy banks. But as the day grew dusky, she realized she had strayed far from the castle, and she didn't know which direction would take her safely home.

The night grew dark around her and the woods were thick with shadows. Guinevere was valiant and had a heart full of courage, but she was afraid of the dark: she knew it hid monsters. Not the usual kinds of monsters: not fire-breathing dragons from the old tales, or ghouls with vicious claws and teeth. These monsters were men who hunted creatures in the darkening woods and killed anything living, to take its skin.

If they caught her, they would drag her away to separate her soul from her body.

She heard their hunting horn, bone-shakingly close, and fled.

She ran and ran.

At last, she stumbled into a starlit clearing in the forest. There, in the middle of the clearing, she found a bear cub. The cub's mother had been killed by the hunters, and the poor little creature was all alone.

But even a motherless cub can be brave and strong.

Little Bear knew his way through the woods. Even though he was small and scared, he led Guinevere home by a secret path, back to Camelot.

Nobody who lived in the castle had slept all night. When the hunting horn in the forest sounded like a howl above the trees, they feared the worst for Guinevere. Everybody gathered in the courtyard, anxiously awaiting her return.

Just before dawn, Guinevere stumbled through the gates, scratched by thorns, tired and blistered and bruised, but safe. Everyone who loved her crowded round.

'How did you escape the hunters?'

'How did you survive?'

'How did you find your way home?'

'It was the Little Bear!' Guinevere told them joyfully. 'He led me home!'

As she turned to thank him, Little Bear disappeared in the dawn light.

Guinevere felt strangely sad. She was glad to be home and safe, but she loved Little Bear dearly. Merlin, the great wizard, saw her heart sadden as she realized she could not keep the Little Bear close, because he was a wild creature, and wild beings of all kinds need freedom.

'Don't worry, Guinevere,' Merlin said to her. 'Little Bear will always be with you to show you the way when you are lost in the dark.'

What Merlin said came true. From that day onwards, whenever Guinevere went wandering in the woods, she would wait until dark, and find Little Bear in the forest clearing. If she was ever lost, he showed her the way home, and he watched over her for the rest of her days.

As Cordelia finished the story, the fireflies winked in and out of light on Sam's head, glowing like the notes of a lullaby come to life. Sam's eyes closed and she heaved a sleepy sigh.

Cordelia felt her heart ache with missing her father.

He would close the book and say, 'So, littlest Hatmaker, Guinevere was never afraid of the dark again.'

'I'm not afraid either, Father!' Cordelia would declare.

But she was afraid of the dark now. Not the deep velvet of night that showed stars in it. She was afraid of the flakes of ruined magic that fell as shadows through the air.

She had found the place her father had sent her to. And she was doing her best to protect the magical places now she was a Mapmaker. But . . .

'There's something I can't see, Father,' she said. 'Something you meant me to see that I haven't seen. Isn't there?'

She felt like Guinevere in the woods, lost in the dark and afraid.

There was a cymbal-crash above the house, a sudden percussion of rain on the roof, and the music of water rushing down gutters. Another storm striking the sky out of nowhere, meeting the earth with an unearthly power.

Once again, rain came and flayed the night.

CHAPTER 28

A shadow closed round Hatmaker House, denser than mere night-dark. It twisted round chimneys and coiled as dreams into Cordelia's sleep.

A Harpy visited darkness on her.

It tore her mother from the deck of a ship, a frenzied writhing of wings and limbs, into the lightning-struck sky.

'Dilly!'

Aunt Ariadne's voice woke Cordelia from her nightmare.

She had fallen asleep next to Sam last night. Someone had come and tucked the quilt round them both as they slept.

'There's a customer downstairs to see you,' Aunt Ariadne told her. 'He said it was something urgent.'

Cordelia looked out of the window to see it was still dark outside. 'In the middle of the night?' she asked in confusion.

'It's morning, Dilly – but another ash storm started at dawn. The sun can hardly shine through at all. And on the day of the Harvest Masque!'

Cordelia eased herself out of bed, careful to leave Sam sleeping. Ash was clotted on the windows, turning the world dark.

'*Another* place burning!'

The customer with the urgent question must be –

'I'm going to check the starlight in the bowl,' Aunt Ariadne called, disappearing up on to the roof. 'I'm afraid it's been ruined again!'

Three seconds later, Cordelia was thundering down the stairs.

Peregrine stood, shredding the feather of his tricorn, in the middle of the shop. A shroud of soot shifted like a shadow around him. He left a dark ghost of it across the floor. He plunged his hands into his pockets and pulled out handfuls of black ash.

'Miss Hatmaker!' he whispered. 'Something terrible has happened!'

On a stretch of the Thames where no island had ever been seen before, not far from Blackfriars Bridge, was a bar of burnt land. Smoke rose from the charred skeleton of a large tree, and the dense reeds that had lined the lagoon were reduced to smouldering scrub. It looked like a sliver of the Underworld, dredged up from below.

A sob rose in Cordelia's throat.

Peregrine rowed the coracle closer. There was no need for the map to show them the secret way in: the magic that had hidden Peregrine's island from the outside world for centuries had gone.

Cordelia drew her cloak closer over her face, squinting at the island as the coracle bumped the shore. Bargemen had stopped their craft mid-river and drifted, mouths agape.

A bargeman's voice carried across the water: 'I wou'n't go on thar, mate!'

Peregrine ignored him, stepping ashore. Ash billowed around him but he didn't seem to care. He staggered on to the island.

Cordelia could not bear to step out of the boat, on to earth that had once been so green and vibrant but was now ruined and lifeless. It was unspeakably sad: the kind of sadness that swallows you whole.

'But . . . how did Witloof get in?' she wondered, shuddering as a flake of shadow ash slipped down her neck. 'How did he find –'

'Cordelia, where is the Westerly Map?' Peregrine called, his voice suddenly desperate. 'This will all stop if we assemble Merlin's Map – your piece is the only one we're waiting for!'

Cordelia shook her head.

'I can't find it anywhere,' she admitted, adding quickly, 'but my friends and I, we've been trying another plan – trying to unite the Makers. That's how we can beat Witloof – we just need to –'

'*No!*' Peregrine wailed. 'No other plan will work! It *has* to be the map! That's the only thing that will stop his senseless destruction!'

'I think it went down with my father's ship,' Cordelia said in a small voice.

'Then it's hopeless!' He sobbed, sinking to his knees beneath the skeletal remains of the Ardourwood Tree. Tears cut lines down the shadows on his face.

'Nothing's ever *hopeless*,' Cordelia argued. 'Not if you have hope! We can catch Witloof coming out of a map – we just need to work together –'

A splash of oars in the water made her look round. She spotted a boat coming downstream. The person in it was cloaked and rowing hard.

'Peregrine!' Cordelia hissed, but he didn't hear her. He was kneeling in the ash at the bottom of the ruined Ardourwood Tree.

The rower of the approaching boat paused to pull his cloak further over his head.

'Very *Witloofy*,' Cordelia said, narrowing her eyes. She shifted position, taking hold of the oars.

She squinted sideways at the boat and saw the figure reach into a bag and pull something out. There was a flash of glass –

'STOP!' Cordelia shouted. She saw a blur of Peregrine turning. But there was no time to wait; she pushed off from the island, the coracle rocking.

Witloof – she was certain it was him – thrashed his oars in the water, pulling away at speed.

'STOP!' Cordelia bellowed. 'WITLOOF!'

The coracle was light and fast, its Fleetwood hull slicing through the water. But her arms, unused to rowing, were burning with the effort.

Suddenly rain came lashing down, so ferocious it roiled the river all around her. The boat bucked, and water sloshed in the bottom. It was as though somebody had emptied a bucket the size of the sky over her head. Then, as quickly as it had started, the rain stopped.

A scouring wind followed, pushing her back downstream as it whistled past.

Cordelia looked over her shoulder. Witloof was still in her sights. But with each stroke he was drawing away. She redoubled her efforts, even though her arms felt as though they were on fire and she could feel blisters bulging on her palms.

The next time she looked over her shoulder, the river behind her was empty.

But across the agitated waves she saw a boat slip under a water gate – a tall, rusty gate bared like rotten teeth over the river.

She steered towards it.

It was like a mouth trying to drink the river – its gullet choked with weeds. In decaying metal letters above it she saw the words:

STORM-EYE HALL

Cordelia guided her boat into the iron jaws.

The weed-choked channel beyond the water gate led to a rotting boathouse.

Cordelia moored the coracle and climbed old stone steps, slick with lichen, up a steep slope through thick trees. The undergrowth was a mess of nettles.

She stole through a vast overgrown garden towards a looming mansion. A hulking stone gargoyle squatted on the roof of the tallest tower, its wings furled.

Inside, it was cold – the kind of cold that goes straight to a body's bones. Light seeped in through grimy windows like leaking water, green and weak. Wet footprints made a trail across the floor of the grand entrance hall and up a stone staircase.

Cordelia wished Goose and Sam were here. Goose's knees would wobble, and Sam would scratch her nose twitchily, and they might be just as scared as she was, but Cordelia would be made braver if they were by her side.

She considered turning tail and running away – she could come back with the others. Three against one were much better odds against Witloof.

But the wet footprints on the stairs were drying. Witloof was here, now, in this very building – and this was her chance to do her duty as a Mapmaker and stop him destroying any more magical places. She had to try.

'Can't be brave if I don't get scared,' she whispered to herself.

She crept across the hall towards the decaying staircase. Curtains of cobwebs hung in the windows and rusting suits of armour slumped by the doors. A rotten oil painting, featuring a dozen villainous-looking aristocrats, hung above a grand staircase. Cordelia's eye was drawn to the bottom corner of the painting: a mean-eyed boy lurked beside a cradle, sneering contemptuously.

She recognized him instantly.

'Witloof!'

It was like his eyes were watching her.

Cordelia tugged a rusty sword from an old suit of armour. Carrying it in both hands, she followed the damp footprints up the decrepit stairs and into a gallery decorated with tattered tapestries. The footprints led to a closed door.

Cordelia listened, heart beating hard. Somebody was moving around inside the room.

Gripping the sword hilt, she kicked the door open and charged through.

Witloof turned in a whirl of cloak.

The sword was too heavy to raise; it fell to the floor with a *clang*. Weaponless, Cordelia launched herself forward, unleashing a battle cry: '*RAAAAH!*'

Her shoulders connected with a soft body – it gave way.

By the time she reached the tail end of her battle cry, Cordelia was sitting firmly on her quarry.

'SURRENDER!' she yelled.

'Get *off* me!' came an indignant voice from inside the cloak.

An indignant voice that did not belong to Witloof.

A hand freed itself from the folds of fabric and swiped the hood aside. A frizz of hair, like a wind-blown cloud, emerged, followed by –

'*You!*' Cordelia cried.

She was surprised to find that she was sitting on Win Fairweather, the woman she had met in the Sargasso Chocolate House. Win wore a fairly unruffled expression, considering she had just been jumped upon.

'Kindly unhand me, Miss Hatmaker,' she requested. 'And, if you possibly could, find somewhere else to sit. There are plenty of chairs.'

'What are you doing here?' Cordelia demanded, scrambling to her feet.

'An odd question, considering you're in my house!' Win peeled herself off the floor.

'This can't be *your* house!' Cordelia said.

'Why on earth can't it?' Win dusted off her rather dusty clothes.

'Because this is Lord Witloof's house. He's in the family portrait on the stairs.'

'You recognized him?' Win asked, motes of dust billowing in the sunlight around her. She fixed her eyes on Cordelia. They were the kind of eyes that could stare down an eagle.

'He is my brother,' she said. 'My real name is Winifred Witloof.'

Cordelia staggered backwards, feeling her face warp with horror.

'Wait!' Win held up a hand.

For a strange moment Cordelia felt Win must be a wizard who had cast a spell to stop her. Then she realized it was the note of desperation in Win's voice that did it.

'Please,' Win whispered. 'I'm not like my brother.'

Cordelia managed to stop herself diving sideways out of the door, but she snatched up the sword and pointed it at Win.

Win strode away from her, into the middle of the huge room.

'You keep the sword and stay there,' Win called from the far end. 'I'll be all the way over here. Now we can talk.'

Cordelia narrowed her eyes. This could be some kind of trick. She poked the door as wide open as she could with the tip of the sword, to make sure she had an escape route.

'Where is your brother?' Cordelia demanded.

'No idea,' Win replied. 'I'm the one offering a reward for information about his whereabouts, remember?'

Cordelia frowned. 'Why *are* you offering that reward?'

'I made a mistake,' Win admitted with a sigh. 'And I'm trying to stop that mistake from getting any worse.'

Something about her mouth made Cordelia believe her. It was the way the words came out: reluctantly.

'What was the mistake?'

Win shuffled her feet in the dust.

'I helped him escape his execution.'

Cordelia's shock must have shown on her face, because Win burst out, 'He's the only family I have left! Witloofs don't abandon each other, no matter what! But I said I would only help him on one condition: that he leave the country and never come back. He agreed, so I unleashed a storm that would distract everyone enough for him to get away.'

She made a sudden movement. Cordelia flinched, jerking the sword. But Win had only thrown her arms round herself in a self-pitying hug.

'But of course he didn't keep his word.' Her shoulders shook slightly. 'I waited for hours with a carriage, ready to smuggle him to the docks, as we'd planned. But he never came. He'd never intended to.'

Cordelia's heart squeezed with sudden pity, but she reminded herself sternly that she needed *answers*. And she was dealing with a *Witloof*. She had to stay on guard.

'What d'you mean, you "unleashed a storm"?' she asked.

Win squared her shoulders and sniffed. 'I got right under the scaffold. I was wearing that excellent hat I'd bought from you only hours earlier, so nobody noticed me. I waited until just before the execution was meant to happen – my brother wanted the storm to strike at the most dramatic moment – and then I smashed a Thunderhead jar. He got away in the chaos.'

This explained the strangeness of that storm! It had erupted, fully formed, out of a –

'*A jar?*' Cordelia repeated. 'But how did you –'

'I can brew weather,' Win said. 'I'm a Weather Brewer.'

Cordelia sensed a defiant kind of shine around the words.

'When we were children, my brother – being the son and heir – was sent to school. I had to stay at home and learn to be a *lady*. Father thought Grandmother was teaching me ladylike things, like embroidery and deportment, but *really* I was learning to stitch sea mists together, and weave bits of rainbow and make lace nets to catch clouds in. It's amazing what you can get away with if you look busy sewing whenever the men poke their heads into the room.'

Cordelia grinned in spite of herself.

'So it's been *you* causing the storms!' she cried. 'I thought it was him!'

Win barked a bitter laugh.

'My brother has only ever used storms for personal gain. Just like all the Witloofs before him.'

She stared moodily at the wall for a moment, then took a deep breath.

'I should tell you, Miss Hatmaker . . . There's a truth about my family that's been secret for centuries.'

She swept an arm around the huge room.

All Cordelia could see was tables covered in junk. Vast paintings of seascapes lined the walls. At the far end of the room, a wide window looked out over the tangled garden, where statues were drowning slowly in the green grip of ivy.

She could not see what 'truth' Win was trying to show her.

'The truth is, the Witloofs are wreckers.'

'Wreckers?' Cordelia repeated. 'You mean *ship wreckers*?'

'Exactly so.'

Win pointed to an enormous painting hanging on the wall, in which a chalk-faced Queen Elizabeth stood on a windswept clifftop. A wiry man was hunched beside her, his eyes trained on the approaching boats.

'That is Wendel Witloof,' Win said. 'My ancestor.'

Behind them, ships flying Spanish colours approached, bristling with cannons and malice.

'Queen Elizabeth needed help – the Spanish were coming with their Armada to attack England. Wendel was a notorious wrecker; his storms had sunk a thousand ships by the time the queen's people sought him out to help defend the realm. Of course, all Making had been banned decades before, by the queen's own father, King Henry, so the choice for Wendel was either to obey or be thrown in the Tower for treasonous Making.'

'But wrecking ships isn't Making!' Cordelia argued.

'My ancestors didn't simply stand on the cliff with a lantern to lure ships on to the rocks: they made the storms that wrecked the ships. Weather Brewing is an ancient kind of Maker magic, and Wendel Witloof was an expert. He captured storms and mixed them up in the most potent combinations he could think of.'

Win pointed at the next painting. It showed Wendel Witloof on a blustery shore, surrounded by what appeared to be a collection of strange fishing equipment. Empty jars stood on the rocks beside him. He held a huge copper funnel and a net hung above him in the sky like a kite. On the horizon, cracked clouds spilled lightning.

'What's he doing?' Cordelia asked.

'Collecting ingredients.'

The look on Wendel's face was like the storm in the distance: there was something charged and dangerous about it. Cordelia could see tiny cracks of lightning reflected in his eyes.

'Wendel Witloof saw his chance for greatness,' Win said. 'He created the most violent storm that had ever been made. He bottled it in very strong glass jars and sent it out, the way the ancient Greeks used to do, into the midst of their enemy's ships. The jars were to be opened exactly when they would cause the most destruction. First lightning, then hurricanes.'

In the next painting, indigo and black smeared the sky. The Spanish ships reared and plunged, caught between the roiling sea and the furious sky. Cordelia could almost taste the saltwater flaying the air. Wendel Witloof stood on the cliffs above, his arms raised as if he was the conductor of a great orchestra.

The following painting was a confusion of fire and waves. Ships were broken open, smashed to splinters and eaten by flames. The artist had taken special care to depict expressions of exquisite terror and suffering on the drowning Spaniards' faces as they were gnashed in the teeth of the sea.

'The Spanish Armada was smashed to pieces. Queen Elizabeth gave a speech telling everyone it was God's doing. Of course, it was *really* all down to a wrecker, but she couldn't admit it: that would have been a scandal! The queen herself using illegal Making! Also, I think she liked to encourage the rumour that God was smiling on *her* specifically. It definitely wound up the Catholics.'

The final painting showed a calm sea. The broken bodies of ships and sailors littered the shoreline as the victorious queen stood magnificent on the cliff, gilded with sunlight pouring down on her from heaven. Wendel was next to her, dressed in velvet finery.

'The queen had to keep Wendel quiet, though,' Win explained. 'She gave him a fortune in gold and made him a lord, but all on one condition: nobody could ever know the truth about the storm that saved England. Wendel agreed. He stopped wrecking ships and took up politics. A different kind of wrecking, you might say.

'Ever since Wendel, the first Lord Witloof, became the queen's Special Advisor for the Destruction of Enemies, the Witloofs have had a place in the royal palace. A Witloof has been behind most diplomatic disasters of the past two centuries. Most recently, of course, my brother tried to wreck the peace talks between England and France.'

'If he wanted to ruin the peace talks, why didn't he just cause a storm?' Cordelia wondered.

'A good question with a simple answer: gold.'

Win's mouth puckered. 'As we grew up, my brother and I became aware that our family fortune was slipping away. It's now entirely gone, lost to the pockets of better gamblers than my father. As the Witloof riches dwindled, my brother's obsession with gold grew.'

'He wanted to get gold by selling cannons!'

'Exactly! My brother had the cannon factory ready. I imagine he aimed to leave diplomacy in tatters, so there would be no choice but to start a war.'

'He very nearly managed it.' Cordelia grimaced. She remembered how close the King of France had been to declaring war on England.

And she remembered something else: Witloof scowling at her on the deck of the Royal Galleon.

There are other ways to make gold. Greater and more terrible ways to do it.

'But *you* stopped him,' Win murmured. 'It makes sense, really. Wreckers are the opposite of Makers: wreckers destroy; Makers create. Perhaps only a Maker can stop a wrecker.'

'But what does this have to do with your brother's dark rain?' Cordelia asked. 'Is it a kind of wrecking weather?'

Win slunk across the room and began sorting through a collection of jars arranged on one of the tables.

'My brother wasn't interested in Weather Brewing,' she muttered. 'He took after our mother's side of the family. *Her* father was a Grimaldi, one of the great Glassmakers of Venice. Whitstable persuaded Grandfather to share the forbidden secrets of creating Leechglass.'

Cordelia gripped the sword hilt, knuckles suddenly white.

'He knows how to make Leechglass?' she gasped. 'I thought the secret was lost!'

Win shook her head. 'The Grimaldi family claimed it was lost, but it wasn't,' she said shortly. 'My brother knows the secret. All *I* know about it is that Leechglass is created by burning a great deal of magic in a blazing Vulcan furnace. Shadow ash always falls whenever Leechglass is being made, because making it destroys magic utterly.'

Win's expression grew dark, as though shadow ash was falling in her head.

'Years ago, once he'd learned how to make it, my brother's experiments choked the top floor of this house with shadow ash, day and night. He burned my mother's entire garden of Gladsome Roses to make a pocket watch. Next, to make a Leechglass knife, he fed my pet Flabbercrest into his furnace, along with my father's entire collection of magical hats. Shadow ash filled the corridors. I'm familiar with the black despair it brings – I had to find ways to clear the air and I discovered nothing but a good strong rainstorm would do it. I often got in trouble as a child, for making it rain indoors.'

Win jutted her jaw and Cordelia thought she could see the defiant child Win had been.

'And, after all this time, nothing much has really changed.' Win tossed a pile of nets aside and moved some delicate glass bottles across the table. 'He's still creating shadow ash and I'm still trying to clean up after him.'

Cordelia finally understood: rather than being part of Witloof's destruction, each storm had actually chased the shadow ash away, scouring the skies and streets. Win must have been constantly on the lookout for signs of it. At the Sargasso, she had disappeared just as the ash began to fall. Minutes later, the storm had cleared the sky.

'He could be making something out of Leechglass,' Cordelia said.

She could not imagine how much Leechglass Witloof could have made with the amount of magic he had burned these past few days.

'Whether he's making something or simply doing it to create chaos and misery, I don't know,' Win said grimly. 'But my guess is that he's going to strike again tonight, at the Harvest Masque.'

Cordelia's stomach swooped. The Harvest Masque would be the perfect place for Witloof to unleash more shadow ash: half of London would be there.

Win pulled a heavy jar across the table, knocking a small glass bottle. It smashed with a tinkle on the floor. A quick, cold wind burst into the room.

'Aah, sorry!' Win exclaimed. 'Broke a Zephyr Vessel!'

The wind twisted Cordelia's hair over her face and swirled her skirt round her legs. The gust spiralled across the dusty floor like a spinning top, polishing a path clean. It messed around in the tattered curtains but exhausted itself quickly, lulling into mutters.

'Sorry about that!' Win smiled. 'Lucky it was only a little one. Not like *this* one!'

She held up a heavy green glass jar. It looked ancient, its cork bung sealed with purple wax.

'This is the last jar of the Armada storm,' she said, her voice trembling with emotion as she hugged it to her chest. 'Wendel made thirteen jars in all, but he only needed twelve. It's been handed down in my family for nearly two hundred years: the storm that brought the Witloofs glory and riches.'

Cordelia realized it wasn't emotion that was making Win's voice shake: it was the force of the storm trapped inside the jar.

'Won't the glass break?' Cordelia asked, grasping her sword, as if it could somehow fight the might of a hurricane.

Win shook her head, teeth clacking.

'The Witloofs have a f-family recipe to make g-glass strong enough to hold e-even the b-biggest st-storms.' She set the jar down on the table. 'It's actually *because* of the ancient Witloof recipe that we ended up with a Grimaldi in the family.' Win's voice was perfectly normal now that she wasn't clutching the shuddering storm. 'Grandfather Grimaldi came to London wanting to learn about the technique of making

Storm Glass, fell in love with my grandmother, and never went back to Venice.'

Cordelia watched as Win strapped a thick leather belt securely round the jar. Then she peered up again at the shipwreck painting. Above a flaming sail, right where a spear of lightning struck out of a bruise-coloured cloud, the wind had taken shape. It was almost invisible – but she could see something . . .

Something that looked like vengeance given wings.

'What *is* that?' Cordelia's voice came out as a croak.

'Ah,' Win said. 'You've spotted her. The murkiest part of my family history . . . It was rumoured that Wendel had help sending the storms out into the midst of the Spanish ships.'

She turned and strode to the end of the room. Cordelia followed.

Win tore the curtains aside.

A creature carved from sea-bitten wood loomed above them. Muscular wings hunched on its back. Hands clutched the air, talons where fingers should be. Writhing hair framed a ferocious face, and a demon-shriek of fangs screamed silently down.

It was a winged creature, clawed and full of fury.

A word, written in her father's hand, flashed in front of Cordelia's eyes. The dotted lines on the sea chart – the circle where the ship had sunk . . .

'Our family ship was named after Wendel's rumoured assistant,' Win said. 'The *Harpy*.'

CLANG.

The sword dropped from Cordelia's hands. She heard Win's voice from far away, reaching her across something vast and dark. Around her, the paintings reeled in a blue blur. The floor bucked like the deck of a sinking ship. She found herself on her knees in the middle of the floor, a truth hard in her head.

Witloof had caused not just one of her family's ships to sink. *He had caused two!*

He had wrecked not only the *Jolly Bonnet*, but also the *Jaunty Bicorn*.

He had caused the wreck that killed her mother.

The dark shape of a ship followed them across the ocean. The ship's snarling figurehead plunged and clawed through the water, sea-foam surging around it, sharp barnacles clinging to its wooden wings. The dark ship *Harpy* hurtled towards the *Jaunty Bicorn*.

The storm struck the Hatmaker ship like disaster out of a blue sky. Lightning threw spears of flame into the rigging. A wind caused a vortex round the mast.

Under a cauldron of black clouds, the Hatmakers' ship came apart. Fire made blazing flags of the sails, shuddered down the mast and ripped the ship right to the keel. The crew were swallowed by the ravening sea.

Stella Hatmaker fought through burning chaos to save her daughter. She emerged through a calamity of fire and water, clutching a hatbox in her arms, and threw it to safety across flames and waves.

Prospero Hatmaker plunged into the roiling sea to catch the hatbox. When he surfaced, his wife was gone. He was alone on the ocean, the tiny Cordelia wet and wriggling in her hatbox beside him. A piece of hull was the only thing left to cling to.

The storm evaporated as quickly as it had come, leaving a broken ship and a heartbroken man behind.

On the blue horizon, the *Harpy* was sailing away.

Win peered anxiously down at Cordelia.

'Are you all right, Miss Hatmaker?'

Cordelia's world had changed.

'Witloof caused the storm that killed my mother,' she said.

A tide of grief rose from some deep she didn't know she had. It swelled through her, dark as heartbreak, and pushed all the air from her chest.

Win had her hands over her face.

'My brother did that?' she whispered. 'To Stella?'

Grief gripped Cordelia's throat. It hurt to speak.

'You – you knew my mother?'

It was clutching for a star when you're drowning at sea.

'My brother was friends with your father once,' Win said. 'They met at university, and your father used to visit us in the summer holidays. One day he announced he'd found the woman of his dreams. Of course I insisted on meeting her. She was . . . she was simply wonderful. Full of stories and laughter, bright as a constellation. His *Little Bear* – that's what he used to call her.'

'Little Bear?'

Something tiny clicked into place in Cordelia's mind, like the smallest part of a clock that suddenly makes everything work perfectly.

'I've got to get home!' she gasped.

'Miss Hatmaker, what in the wide sky is the matter?'

'No time to explain!'

Cordelia knew where the Westerly Map was. It was not at the bottom of the sea! Her father had given it to her the day he left for his last voyage. It was in Hatmaker House: it had been there all along. She had held it in her hands only yesterday!

Win hurried behind her, down to the boathouse.

Cordelia shoved the coracle out on to the water and clambered in. Win broke open another Zephyr Vessel on the shore. The wind caught the boat and urged it along.

'SEE YOU AT THE MASQUE!' Win shouted. 'Be ready for ANYTHING!'

'YES!' Cordelia yelled back, wrestling with the oars. 'I WILL BE!'

The tower of Storm-Eye Hall disappeared behind the dark trees.

Cordelia was so intent on rowing the boat, she didn't notice that the great winged gargoyle had gone from the roof.

The wind pushed her down the Thames much quicker than she'd rowed up it, wind and water conspiring to get her back as fast as possible.

Her belly was filled with lightning-strikes and a great thunderhead of heartbreak swelled her chest. *Witloof killed my mother. And he tried to kill my father.*

She did not allow the thought *Perhaps he succeeded* to catch up with her – she rowed as hard as she could to get away from it.

She contained a storm: clouds that couldn't break yet. There was too much to do. *Rain, come later.*

Peregrine, stranded on his island in the shadow of the charred tree, saw her return.

She hailed him frantically, and he clambered into the boat. There was no time to apologize for abandoning him.

'I know where it is!' she panted. 'The map!'

His face, which had been shrouded in shadows, was suddenly lit with a small ray of hope.

'Oh, Miss Hatmaker, are you certain?' he said.

'Almost completely!'

The boat bumped across the waves as they rowed to the bank.

'All may yet be saved!' Peregrine cried. 'I shall inform the other Mapmakers right away – the ceremony at the Library of Maps can take place at midnight!'

Cordelia found the age-battered copy of *The Mythmaker* lying on Sam's bed where she had left it. Grateful that her family were occupied in the shop, selling hats to last-minute masque revellers, she scrambled up the ladder to her room and threw herself on to her bed.

The Mythmaker had a leather cover worn smooth with age, and it whispered adventures from every page. The book looked the same as ever, felt the same as ever, *smelled* the same as ever . . . But Cordelia's nose tingled, the way it did when there was big magic close by.

Her father had handed this book to her the day he left for his last voyage – the voyage from which he'd never returned.

'Look for hidden messages in stories, littlest Hatmaker,' he had said. 'They are the stars that can lead you through life.'

Every tale in *The Mythmaker* thrilled with magic, with giants and dragons and wizards. There was even a story about how Merlin had made Stonehenge – the very place where the Mapmakers believed he had hidden the Elixir Oak!

Cordelia examined the book. Its spine was ridged, like vertebrae stacked on top of each other. Inside the back cover, scratched into the leather in the bottom corner, was a tiny face. His beard curled in wisps, his eyes were wide, his hair wild.

The North Wind!

He appeared to be trying to blow the cover off the book.

The very corner of the cover was loose.

Cordelia pulled it.

With a soft creak of old leather, the back cover came away.

Hidden in the curve of the spine, a small crystal vial was nestled in a bed of dried moss. It looked so at home there that Cordelia realized this must be where her father had *always* kept it hidden, inside a storybook.

Hardly breathing, she lifted the vial out of its hiding place. It was filled with gleaming water.

'This is it!' she whispered. The missing piece of Merlin's Map had been under her bed all this time, hidden among her treasures.

Two minutes later, Gertrude, the pale-grey Quest Pigeon, was cutting a path above London's rooftops towards

Blackfriars Bridge, a note to Peregrine in a tiny bottle tied to her leg.

'Cor?' It was Sam, poking her head round the door. Cordelia clutched the crystal vial to her chest, hiding it.

'Where ya bin, Cor?' Sam grinned. 'It's almost time for the masque!'

Cordelia felt a tickle of excitement in her belly. 'Time to get ready!'

'Whatcha gonna wear?' Sam asked. 'You never said.'

Cordelia smiled.

'It's a surprise.'

CHAPTER 32

Great-aunt Petronella had announced that she preferred moon-bathing by her observatory window to having her bones jangled at Vauxhall. Cordelia slipped into the Alchemy Parlour to say goodbye before she left for the masque.

The lilac fire flickered and the spirit chimes clinked. Great-aunt Petronella was sitting by the window, skirts bunched up above her knees, her pale legs stretched out in the moonlight.

'Oh, Dilly!' she exclaimed. 'You are a vision to behold!'

Cordelia glowed.

Her mother's dress had only taken a little altering. She had done it with Glamour Spider thread – turning the sleeves back and making the hem shorter so she didn't trip. And she had patched the threadbare bits with tiny Evocation Shells, which glimmered as she moved.

She wore the shell portrait of her mother, the broken chain replaced with a turquoise ribbon to match her dress. A velvet pouch also hung round her neck, containing one part of Merlin's Map. Stuck through her Hawkish-eyes Hat was her aquamarine hatpin.

'Off you go, little Hatmaker,' Great-aunt Petronella croaked. 'Out into the big world.'

The Thames was crowded with boats, and the boats were crowded with Londoners, all wearing their fanciest outfits as they sailed through the dusk to the biggest party of the year.

Some boats were hung with lanterns and transformed into velvety bowers to transport their owners along to the pleasure gardens. Others were leaky tubs being rowed quickly, with the aim of arriving at the destination before the boat sank.

The Hatmakers' boat contained a motley collection of characters: Queen Elizabeth was wedged between a unicorn and a Roman emperor, her enormous lace ruff tickling them both. A fairy with a dozen living stars flitting around her trailed her fingers in the river. The boat was being steered by an elephant, whose trunk occasionally got in the way of the rudder. A girl in a dress mended with spider silk admired them all affectionately from the prow.

Cook twitched her ruff and the Roman emperor sneezed.

'Oh my, Cook! Your lace gets lacier every year!' said Aunt Ariadne, adjusting her toga.

Uncle Tiberius twiddled his narwhal tusk. He made a very fine unicorn.

Cordelia smiled. Everyone looked wondrous, and felt that way too: that is the magic of dressing up. The Harvest Masque was a night when cooks could be queens, and orphans could be fairies. It was a night when anything seemed possible.

The Elysian Eagle feather in Cordelia's Hawkish-eyes Hat made her vision extra sharp. She would be the first to spot Witloof if he appeared at the masque. If she couldn't catch him then and there, at least Win would be able to blow away the shadow ash he created.

Merlin's magic will come alive tonight and we'll be able to stop Witloof in his tracks!

Cordelia spotted Gertrude fluttering through the dusk.

Jones got his trunk tangled again. Everyone looked round as the boat rocked, so nobody saw Gertrude land on Cordelia's hand. Cordelia slipped the tiny scroll from the bird's leg and ushered her back into the sky.

Midnight.

That was all the message said.

Perfect. There were to be fireworks at half past eleven, so Cordelia could use them as a distraction and slip away to the Library of Maps while everyone's eyes were turned skyward.

'Look! Look!' Sam's gauzy wings fluttered as she pointed.

They were coming round the bend in the river. Vauxhall was alive with lights and music; the full moon hung above.

As the Hatmakers' boat moored up, they were greeted by a choir of mermaids sitting on rocks, wailing strange songs from the deep. (These mermaids were really a rather chilly collection of St Paul's choirboys, wearing fishtails and seaweed wigs.)

'We're guests of honour,' Aunt Ariadne reminded Cordelia and Sam, as they climbed out of the boat on to a velvet carpet. 'Let's remember to behave that way!'

Fire-eaters and sword jugglers made a bright corridor for the Hatmakers to walk down, and they arrived at the edge of a continent of wonder. The lawns were alive with dancing. Music wove through the air like sweet strains of sunlight.

They made their way through the crowds, past jugglers and under the legs of stilt-walkers. Dancers in candyfloss wigs whirled streamers through the air, and tumblers bounded through flaming hoops.

At the dancing lawn, Cook was pulled into a waltz by a jester, and Jones was met by a man dressed as a giraffe, who took him gallivanting off into the party.

Vauxhall was a vast maze of gardens and groves, of miniature palaces tucked between overgrown hedges, formal lawns unfurling in squares of green velvet, glimmering fountains and silvery glades.

The Hatmakers walked along the edge of a sparkling lake, where ladies dressed as enormous flowers floated on boats shaped like leaves. Cordelia's hat helped her notice everything – the curl of their laughing mouths, and the gold flecks painted on their petals. But there was no sign of Witloof.

They ventured through labyrinths and grottos, across lantern-lit plazas and past secluded bowers. Magic hung around Vauxhall like a garland.

In the spangled dark of the Ardourwood Grove, Beguiling Blackbirds sang songs to enchant the soul. Carbuncle Beetles idled along the stalks of Nonpareil Bushes, bearing berries that gleamed like gems.

In the Starflower Meadow, a pair of enormous silk balloons floated above the crowd, a tightrope suspended between them. Acrobats sauntered along it, turning somersaults high above the breathless audience. They swung from the ladders that dangled beneath the balloons, flying through the air as though gravity hadn't been discovered up there.

Amid the throng, Cordelia spotted a magnificent miniature ship in full sail, determinedly nosing its way across a sea of wigs and hats. The ship seemed to be in pursuit of an admiral wearing an important-looking bicorn.

'It's your Ship Hat, Uncle!'

Beneath the gliding ship, Janet Crust paddled, her legs as frantic as a duck's.

'Prithee, Admiral Ransom!'

A herald dressed as a peacock ushered them away up the avenue towards the Grand Pavilion. Fountains arced over their heads in time with the music and torches blazed all around.

Heads turned as the Hatmakers walked up the pavilion steps. Ladies waved; fops bowed with extra flourish.

'Make way for the honoured Makers!'

Inside, seated on thrones surrounded by lanterns, under a silk-swagged ceiling, were a swan and a lion side by side.

'Your Majesty.' The Hatmakers bowed and curtsied to the lion.

'Welcome, Hatmakers!' the king boomed, his Ochre-grass mane rustling regally.

The Hatmakers turned to the swan, sinking into bows and curtsies. 'Your Highness.'

The swan smiled wanly, dipping her long neck.

'We are honoured to have all the Makers here tonight!' the king exclaimed, getting a mouthful of his own mane.

As Aunt Ariadne and Uncle Tiberius made modest noises in their throats, Cordelia sidled up to the princess. Her face seemed even thinner than it had a few days ago.

'Good evening, Cordelia Hatmaker and Sam Lightfinger,' the princess murmured.

'Oh, this isn't Sam Lightfinger!' Cordelia declared, with a fop-like flourish. 'This is Queen Titania of the Forest Lights.'

Sam's ears lit up bright red. The fireflies had hidden behind them, giving them a rosy glow.

'Show her your fireflies, Sam,' Cordelia encouraged.

'Please, Queen Titania!' the princess begged.

Sam coaxed the fireflies out from behind her ears. They trailed after her fingers in a bright bobbling line, making swirls and looping the loop. As Sam drew hearts and stars with firefly light, something about the princess changed. It was as though a flame was waking within her.

'This is truly magic!' she gasped.

Sam froze. The fireflies scattered and re-formed in a knot of light on her shoulder.

'Yer not gonna throw me in the Clink, are ya?' she asked fearfully.

'Why ever would I do that?' the princess asked.

'For . . . for messing with magic when I ain't a Maker.'

The princess smiled, the kind of smile that breaks clouds apart.

'You have made my heart light again!' she murmured. 'You deserve a reward, not a punishment. Nobody who makes magic to lighten hearts should be jailed.'

'I agree!' Cordelia said fervently.

'Perhaps it is time to change those old laws,' the princess said, gazing at the fireflies, which fizzed around Sam like tiny fireworks come to life.

Sam began to dance with them again. The princess laughed with delight as they spiralled around her.

Cordelia looked across the pavilion. All the Maker families were there, as usual casting dark glances at each other. The words *Makers, Unite!* flickered like a guttering candle in Cordelia's mind.

'Not a chance,' she muttered ruefully, catching a scowl from a medieval knight who turned out to be Vera Glovemaker.

At least we don't have to rely on the Makers working together to stop Witloof.

She saw the Cloakmakers, dressed as a family of bright-winged butterflies (except the teenage son, who appeared to have come as a bat, all in black). Their faces were a jealous kind of colour as they watched the Hatmakers hold court with the king and the princess. The Glovemakers, looming beside the feast table, were dressed as a troupe of medieval knights, wearing shiny armour and spiked helmets. One knight raised a metal hand to wave at Cordelia. It was Bernard! Before Cordelia could wave back, the other knights slapped his hand down, glowering.

Near the orchestra, Cordelia spotted a self-conscious-looking cherub lurking behind a potted palm. His halo was wonky, and he wore a very small loin cloth that left his legs and chest bare, but his wings were resplendent with snowy feathers.

She trotted over to him.

'Hello, Goose!'

'Hello, Cordelia. You look nice.'

She grinned. 'Thanks!'

'Mother made me wear this.' He indicated his loin cloth ruefully. 'I'm meant to be Cupid. She's come as Venus.'

'At least you've got a bow and arrow,' Cordelia consoled him.

Goose clutched his rather pathetic weapon, throwing a nervy look at the Glovemakers.

'I wish they'd leave the feast table for a minute,' he muttered. 'I'm hungry! But, actually, perhaps it's better they're where we can see them. There's plenty of dark corners where they could lurk, ready to get us.'

'It isn't the Glovemakers we should be worried about, Goose,' Cordelia said. 'There are plenty of dark corners for *Witloof* to be lurking in.'

But her sharp eyes saw nothing but merriment all around them. It was hard to believe anything bad could happen in a world so filled with light and music.

Across the pavilion, Cordelia noticed a rather sullen Venus, staring daggers at Uncle Tiberius. Perhaps it was her Hawkish-eyes Hat, but Cordelia thought she noticed something new about Nigella Bootmaker's expression tonight as she glared at Uncle Tiberius. *Regret?*

The Moon appeared from behind a curtain, tottering on silvery legs and beckoning.

'Sir Hugo!' Cordelia grinned, towing Goose over.

'My good man, a *loin cloth*?' Sir Hugo asked Goose, aghast. 'On a night like tonight?'

'My mother has a very strange sense of humour,' Goose said, shivering resentfully.

'Do indulge me for a moment, Miss Hatmaker,' Sir Hugo begged.

He bustled Cordelia behind the curtain, out of sight of the crowd, into his makeshift dressing room.

'How do I look?' the actor asked anxiously, doing a twirl.

He wore silver stockings, pearly pantaloons, a doublet woven with shining threads, and the magnificent Moon Headdress Cordelia had made.

'Resplendent!' she confirmed. (She had known he would ask this question and had looked up a new word in the dictionary for the occasion.)

Sir Hugo seemed very pleased with 'resplendent'.

'There are some who say I wear the halo better than my namesake.' He cast an envious glance skyward. The moon smiled serenely down at him, unfazed by her earthly competitor.

'I'm sure your Moon Dance will be beautiful,' Cordelia assured him.

'I intend to outshine my lunar friend –' Sir Hugo narrowed his eyes at the moon – 'so the princess will only have eyes for me.'

He peeped through a gap in the curtains.

'Who is that vision in wings?' he demanded.

The princess was still absorbed by Sam's firefly dance. Indeed, a small crowd had been drawn towards the magic Sam was making.

'Um – that's Titania,' Cordelia said.

'My Moon will put even the Queen of the Fairies in the shade!' Sir Hugo vowed. 'I shall astonish Her Highness with the greatest Moon ever seen at Vauxhall!'

Back in the middle of the pavilion, Hatmaker and Bootmaker ignored the astonished goggling of the other Makers as they shook hands with Old Father Time and his two grandchildren. Hop, dressed as a grandfather clock, blushed when Goose complimented him on his pendulum.

'Ask me the time!' Tick cried, circling his arms like the hands of a wound-up watch.

'What time is it?' Cordelia enquired.

'Time to see the acrobats!' Tick announced.

'I shall stay here and rest my weary bones.' Old Father Time winked as he helped himself to a cloudbun from the tray of a passing waiter.

Cordelia and Goose allowed themselves to be cajoled by the little pocket watch (and accompanied by the much statelier grandfather clock) out on to the front steps of the pavilion.

Cordelia noticed raised eyebrows and whispering lips all around them.

'D'you think we're causing a scandal being seen with the Watchmakers?' Goose murmured.

'Yes!' Cordelia declared. 'And I hope everyone's *very* scandalized!'

From the front steps they had a spectacular view down the avenue to the silk hot-air balloons. Out across the pleasure gardens, the sounds of partying had a distinctly tipsy lilt. Cordelia observed teeth biting strawberries, sweat on the necks of the acrobats, and a friendly wrestling match happening in some bushes. But there was no sinister black ash sifting through the sky. Perhaps it had been foolish to think Witloof would appear here. Vauxhall was exuberant with lights and music, too bright a place for a shadow to fall.

'*OOOH!*' The crowd gasped as an acrobat turned a triple somersault high in the air.

Tick demanded to be picked up. Obligingly, Goose and Hop hoisted him between them.

Cordelia noticed Charity Cloakmaker craning to see over the crowd.

'Cuthbert, I want to *see*!' she whined. 'Can we go closer?'

'I'm gonna get some more ssh-sshampagne!' her brother slurred, flicking his batwing cape.

'Mama said you had to look after me!' Charity insisted.

But Cuthbert Cloakmaker reeled away. Charity peered longingly at the acrobats, before catching sight of Cordelia.

Cordelia raised her hand to wave, but, in a flurry of multicolour cape, Charity fled.

'*Makers, Unite*,' Cordelia muttered wryly.

Her belly clenched – someone wearing a dark cloak and a grim expression was slipping through the crowd.

Witloof!

Then she realized it was Win. She was making for the pavilion, hampered by a bulky bag slung across her chest.

'Any sign of him?' Win asked, arriving at Cordelia's side.

'None.'

The bag clinked as Win shifted it on her shoulder. 'I've brought every weather bottle I have left,' she said.

A brassy tooting of trumpets caused every head to turn. 'The Moon Dance is about to begin!' a herald cried.

A melody sang out across the grounds. Cordelia recognized the overture to Sir Hugo's Moon ballet.

'We shall toast the Harvest Moon in the traditional way!' the king boomed from his throne. 'Bring out the honey mead!'

A troupe of waiters dressed as penguins waddled out to offer everyone in the pavilion icy glass goblets of golden mead. Cordelia, remembering the sour ale at the Compass and Main, wrinkled her nose and refused. All the grown-up Makers accepted enthusiastically.

Sam came running towards them, fireflies a blur of light behind her, holding a goblet of mead like a trophy. 'Look what I got, Cor!'

'*Oooh!*' The crowd pointed and gasped. On a platform held high in the arms of a silver birch, Sir Hugo emerged like the moon coming out above the treetops.

'To the Harvest Moon!' the king bellowed.

'*The Harvest Moon!*' the crowds chorused. All the Makers raised their glasses in tribute. Cordelia felt pride swell with the music. Sir Hugo did, indeed, look resplendent.

Every face was turned towards him like a thousand Moonflowers drawn to his light. The music grew higher and louder. Sir Hugo twirled ecstatically, shaking stardust from his shoulders.

But before he could do his first *grand jeté*, the sweet music turned sour: it became a wail.

Win gaped in horror and then snatched the goblet from Sam's hand.

'Leechglass!' Win cried.

The wail persisted into a screech, a deafening intensity of sound. All around Cordelia, faces crumpled as the shattering music trembled the air.

'I shall astonish Her Highness with the greatest Moon ever seen at Vauxhall!'

The glass in Win's hand burst apart.

The terrible wailing stopped.

With the tinkle of a thousand falling icicles, shards of glass fell from the Makers' hands.

A triumphant laugh rang out in the sky.

Something dark circled above, just beyond the reach of the light.

Uneasy murmurs winnowed through the crowd below.

In the pavilion, the king frowned at his bleeding paw. The princess's swan feathers were suddenly speckled. Dazed Makers gazed at their hands, flecked with red. Shattered glass glinted around their feet.

Cordelia felt a chill prickle her skin.

The Makers were not merely dazed; it was as though they had eyes made of glass.

'Leechglass!' she whispered. 'It's cut them all!'

Win lurched towards her, fumbling with her bag. 'Take – it!' she rasped, breath coming out as a frozen cloud. '*Go!*'

'Win, you're hurt too!'

A *swoosh* shivered the air above their heads.

Cordelia whipped round to see Witloof appear on the treetop stage beside Sir Hugo. A shape streaked into the sky above him, smearing dark over the stars.

'Some of the Makers missed out on the toast!' Witloof crowed.

Sir Hugo unclenched himself from a fearful crouch to swell into a righteous blaze beside Witloof.

'GET OFF MY STAGE!' he bawled.

Witloof took a glass dagger from his belt and flicked the actor's cheek with its tip. Sir Hugo looked astonished. In the silver glow of his moon headdress, his eyes turned icy.

'TAKE THE MAKERS – ALL OF THEM!' Witloof commanded.

The words broke a spell. Panic ripped through the crowd below, breaking it apart. People ran, screaming.

A shape made of uproar and hurricanes shot through the air.

There was a blur of darkness over the pavilion and Mrs Cloakmaker was snatched into the sky.

'*MAMA!*' Charity Cloakmaker howled.

Cordelia didn't stop to think – she dashed into the pavilion, broken glass crunching under her feet, and found herself surrounded by frozen Makers.

'*Aunt!*' she cried. '*Uncle!*'

They gazed at her with unseeing eyes.

A bolt of darkness jolted the air and Uncle Tiberius was dragged upwards into the night.

Cordelia stared in horror at the empty place where he had been.

'*Cuthbert! Why are you all cold?*'

A wail shook Cordelia back into action. She found Charity Cloakmaker clinging to her brother.

'We've got to get out of here!' Cordelia hissed.

Charity simply sobbed and clung to Cuthbert.

Suddenly the whirlwind of darkness returned, seizing Mrs Bootmaker.

'HELP!' Cordelia cried, trying to drag Charity away.

A knight in shining armour clanked out from under the feast table. Another followed. It was Bernard Glovemaker and his twin, their faces stark with shock.

'We can't leave her!' Cordelia groaned.

Bernard and Buster swept Charity up in her cloak as though she was a butterfly in an enormous cocoon.

Cordelia grabbed Bernard's arm. 'Where are your sisters?'

'Glass,' he gasped.

Just as Cordelia turned to see Violet and Vera staring blankly, their fingers bleeding from Leechglass cuts, a shock of living darkness snatched them both into the air. Cordelia ran.

On the pavilion steps, she collided with Sam, Goose and the Watchmakers.

'Quick!' Cordelia shouted, dragging the weather bag out of Win's stiff hands and slinging it over her shoulder.

'FOLLOW ME!' Sam yelled.

The children raced down the steps, past the arcing fountains and blazing torches. Cordelia pounded along behind Sam, dragging Goose after her. Tick swung between Goose and Grasshopper, his feet barely touching the ground. Charity's yelps were muffled within her cloak as the Glovemaker boys brought up the rear.

The crowd was a panicked swirl. The children collided with a frenzy of fops and scattered a madness of clowns.

Janet Crust cowered in a flowerbed at the edge of the avenue, her head buried in a bush, Ship Hat upended.

A rush of storm-bringing wings made Cordelia throw herself flat to the ground. When she looked up, their way was blocked by Witloof, brandishing his Leechglass knife.

'NO, YOU DON'T!' Goose roared.

He grabbed Janet Crust and yanked her upright.

The knife carved a deadly arc inches from their faces.

Boom!

There was a dazzle of sparks as Goose fired the tiny cannons on Janet's hat, peppering Witloof in the face. He lurched away with a howl of rage, clutching his eyes.

The dark shape descended once more, dragging Witloof up into the night.

'You saved us, Goose!' Cordelia gasped.

Goose attempted to look modest as he pulled her to her feet.

'This way!' Sam cried, leading them onwards.

They reached the edge of the Starflower Meadow but the woods and gardens were choked with fleeing people.

'Which way do we go?' Cordelia asked.

'Up!' Sam pointed.

Above them, the hot-air balloons rocked in the wind, abandoned by the acrobats. Sam grabbed the rope ladder, leaping upwards.

'You're not serious?' Goose spluttered.

A scream pierced the night, keen as the cry of a hunting bird.

'It's the only way out!' she called down. 'We're easy prey down here!'

Tick scrambled up the ladder behind Sam. Cordelia gave him a boost, making way for the Glovemakers, who hauled their wriggling cargo up next – Charity's objections could be heard loudly from the folds of her cloak.

Hop slid out of his costume, reducing himself to a boy in black stockings and shirt, with a clock painted on his face, and sprang upwards.

Goose grabbed the ladder as if he was wrestling a bear, and scrabbled up clumsily.

Cordelia mounted the ladder last.

Halfway up, a silver helmet sailed past her, followed by a pair of gauntlets. The knights were shedding the extra weight of their costumes.

Many hands hauled Cordelia to safety in the basket. She dragged Win's bag behind her.

Above them, the great bulk of the silk balloon strained and creaked.

Sam seized one of the Glovemakers' swords and sawed at the tightrope tied to the basket. It frayed and broke – the balloon jerked, freed from its twin.

'Sandbags!' Sam panted.

Goose and the Glovemakers heaved three sandbags over the edge.

The balloon rushed upwards, as though eager to meet the moon face to face. Everyone was thrown to the bottom of the basket.

Cordelia dragged herself up to peer over the side.

She saw the pleasure gardens telescope away as they rose. They were five times higher than the tallest trees. The world was transformed when seen from the sky.

Goose, trembling, pulled himself up beside her.

'This is *amazing*!' he cried.

He promptly vomited spectacularly into the night.

And Cordelia found she was laughing, defiant with joy and sheer *aliveness* and the rush of flying upwards.

The balloon rushed upwards, as though eager to meet the moon face to face.

'*WHEEEEEEEEEEEE!*' she shrieked like a wild hawk. '*AIIIIIIIIIIIIIIIII!*'

And suddenly all of them were yelling into the night, wild with escapes and the thrill of riding the wayward air.

The lights of London blurred beneath them. The river was a twist of silver away to their left.

Cordelia stared over the angular mountain range of the city's rooftops. She saw the great dark swathe of the park, the definite line of Oxford Street cutting a canyon through the buildings, the moon-burnished dome of St Paul's.

And above the treetops of Vauxhall a creature made of nightmares and storms circled, searching.

'*Harpy!*' Cordelia whispered.

It was not only the name of Witloof's ship: it was also the name of his secret weapon.

It must have been the Harpy that Witloof had spoken to through his tower window the night before his execution. The Harpy must have stolen the maps from the library, and snatched Witloof into the sky from the scaffold amid the confusion of the storm that Win had unleashed.

Cordelia clenched her fists as Jack's words came back to her.

The wind had wings and claws.

It had been the Harpy that had snatched her father from the deck of his ship and torn him into the sky –

'Cordelia?' Goose was beside her, frowning in concern. 'Are you all right?'

This was no time to think about her father.

'Our families have been cut with Leechglass,' she said urgently. 'They need the Essence of Magic, otherwise . . .'

She could not finish the sentence.

Otherwise they'll die.

Like the Watchmaker's daughter.

Everyone was staring at her: Goose, Sam and Hop, Tick (still in his pocket-watch costume) and the two Glovemaker boys – now armourless knights. Even Charity peered out from her cloak. Everyone's face was fearful and brave.

'I need to get to the library!' Cordelia announced.

'The *library*?' Goose spluttered. 'Now's not the time to get lost in a book!'

The basket bumped the air, wind whistling through the gaps.

'There *is* a way to stop Witloof and save our families,' Cordelia told them. She tried not to think about Uncle Tiberius and Aunt Ariadne, glass-eyed and staring. 'To make sure it happens, I've got to get to a library near Blackfriars Bridge before midnight.'

As if on cue in a Drury Lane drama, chimes sounded beneath their feet. From way up in the air, they heard all the voices of London's bells, ringing deep and silvery across the city.

'Fifteen minutes to midnight!' Cordelia cried.

'We've got lift,' Hop said, studying the complicated arrangement of ropes and pulleys strung above their heads. 'But not thrust!'

'What d'you mean?' Cordelia asked.

'We can go *up* by stoking the fire in the basket,' Hop explained. 'But we can't steer. We'll just be blown by the wind until we run out of fire and float back down to earth.'

Sam scrabbled her arms, trying to doggy-paddle through the air. Goose joined in, flapping his Cupid wings.

As Cordelia leaned out to help, Win's bag bumped against her leg. She could feel the whole thing shuddering – the Armada storm must be inside.

That storm would be far too strong – dangerously so: it would hurl them miles across the sky. But perhaps there was something – *yes*!

She found a Zephyr Vessel – a twist of glass as big as a spinning top.

'Hold on!' she warned.

She smashed the glass against the outside of the basket. With a whoosh, the wind burst free.

'*Whoooooo!*'

Cordelia heard her own voice unspool from her mouth as the balloon and its passengers were rushed towards the glimmering river.

Riding the sky was like riding a highly strung horse.

She found another Zephyr Vessel – this one bigger.

'Lean towards the river!' she yelled.

The Glovemakers pulled Charity with them as everyone leaned.

The basket dipped sickeningly.

'Hold on!'

Air burst in a great fountain and the wind blew them with breath-stealing speed. Soon the river glimmered far below. From their great height, Blackfriars Bridge looked like a carved wooden toy.

'Glovemakers!' Hop called. 'Empty the flame basket!'

Embers fell like tiny fireworks over the edge.

The balloon dropped with a swoop and a stray spark brushed the balloon like a Firebird's wingtip.

In an instant, the balloon was ablaze. The silk was so fine the flame ate through it in seconds.

Basket and humans plummeted. The bridge sped closer, getting bigger – now life-size and horribly solid –

'JUMP!' Sam roared, launching herself into the dark.

In a whirl of night and flame, Cordelia leaped, pulling Charity with her.

The river rose up to swallow them in its freezing jaws and suddenly the world was green and slow and silent. Bubbles rose all around Cordelia like stars drifting upwards. She pulled Charity through the water, following the path of the stars.

They broke the surface, gasping for air.

The flaming silk drifted dreamily down and extinguished itself in the river.

Charity flailed; she seemed most displeased with the situation. Some cursing indicated that the Glovemakers did not appreciate the wet landing the river had afforded them either.

'Cook wanted me to have a bath!' Sam spluttered cheerfully, surfacing nearby. 'Now I'll tell her I've had enough of a bath to last me a year.'

'I think you're more likely to need a bath now than ever before.' Cordelia grimaced: the river was not exactly clean.

Tick's costume proved to be buoyant. He and Hop floated past Cordelia as she peered around, trying to get her bearings. Blackfriars Bridge loomed above them, dark against the night sky. They had been extremely lucky: they were very close to the hidden mouth of the Fleet.

'*Goose!*' Cordelia called.

'*H-here!*' came the answer.

She swam towards the sound of his voice and saw Goose clinging to a great chain hanging from the bridge, the river tugging insistently at his cherub's wings, as though it wanted to show him something further downstream.

Profoundly grateful that her father had taught her to swim in the Serpentine, Cordelia grabbed hold of Goose's sodden wings in one hand and Charity's cloak in the other and struck out for the river wall.

'This way!' she called to the others.

The river was determined to take them downstream – they had to swim hard against it. Cordelia could see the dark blur that was the ivy hiding the mouth of the River Fleet. The current almost swept her right past it, but she clutched the weeds and her feet found the bottom foothold.

The grating creaked open and she pushed Charity up into the tunnel. It was rather like trying to manoeuvre an uncooperative octopus. Cordelia clambered up after her, and one by one the others followed – Tick was hauled up by his watch chain.

Cordelia counted everyone into the tunnel: 'Two Glovemakers, two Watchmakers, a Cloakmaker, a Bootmaker and a Lightfinger.'

'And a Hatmaker,' Goose added.

'And me,' Cordelia confirmed.

Charity hiccuped, sitting miserably up to her elbows in rushing water.

The Fleet nosed curiously around them. It was colder, but fresher, than the Thames. It washed the stink of the big river off them.

There was no time to waste, but Cordelia found herself hesitating.

Peregrine had said that if she shared the secret of the Mapmakers, she would be expelled from the society. She would have to give up Merlin's Map and give up the responsibility that her father had entrusted to her.

'I – I'm meant to do this alone,' she said to the others.

'What do you mean? *You're* the one who told us Makers to unite!' Goose cried.

The silence that followed was the kind that weighs heavy. The kind it's impossible to budge.

Goose was right. And Cordelia knew she would never have got this far without her friends – without their brilliance, their bravery, their stubbornness and courage. She desperately did not want to get shut out of the Secret Society of Mapmakers, but there would be *no* society if she failed. And she would already have failed if it wasn't for her friends.

The Fleet became urgent, tugging at her legs.

'Right,' Cordelia said. 'I'm not meant to tell *anyone* about this place – it's a huge secret. But I'll take you with me. You'll have to hide at first. Afterwards, you can come out and I'll try to explain everything. Be prepared: it will require you all to be sworn to absolute secrecy.'

Cordelia whispered to the Fleet as she set off down the tunnel, leading the crowd of young Makers towards the Library of Maps.

'Remember me, Fleet? These are my friends. I know they're not meant to be here –'

The river slapped the walls, hurling itself against the stone.

'But they want to help protect the magic!' she went on quickly. 'I've brought a piece of Merlin's Map!'

With a sudden swell, the river picked them up and towed them up the tunnel. It spat the young Makers out into the vaulted cavern of the library, depositing them in a pile on the steps.

'Keep low and quiet!' Cordelia instructed the band of bedraggled children.

They nodded, wonder scrawled across their faces.

Cordelia climbed the steps on wobbly legs.

'Thank you, Fleet,' she said politely.

Tonight, the library seemed even more mysterious than the first time she had seen it. The air itself seemed to be tense and trembling.

If a room could hold its breath, Cordelia thought, *this is what it would feel like*.

'Miss Hatmaker!' Peregrine appeared from behind the waterfall with an armful of green candles. 'You are the first to arrive!'

As he busied himself at the round table, Cordelia took the chance and beckoned her friends to come closer. They scrambled up the steps and slipped behind a pillar, into the deep shadow.

'Stay here till it's time to come out,' Cordelia whispered.

She hurried over to Peregrine, who was arranging the candles around rune-carved stones laid across the great table.

She pulled out the crystal vial.

'Oh, Miss Hatmaker! You found it!' Peregrine cried, eyes filling with tears.

'Witloof has hurt all the Makers with Leechglass!' Cordelia told him. 'We need to get them the Essence of Magic as soon as we possibly can. Can we set out for Stonehenge immediately after the ceremony's finished?'

'Yes, yes!' Peregrine said distractedly, placing the final candle. 'We will do what must be done. It's all to save the magic.'

He took a mask from his desk. It was made of ribbons of living water woven together. It rippled and shimmered as Peregrine held it out.

'When the Mapmakers meet, it is always in disguise,' he explained. 'Yet another form of secrecy that has protected us for centuries. Only the librarian knows the identity of all the Mapmakers.'

Cordelia took the mask and tied two ribbons behind her ears. It covered her face, liquid and cool against her skin.

Peregrine gripped her shoulders very tight and leaned down to look into her eyes.

'Miss Hatmaker, you must believe me. This is the only way I can think of to stop all the senseless destruction Witloof's causing!'

She smiled reassuringly at him, though the mask obscured her features. 'It's going to be all right.'

Peregrine put on his own mask. It was made of rocks, which shifted like miniature mountains when he spoke. 'Once the other two Mapmakers arrive with the Easterly and the Southerly Maps, we can begin. Please take your seat at the table.'

Cordelia sat down. The wooden seat was huge around her, its arms worn with a thousand years of use. The table had a thousand growth rings, like ripples in a pond.

She could not stop her hands trembling, so she clutched the crystal vial tight: a piece of Merlin's Map.

The map, when complete, would show the way to a hidden doorway in Stonehenge: the doorway that led to the Elixir Oak that pulled the Essence of Magic up into its sap. The Essence of Magic would stop Witloof and save the Makers.

Peregrine had never explained exactly *how* the Essence of Magic would stop Witloof. She opened her mouth to ask him, but he turned his head anxiously towards the tunnel.

'The river is rising! The next Mapmaker is approaching.'

Two Mapmakers appeared together, borne on the water.

One wore a mask that enveloped his head in plumes of airy cloud; the other's mask was made of Firebird feathers and shone flame bright. He stared curiously at Cordelia. She could see his eyes gleaming as they nodded in greeting.

He's probably wondering who I am, she thought. *Peregrine said there's never been a younger Mapmaker than me.*

Peregrine sat down. His voice was heavy with the solemnity of the occasion.

'Mapmakers!' he intoned. 'Tonight, we gather to make the Map that Merlin divided.'

He struck a gong. The green candles ignited, casting an otherwordly glow over the table.

The rune stones hummed an ancient song.

'We hold the four quarters. Asunder, they are nothing of consequence,' Peregrine said. 'But, united, they make a map that leads to the heart of the land's magic.'

He lifted a blank stone tablet, the size of a large book.

'North!' he declared.

He placed it in the middle of the table.

'East!'

The cloud-masked Mapmaker produced a long strand of moss, knotted in the middle. It moved gently in an unseen breeze.

'South!'

The flame-faced Mapmaker brought out two lightning stones – they flashed and cracked in his gloves.

'West!' Peregrine's command was sharp.

Cordelia unclenched her hand. The water within the crystal vial glimmered as though it was keeping a great secret.

The holder of the Easterly Map untied the strand of moss. A wind uncaught from it and whispered towards the stone tablet.

The Southern Mapmaker struck his lightning stones together and a fist of fire clenched in the air.

Cordelia, somehow, knew what to do.

She pulled the stopper from the crystal vial and tipped the starry water over the glistering bundle of fire and air.

In water, flame and air, the stone tablet was consumed. Cordelia peered into the blaze. There was something glowing in the heart of it.

As flame and water evaporated, suddenly the map was revealed.

Bright lines were etched in the stone, converging in a whorl like a snail shell. The circle in the very centre gleamed like a new-forged coin.

'It is done,' Peregrine said, picking up the map. He seemed strangely defeated. 'Merlin's Map is made.'

'Most excellent!' A voice sliced like steel through the room. 'Now give me the map or I will set fire to this entire library.'

CHAPTER 36

The flame-faced Mapmaker took off his mask.

It was Witloof.

All the air left Cordelia's lungs. She lurched to her feet. Witloof's eyes glinted, hard and sharp in the middle of the spinning room.

'No!' Cordelia growled. 'I won't let you take it!'

She tore off her mask to stare defiantly into his sneering face.

'Yet you have practically handed it to me already,' Witloof said. 'We couldn't have made the map without you, could we?'

'We'll *never* give it to you!' Cordelia declared, stepping between Peregrine and Witloof.

'Come now, Miss Hatmaker, do you really think you have a choice? My Harpy *allowed* you to escape the masque and come here. You've done *exactly* what I wanted, though you were slower finding your father's piece of the map than I would have liked. Waiting for you has been tedious, but I don't need to wait a moment longer. Merlin's Map is mine.'

'Help!' Cordelia begged the cloud-masked Mapmaker, still sitting at the table.

Witloof laughed. 'He can't help you. He's *helpless*.'

The Mapmaker groaned quietly, and Cordelia saw a flash of icy eyes.

'One touch of my Leechglass knife took care of him,' Witloof said with a cruel smile. 'And the only thing that cures a cut from Leechglass is the Essence of Magic.'

With a tooth-tingling swish, the villain pulled the glass blade from his belt. It was jagged-sharp, glinting in the light from the river.

'Give me the map.'

'NO!' Cordelia bellowed.

'No?' Calmly, Witloof returned the blade to his belt and then took out a jar from his cloak. It contained a spike of Lightning Strife.

Peregrine moaned in despair, gripping the stone map.

The Fleet sloshed, agitated.

'So, you choose fire, Peregrine?' Witloof asked. 'I'll burn this place to ashes.'

'*No!*' Peregrine cried. 'You *promised*!'

'And *you* promised *me*,' Witloof replied.

Peregrine gave a low sob.

'*Promised?*' Cordelia felt everything shift around her. She stared at the librarian.

'I had no choice!' Peregrine wept.

He stumbled to his desk and, with a shaking hand, pulled out a torn piece of paper.

UNLESS YOU GIVE ME MERLIN'S MAP – W.W.

Cordelia recognized the scrawl. It looked exactly like the note Peregrine had shown her when she had first found the library.

I will destroy every precious magical place – the note had read – *unless you give me Merlin's Map*.

The dreadfulness of what Peregrine had done made her dizzy.

'You told me making Merlin's Map would stop the destruction – but it was only because Witloof was blackmailing you!' she cried. 'It wasn't anything to do with the Elixir Oak, was it? It was because he said he'd only stop destroying things if you gave him the map. You lied! You tricked me into this!'

Peregrine turned his face to the library.

'It was the only way,' he said. 'So many precious places! And I am meant to be their guardian.'

Trembling, Peregrine held out Merlin's Map.

Cordelia dived for it, but the rough stone was snatched out of her grasp.

Witloof had Merlin's Map. His face was alight with triumph.

'He'll destroy the heart of the magic!' Cordelia yelled. 'Then magic *everywhere* will die.'

A tear ran down Peregrine's long nose. 'But the key is lost,' he said, a desperate light flickering in his eyes. 'So I haven't done the worst thing! Remember, you can't get through the doorway without the key. He can stand in Stonehenge as long as he likes; without the key he'll never –'

'Ah, but I *have* the key,' Witloof said, patting his chest pocket. 'I got hold of it years ago and I have it here, safe in my pocket.'

Out of the corner of her eye, Cordelia saw something Witloof had not reckoned for: something many-legged creeping up behind him.

'Thank you for giving me this map.' Witloof smiled at Peregrine. 'I know I said I'd stop burning things once you gave it to me, but I really don't think you'll be needing this library any more.'

He hurled the jar of Lightning Strife into the nearest shelves. Fire swallowed the maps in a blaze of flame.

'NOOOO!' Peregrine screamed.

'AAAAAARGH!' In a confusion of arms and legs and yells, a troupe of children launched themselves at Witloof.

He staggered backwards, struggling to grab his Leechglass knife, and crashed into the round table. Cordelia leaped to help her friends – and swerved to escape the glass blade.

The Glovemakers had attached themselves to Witloof like a pair of trousers – one on each leg. Hop and Tick each clung to an arm, Sam was clamped on his back, and Charity held him round the middle. Goose clung to a foot with the doggedness of a tightly laced boot.

Witloof swung savagely, roaring in fury.

Cordelia dodged the swipes of the knife as maps made of bark and moss fell burning all around them. Water maps went up in clouds of steam, shells cracked in the heat, rock maps shattered, and flowers blackened.

'Peregrine!' she cried.

Peregrine was desperately bailing water from the Fleet as flames gobbled their way up the shelves. Bitter smoke spiralled from the burning maps.

'FLEET!' Peregrine howled. 'HELP!'

The waterfall's roar got stronger. The river was rising.

Witloof struggled to free himself from the swarm of children. Cordelia couldn't get close – every time she tried to grab Merlin's Map, the knife bit the air in front of her face.

'You did this!' Peregrine growled, turning on Witloof. '*You!*'

Propelled by righteous fury, he flung himself at Witloof. The knife drew a bright stripe in the air and Peregrine toppled to the floor.

The children's hold on Witloof went slack. They backed away from him and his knife in horror.

'*Peregrine!*' Cordelia threw herself to the floor beside him.

His eyes were glassy. There was a deep stain on his jacket, and starry water ran red over Cordelia's hands.

'Merlin's Map is mine!' Witloof sneered.

'No, it *isn't*!' came a valiant scrap of a yell. Small fingers reached up and snatched the map out of Witloof's hand.

'Impudent imp!' Witloof shrieked, lunging for Tick.

In a flurry of cherub's feathers, Goose pushed Tick out of the way. There was a yell, and the crunch of the knife hitting stone.

The Fleet rose in full fury, flayed into rageful claws and teeth. It snatched Witloof in enormous jaws. He was caught like a ragdoll in a riptide as the river tore him away down the tunnel.

Goose had the map. His face was stark – shocked at what he'd done.

The waterfall became deafening, pouring itself into the library. It curled into liquid streamers and lashed the flames, extinguishing them.

Through smoke and darkness, Cordelia saw Peregrine being lifted by the river. His eyes were closed, the water rocking him like he was a sleeping child.

'*Peregrine?*' she cried.

But the river carried him away.

Water washed the tears from Cordelia's cheeks.

Water was everywhere – hammering down from above, rising around their knees.

'Cor!' Sam called, hauling Tick and Charity on to the round table as the Fleet swelled higher. 'What do we do now?'

Win's weather bag bumped into Cordelia. She grabbed it and scrambled up beside them, pulling Goose with her. The Glovemakers yanked Hop up between them.

Starry water churned around them like a stormy sea.

'We've got to get down the tunnel before the whole place floods!' Cordelia bellowed.

But the river had other ideas. It threw its arms round the children and lifted them up.

It was a bone-shaking, lung-crushing experience that lasted several seconds and also a lifetime. The river surged the children up through the waterfall, up through a pillar of dense, breath-stealing water.

Cordelia's head broke the surface and she gasped lungfuls of air. Beside her, Glovemakers, Watchmakers, Cloakmaker, Bootmaker and Lightfinger appeared, all gulping grateful breaths.

They were in a tunnel – low and narrow. They had been borne up the waterfall like a school of salmon, and were being carried further upstream – away from danger. They were bedraggled and soul-shaken, but alive.

'Thank you, Fleet,' Cordelia said.

The river playfully swirled her round.

It jostled the children, bumping them against each other, but it would not let them sink. They bobbed like pieces of flotsam. Even Goose, clutching the stone map, did not disappear beneath the surface. He looked astonished, his cherub's wings splayed behind him as they surged along.

Cordelia felt the person beside her slip a hand into hers. It was Charity Cloakmaker. She gave the hand a squeeze.

'Wh-where are we going?' Hop called. His voice echoed in the stone tunnel.

'No idea!' Cordelia called back.

'*Wheee!*' Tick squealed in delight as the river whirled him in circles.

The tunnel got lower and lower.

'Ouch!' A Glovemaker bumped his head on the rocky ceiling.

Just as Cordelia began to wonder whether there would soon be space to breathe, she was plunged under the surface in a roiling froth of bubbles. There was a metallic clank, a rush of air and light –

Cordelia landed with a thud on dry ground. She rolled over, getting tangled in the strap of Win's weather bag. Charity, Goose, Sam, Hop, Tick and the Glovemakers arrived beside her.

They were lying on a pavement in High Holborn. With a *splosh*, the Fleet drew itself back down a narrow vent in the road.

Everyone got up, wobbling on clumsy limbs. Everyone except Goose. He was lying on his side, wings ruined, hugging the map to his bare chest.

'Goose!' Cordelia grinned, tottering over to him. 'You saved the map!'

'C-Cor-delia,' he said, shivering. 'Why's it so c-cold?'

Cordelia felt the grin slip off her face. She reached out and touched her friend. He was shockingly cold. Then she saw it: the tiniest shard of glass winked in his shoulder: the tip of Witloof's knife.

'Goose!' she gasped, grasping his hand. His fingers were stiff, his eyes turning glassy.

Cordelia turned to the others, ranged around her like a Greek chorus, watching in horror.

'Leechglass,' she croaked.

Goose was losing himself, the light in his eyes disappearing.

'*Goose, no!*' Cordelia pleaded. 'Come back!'

A sound to shiver bones rang above them: an otherworldly cry, somewhere in the sky. The Harpy.

'We gotta run!' Sam hissed.

But Cordelia threw herself protectively over Goose.

'I won't leave him!'

'We'll carry him,' the Glovemakers said together.

'Here.' Charity held out her cloak. It was soaking and ragged, but it would do.

Together, the children moved Goose on to the cloak. The Glovemakers hoisted him up, slung between them.

Cordelia felt a sob tremble in her throat. She gripped Sam's hand so tight she felt the bones of their fingers almost meet.

The Harpy keened again.

'Stick to the shadows,' Sam whispered. 'C'mon! I know the back ways home.'

The moonlight was treacherous; shadows were safer. Sam led them into a black crack between moon-silver buildings. The shadows hid them as they ran.

The Harpy's cry pierced the air, circling. Searching.

They dashed across an avenue of moonlight into a valley of shadow, slipping along the back streets, dark shapes flitting through the dark.

London was deserted; its buildings stared with blind eyes.

Great-aunt Petronella will know what to do, Cordelia told herself. *She'll have something up her sleeve*.

St Auspice's spire reared above them.

'Almost there!' Sam whispered.

They just had to cross the moonlit plain of Cavendish Square to get to Wimpole Street, but Charity grabbed Cordelia's arm, pointing wordlessly.

With a churning of powerful wings, the Harpy surged across the sky. In the silver and black night, Cordelia got her first clear view of it: a creature made of dread and storms.

It landed on the steeple of St Auspice's Church, like a gargoyle come to life. They heard the squeal of its claws on the tiles, the scrape of its ragged breath, the heartbeat-thud of its wings.

It raised its face, shaking a shock of storm-wild hair, and unleashed a furious scream. Cordelia's skin erupted in goosebumps.

The children cowered in the shadows as the Harpy's blazing eyes seared the darkness. Cordelia felt the Makers pressing in around her. Nobody breathed.

Striking lightning from its wings, the Harpy clawed its way back into the sky, disappearing beyond the rooftops in a rumble of thunder.

They all breathed again.

'Let's go!'

The children charged out into the wide expanse of Cavendish Square.

The moonlight was painfully bright – Cordelia felt as though they were running across a well-lit stage. Wimpole Street was up ahead. As they reached the edge of the shadows a skin-prickling screech split the night.

The Harpy had seen them.

They tore round the corner, racing for Hatmaker House as the Harpy swept down through the sky, a nightmare given flesh and wings.

'*Ooof!*' Cordelia crashed into the front door.

The Harpy closed in, its wings whipping up dust from the street.

Cordelia fumbled with the handle – the door burst open – the children fell inside, splaying over the hallway tiles.

Cordelia lurched to her feet. She glimpsed a face, blazing with fury, a wide scream of a mouth – and slammed the door.

BOOM.

The door shuddered.

BOOM.

The Harpy hurled itself against the door again.

BOOM.

Cordelia turned the Salvus Iron Key in the lock.

'It can't get in,' she panted. 'Not for a while, anyway.'

The others looked doubtful as the Harpy's screech rattled the window. They saw its raging face distorted in the glass.

Cordelia pulled aside the cloak to look at Goose. His eyes stared strangely.

'Goose!' she said. 'I'm going to save you.'

'You mean *we're* going to save you!' Tick's voice was high.

Looking at his determined face, Cordelia found herself achingly grateful for her friends.

With a furious howl, the Harpy took off into the night.

Sam frowned. 'Probably gone to get Witloof. We gotta hurry.'

Although the Glovemakers were exhausted, they carried Goose up the spiral stairs to Great-aunt Petronella's Alchemy

Parlour. Everyone helped. Cordelia could feel the cold of Goose's skin, even through the cloak.

Great-aunt Petronella had fallen asleep, moon-bathing in her window.

'Great-aunt!' Cordelia gasped, shaking her shoulder. 'It's an emergency!'

The ancient lady was awake in an instant, eyes wide in the lilac firelight.

She blinked at the Glovemakers, Watchmakers and Cloakmaker crowding into her parlour. They all stared at the lady hunched in her chair, bare legs stretched in front of her.

Hop bowed. The others bobbed.

Great-aunt Petronella surveyed them critically.

'You may have heard rumours that I use the tears of Cloakmakers in my potions,' she rasped. 'Or that I eat Glovemakers' fingernails.'

The children muttered and shuffled.

'Don't worry.' The ancient lady's eyes twinkled. 'Never on a full moon!'

'There's no time for jokes,' Cordelia chided. 'All the Makers have been cut by Leechglass – Aunt and Uncle and everyone.'

She grasped Goose's hand. It was shockingly cold.

'And Goose!'

'We need light,' Great-aunt Petronella commanded. 'Put some Ardourwood branches on the fire, Dilly, and some leaves of Radiant Bay.'

Cordelia piled the sweet-smelling branches on the fire and red tongues of flame licked up the chimney. She threw on Radiant Bay leaves that crackled gold.

'Lay him on the chaise!' Great-aunt Petronella ordered.

The Glovemakers jumped to it. Sam dragged Great-aunt Petronella's heavy chair round so she could inspect Goose.

'This boy needs as much light as possible,' she said at once. 'The strongest we've got.'

Sam pulled off her hat, and her tiny troupe of Dulcet Fireflies emerged, bringing their soft hum of light into the room. They settled on Goose's face, showing how pale he was.

Cordelia flung open a cupboard. Different notes of light fell on her with musical chimes.

'Starlight – Moonlight – *Sunlight!*' She grabbed handfuls of the tiny bottles.

Great-aunt Petronella trickled liquid sunshine between Goose's lips.

His glassy stare waned.

'Cor – delia,' he murmured.

'Goose!' Tears splashed from Cordelia's eyes on to his face. '*Goose!*'

Great-aunt Petronella trickled another drop of molten gold between his lips. 'This will keep the soul cold at bay.'

'*At bay?*' Cordelia repeated. 'Not *cure* him?'

But she already knew the truth. There was only one thing that could cure a cut from Leechglass: the Essence of Magic.

Goose was still holding Merlin's Map – the map to the Elixir Oak. She prised it from between his stiff fingers.

The map etched in the stone shone copper-bright: a whorl like a snail shell encircled by another ring. There were strange angular lines traced around the outer circle. In the very corner of the map, there was a compass rose and an arrow pointing east, with the word LONDINIUM scratched beside it.

'It's Stonehenge,' she told the others. 'This map shows the doorway to the Elixir Oak – its sap runs with the Essence of Magic – but – but . . .'

She trailed off. Her friends' faces flickered between hope and despair in the firelight.

'But what?' Hop prompted.

'To get through the door we need the key,' she told them. 'And Witloof's got it.'

There was a crushing silence.

'Actually,' said Sam, sticking her hand in her pocket, 'I stole it outta his jacket in the scuffle.'

She produced a heavy brass key.

One of Sam's wings was tattered, and all the glister of her fairy costume had been scoured away by fire and flood, but to Cordelia she was the most magical being alive.

'We have the map and the key!' Cordelia gasped. 'We have everything we need!'

She squeezed Goose's cold hand. His eyes had a little shine in them.

'For our families?' His voice was whisper-weak.

'We'll get to Stonehenge as fast as we can and get the Essence of Magic,' Cordelia reassured him. 'Everything will be all right.'

Sam took the map, frowning.

'We've got a carriage – how long will the journey take?' Cordelia gabbled. 'We've still got some of Win's weather, but I'm not sure that'll help on land.'

'I recognize these lines,' Sam muttered, tracing a finger over the angular lines etched around the circle.

'We need as much light as we can carry!' Hop added.

'And bottles, to bring the Essence of Magic back for everyone else!' Charity piped up.

But Sam was still staring at the map.

'This ain't Stonehenge,' she said, grabbing Cordelia's arm. 'This is the Guildhall!'

It took several seconds for the information to sink in.

'The *Guildhall*?' Cordelia repeated.

'See these lines?' Sam pointed at the pattern on Merlin's Map. 'I saw 'em in the stone – they were under all the plaster that fell off when I was trying to get away from that lot.' She nodded at the Glovemakers. Buster and Bernard blushed. 'I held on to the grooves to keep from falling. Ya don't forget a thing when it's saved ya from breaking yer neck.'

'But Peregrine told me Stonehenge is where the Elixir Oak is hidden.' Cordelia frowned. 'That's what the legend says.'

Great-aunt Petronella looked up from dripping more sunlight into Goose's mouth.

'Legends can be very misty,' she said. 'Sometimes the mist is there on purpose, to hide the truth.'

Hop tapped the arrow pointing east, with the word LONDINIUM next to it.

'But the place the map shows isn't *in* London: it's clearly west of London,' he said. 'Like Stonehenge.'

Cordelia was struck with inspiration the way some people are struck by thunderbolts.

'This map was made a thousand years ago! "Londinium" *would* have been away to the east! The city was much smaller then!'

'And the Guildhall's built on a stone circle!' Charity added. 'Mama told me Henry the Eighth built it over an ancient magical site!'

'Indeed he did!' Great-aunt Petronella crowed. 'The old rascal!'

Cordelia felt as though she had lurched on one gust of wind halfway across the country – from Stonehenge to the Guildhall.

Could the Guildhall be built over the place where Merlin had hidden the source of magic? The wall beneath the plaster had looked like rock . . . Was there an ancient stone circle, hidden inside the walls?

'There's only one way to find out,' Cordelia said. 'We go to the Guildhall and try to find the hidden door.'

'But we can't get there!' Charity wailed. 'Not with that horrible *thing* outside!'

Great-aunt Petronella held up a hand, commanding silence.

'Take me downstairs,' she said. 'It's time to show you a secret.'

The children set the ancient lady's armchair down in the hallway.

She pointed to the grandfather clock that stood against the wall like a shy person hoping not to be noticed at a party. Cordelia wondered if her great-aunt had been moonstruck from too much moon-bathing.

'Turn the hands to midnight,' Great-aunt Petronella said.

Hop stepped up to the clock respectfully. He gently laid a finger on its face, tracing a circle to drag the hands round to midnight. As soon as the two hands met, the clock moved. It shrugged forward stiffly and slid along the wall, revealing a dark rectangular hole.

'This tunnel links all the Makers' houses to the Guildhall,' Great-aunt Petronella said.

The Watchmakers, Cloakmaker and Glovemakers gasped.

'See!' Cordelia said triumphantly. 'We were always meant to be friends! Enemies wouldn't have a secret tunnel linking their houses, would they?'

Tick and Hop beamed. The Glovemakers grinned. Even Charity managed a smile.

While Sam and the Watchmakers carried Great-aunt Petronella to the warmth of the kitchen fireside, the

Glovemakers gathered Goose up in the cloak again. Then Cordelia grabbed a candle off the hall table and went down into the tunnel. Win's bag bumped against her legs, now filled with bottles of light, along with the jars of weather.

Sam was right behind her. That much was good to know: it was better to go into the dark with a friend at your back and a light in your hand.

The air was close and cold. Rough brick bit Cordelia's shoulders as she felt her way down dozens of stairs.

There was an ancient feel to the air at the bottom. The tunnel unspooled for a thousand steps before she came to a fork. To the right, a shield with seven stars showed the way to the Guildhall. To the left, there was a brass boot mounted on the wall.

'That must lead to the Bootmakers,' she murmured. It made her fiercely glad to know that, beneath it all, under the mess of the city, like a shortcut through time, the Makers were joined together. They always had been, even when they didn't know it.

'How's Goose?' she called over her shoulder.

'Charity's giving him some more light!' came Buster's reply.

Cordelia hurried onwards through the dense dark, with only the restless flame of the candle to light her way.

Two more tunnels turned off to the left, a brass glove and a silver cloak showing where they led.

The next sign was a cane.

Of course. The Canemakers still belonged to the Makers' Guild when this tunnel was built! Cordelia realized. This tunnel was far older than any of the quarrels that had divided the Makers.

The final sign was a golden watch.

'We're almost there, I reckon!' Cordelia called.

Two minutes later, the candle flame grew agitated. Hot wax dripped on Cordelia's hand. There was a lick of air across her face – and a sharp pain in her shin. She had hit it on the bottom step of a flight of stairs.

The candle cast shadows like dark spells around her as she climbed up. At the top there was a wooden door with a handle worn shiny by centuries of use.

With a creak, the door groaned open.

She emerged through a section of carved wooden panelling. The door was so skilfully made that, when closed, it would be completely invisible. Intricate vines and roses fitted together perfectly, hiding the door from sight. No wonder the secret tunnel had been forgotten.

The circular Great Chamber of the Guildhall was as wide as open arms before Cordelia. She stared around. Could there be massive stone slabs hidden within the walls?

The others stumbled in, gazing around the Guildhall as if the place amazed them simply because they'd come in by a different route.

Cordelia grabbed Goose's hand as the Glovemakers carried him out of the tunnel. His skin was icy and his eyes were dim. She dug in Win's weather bag and pulled out a tiny bottle.

'We're down to the last bit of sunlight. There's moonlight and starlight but they won't help for long.'

Charity gathered a pile of cloaks from the mess left by the Glovemakers' jousting tourney. Tick kicked a jumble of jewel-encrusted Canemaker sticks out of the way. The Glovemakers laid Goose gently on the cloaks.

Sam whistled. Like a blob of liquid sunshine, a thousand Dulcet Fireflies swam through the air to hover over the Bootmaker, cloaking him in a raiment of light.

Cordelia trickled a little sunlight into Goose's mouth and his eyes flickered.

'We need to find the doorway now!' she burst out. 'Where's the map?'

Tick presented it to her (it had been his job to bring it through the tunnel because he was too small to help carry Goose).

Something strange had happened to the map. Its glowing lines were trailing light upwards, swaying like tendrils of luminant seaweed. Cordelia raised it level with her nose, squinting. At first, the wavering lines were all criss-crossing confusion. But she turned and suddenly the lines lined up with the Guildhall windows.

The windows must be in the gaps between the standing stones! she realized.

'But where's the doorway?' she wondered aloud.

It did not appear to be on the map.

The others set about trying to find it. Several hundred fireflies flitted into the vast dark like living stars, to light the way for the children. Hop lifted a flap of ancient tapestry, but found only smooth wall behind it. Sam moved paintings and Tick attempted to pull the wood panelling apart. The Glovemakers tried to prise open the iron doors of the Menacing Cabinet.

'Not in there!' Cordelia said quickly. The last thing they needed was loose Menacing ingredients causing chaos as they searched.

She carefully lined the map up with the gold words inscribed on the wall, and saw –

'There are more words further round!' She hurried over to Sam. 'They must be important.'

Sam climbed up, swung on to the plaster garland high above their heads and began kicking it.

Cordelia frowned down at the parquet floor. It fitted together like a jigsaw of wooden blocks, arranged in a spiral pattern.

'The doorway must be here somewhere,' Cordelia said.

'But how do we get to it?' Bernard wondered.

Cordelia dug her nails between the blocks of parquet, but she couldn't pull them loose.

'I think Merlin left instructions!' Sam called down. She had kicked away more plaster to reveal new golden words. She sat proudly above them, perched on the windowsill.

MAKERS, UNITE! MAGIC, IGNITE!

'That's not instructions!' Buster scoffed. 'That's decoration.'

'It's on the map, actually,' Hop argued calmly. 'It's a translation of the carved lines, see?'

'*Makers, Unite! Magic, Ignite!*' Cordelia murmured. She felt a jolt of excitement, right in her belly, and her nose tingled with the magic of the words. 'So, we unite!'

Cordelia hurried over to Goose and took his hand. His fingers were freezing.

'It's going to work, Goose,' she whispered.

Everyone looked very serious and a little self-conscious as they formed a circle. Buster didn't seem keen to hold hands with Cordelia, but she squeezed his hand tight anyway.

Bernard joined hands with Charity, completing the circle.

Everyone looked at Cordelia.

'Um, well – we've united,' she said.

They looked around expectantly, hoping the door would appear.

It didn't.

'We could *say* it?' Tick suggested.

Cordelia cleared her throat.

'*Makers, Unite!*' she cried. '*Magic, Ignite!*'

The others joined in.

'*Makers, Unite! Magic, Ignite!*' they chanted. '*Makers, Unite! Magic, Ignite!*'

It felt like good ideas, compliments and songs were being passed between them quicker than light moves. Everyone's innermost magic sang through their fingers, joining together in joyful noise. Cordelia couldn't tell if the great hum of excitement was coming from the centre of the circle or the centre of her chest.

'*Makers, Unite! Magic, Ignite! Makers, Unite! Magic, Ignite!*'

The floor juddered like a carriage going over cobblestones. The children felt it in their feet.

'*MAKERS, UNITE! MAGIC, IGNITE!*' they shouted in one voice.

Something was trying to break through the floor. It rattled and jolted, causing the parquet to jump and jostle.

But it didn't work.

The good feelings passing from hand to hand got too hot to hold, and the circle broke apart.

'What's wrong?' Hop panted, as Tick wailed and blew on his fingers.

'Why didn't it work?' Bernard flapped his hands.

'We're close!' Cordelia could feel it. 'But there's something missing.'

Whether it was the magic of the Guildhall or the aftershock of the rumbling beneath their feet, none of them would ever be quite certain. But at that moment the jumble of discarded Canemaker canes slipped and rolled, clattering, across the floor.

One particularly tenacious cane rolled furthest, to nudge Cordelia's toe. And she realized.

'We're missing a Maker!'

As she had done two days before, during a rather more hostile meeting of the Makers, Cordelia pointed out the family crests with their seven stars hanging above each of the workshop doors.

'The seventh star is to show we're strongest when we work together,' she reminded the others. 'So I think we need someone from all six Maker families to be in the circle.'

'But there's only five Maker families!' Buster objected.

'That's not actually true,' Cordelia told him. 'You're forgetting the Canemakers.'

'Luckily,' Sam added, from her perch above them, 'we know where to find the last Canemaker.'

Makers had not worked together this way in decades, and between them they devised a plan.

The words *Makers, Unite! Magic, Ignite!* twinkled above the children as they ran back and forth between workshops, sharing secrets and ingredients that had been jealously guarded for years.

'Here!' Charity called, appearing with a liquid indigo cloak streaming behind her. 'This'll do nicely for you, Bernard! It's made of Murk Moth silk.'

Bernard swept the cape round his shoulders and became instantly vaguer.

'Add this hat!' Cordelia suggested, dusting off an ancient Blear Bonnet. 'You'll be almost impossible to spot!'

Bernard put the bonnet on. He immediately became less evident.

Sam emerged from the Bootmaker workshop with a tangle of ribbons.

'I fink these are Running Ribbons,' she announced. 'Could be useful for lacing up boots so we can go faster.'

Tick grabbed the ribbons. 'I'm good at untangling things!'

'Here's an old pair of Moufle Gloves!' Buster chucked them to Sam. 'They'll be useful for any lock-picking you might have to do.'

Sam pulled them on.

The Makers raided all the workshops in the Guildhall, adding feathers from the Hatmaker workshop to cloaks, chains from the Watchmaker workshop to gloves, and ribbons from the Glovemaker workshop to hats. They worked until they had made four outfits cunning enough to disguise the heroes on their perilous expedition.

Cordelia, Sam, Buster and Bernard each pulled on a concealing cloak, and a hat to make them quick-witted and good at sneaking (Cordelia had stuck a few dried Vigil Weeds in the hatbands to help them stay alert). They wore gloves to keep their hands steady, and quicksilver watch chains to make them speedy. Their feet tingled in shoes newly laced with Running Ribbons. They did look rather eccentric, as several centuries' worth of fashion converged on them at once, but they felt ready.

Goose's eyes were dull by the time Cordelia knelt beside him to say goodbye.

'We'll be back as soon as we can,' she promised.

Charity and Hop had agreed to stay behind and take care of Goose. Tick had *not* agreed to stay behind, loudly insisting that he wanted to go too. But Hop had forbidden it (Cordelia privately thought this was for the best). That did not stop Tick trying to sneak out with them under a pilfered Bufflehead Hat, but Hop spotted him at once and held him firmly by the collar while the others slipped away.

When they stepped out of the Guildhall, it should have been dawn. But the day had dawned dark. The *Starless Days*, Peregrine had called them: days, long past, when there was so much destruction of magic it blackened the skies.

Ash swirled through the air and settled in drifts over the streets, making a nightmarish landscape of familiar places as they stole across the empty city. The Harpy did not appear above them, though they heard its wail on the wind.

The Tower loomed darker than Cordelia had ever seen it, cloaked in the murk of burnt magic.

They pummelled on the gate and the small viewing window was flung open.

'Whatcha want?' a gruff voice demanded.

'We're here to visit a prisoner,' Cordelia answered politely, taking off her bonnet so the eyes peering through the window could focus on her.

The window slammed shut.

'No visits today!' came the muffled answer.

'We're bringing food!' Cordelia sang loudly.

'What? No, we're not!' Bernard muttered.

But it worked. The little door within the big gate slammed open.

'Gimme it.' The guard reached for Cordelia's basket.

Sam jammed a nightcap on his head, and he was asleep before he hit the ground.

The way to the Traitors' Tower was clear. They slipped across the courtyard and along the dreary corridor. Their gloves helped them turn every door handle silently and their boot ribbons carried them quickly up the stairs. They made excellent thieves, there to steal someone to freedom.

They found Delilah Canemaker huddled in the corner of her cell.

'We're here to rescue you!' Cordelia called, shaking off her cloak.

Delilah flew to the bars, face ablaze. '*Rescue!*' she whispered fiercely.

The others shuffled backwards. Even Cordelia felt a flicker of alarm at the fire in the Canemaker's eyes.

'We need your help,' she said steadily.

Sam produced the keys she'd stolen from the guard, and Delilah Canemaker watched intently as they tried them in the lock. None of them worked.

'Here!' Cordelia said, pulling her hatpin from her hair and handing it to Sam.

'These Moufle Gloves are brilliant,' Sam said, winking at Buster.

Buster squared his shoulders proudly.

Three seconds later, the lock clicked.

Delilah left her cell like a queen stepping out of a carriage.

'TRESPASSERS!'

A guard loomed in the doorway.

The Glovemaker twins moved as one. They grabbed the guard's arms, but he was too strong for them. He hurled Buster aside and elbowed Bernard in the chest. Both boys fell to the floor, groaning. The guard aimed a thwack at Sam.

Cordelia reached into her basket and drew out a heavy watch. The guard grabbed at her as she lurched forward, hooking the watch on to his jacket.

The effect was instantaneous.

'It's a Leaden Time Watch, made to slow things down for the wearer when the world feels like it's moving too fast,' Hop had explained when he'd slipped it into the basket back at the Guildhall.

The guard's movements became slower with every tick of the clock. He turned with comical slowness, eyes bulging in surprise, as Cordelia pulled herself free of his grip. He opened his mouth. His voice came out deep and blunt.

'STO–'

The Glovemakers jumped to their feet.

Sam wiped her bleeding nose.

Delilah stamped on his foot.

And they all rushed out of the door before he finished the word.

'–OP!'

The guard in the gatehouse was snoring as Sam slipped his keys back on to his belt.

Delilah stared out at the world – it was a long time since she had been free in it.

'We're taking you to the Guildhall,' Cordelia told her.

Delilah's face darkened. 'Am I your prisoner?'

Cordelia saw Bernard and Buster exchange glances. They'd be ready to catch Delilah if she tried to run. But that would not be Makers uniting; that would not ignite magic. It would just ignite more strife.

'We need your help at the Guildhall because you're a Maker,' Cordelia explained. 'Please?'

Delilah studied her for several moments.

'I *am* a Maker,' she said quietly. 'And I'll help you.'

'Thank you!' Cordelia found she had been holding her breath. 'Thank you!'

'Ready for the run back?' Sam asked.

Cordelia realized they had forgotten one important thing: there was no disguise for Delilah. She wore a ragged dress and tattered shoes, and nothing to stop her being spotted by the Harpy.

Cordelia quickly untied her Running Ribbons and cut them in half, using a halberd mounted on the wall. She tied two of them round Delilah's shoes and laced up her own boots with the shortened bits of ribbon. Then she ripped her cloak in half and draped one piece over Delilah's shoulders. Finally, she pulled her bonnet off and tied it on Delilah's head.

'Ready.'

Everything went smoothly until they turned up Bond Street.

Cordelia and Delilah were falling behind the others: the Running Ribbons were fraying. Delilah tripped as Buster and Bernard turned into the alleyway.

'Wait!' Cordelia called.

Sam skidded round. 'Cor!' she shouted, pointing up at the sky.

The crackle of lightning made Cordelia's skin prickle. She turned to see the Harpy descending, swelling the storm around it with every beat of its wings.

Sam and Cordelia grabbed Delilah's hands. They raced down the alley and across the shabby square. The Harpy surged above them, wings striking the air like thunderclaps.

They hurtled into the Guildhall. Bernard and Buster slammed the door shut behind them. A screech of rage was muffled by the door.

Cordelia threw herself to a window to see the Harpy peel upwards into the sky.

'It'll be bringing Witloof,' she panted. 'We don't have much time.'

'*Makers, Unite! Magic, Ignite!*'

This time, the magic was alive like a waterfall, like lightning and laughing. Delilah's and Goose's hands were firmly in Cordelia's and the magic that passed between the Makers was older than time and stronger than sunlight.

It moved the ground beneath their feet.

The floor broke open.

A doorway erupted from below, weaving itself into being. It was no ordinary door – it was made of moss and vines and magic, of roots and ivy and starlight. It brought with it a smell of earth and wild air.

A long crack split the floor beneath their feet in a great circle, and the Makers scattered. Cordelia dragged Goose out of the way as vines of light snaked from the rupture, climbing upwards. Below, ancient stone steps unfurled in a spiral beyond the doorway. At the bottom was a huge tree stump, so old its middle had rotted hollow. It looked like a jagged mouth emerging from the earth.

A prehistoric kind of silence fell.

Cordelia gazed past the twisting vines of light, down into the sunken secret place.

In Merlin's time, Peregrine had said, *the roots of the Elixir Oak went so deep they reached the source of magic itself.* Thirteen centuries later, only a stump remained. But something glimmered within its hollow.

Cordelia's nose tingled, the way it always did when there was big magic close by.

'This is it!' she whispered.

'It's not very . . . *pretty*,' Charity quavered.

'Some magic isn't pretty,' Cordelia told her kindly. 'Wild magic doesn't need to be *pretty*: it's something much more interesting than that. Same as people.'

'Cor,' Sam murmured. 'Your freckles – they look different.'

Everyone stared at Cordelia.

'Yeah!' Bernard agreed. 'Like little specks of light.'

'I always get nose-tingles near big magic!' she explained, trying to look cross-eyed down her own nose.

She seized the brass key from Sam.

'C'mon! Let's open it!'

The doorway, an intricate tapestry of roots and leaves and stones and stars, towered above them. It was ancient and – Cordelia shivered – fearsome.

She peered at the door, from what felt like a respectful distance. 'But . . . where do I put the key?'

There was no keyhole.

Peregrine's words came back to her: *The legend insists that the one who keeps the key will never see it, even though it is right before their eyes.*

Cordelia stared at the brass key in her hand. She could see it clearly. Did that mean it wasn't the right key?

'HAH!' A cold laugh sounded behind them. 'You thought that old *door key* was the key to Merlin's magic?'

Witloof stood at the entrance to the Great Chamber. His Harpy, hunched behind him, had the wingspan of a dragon. Cordelia's stomach clenched with fear. The Makers bunched behind her.

'That's merely the key to Storm-Eye Hall. I have the *real* key right here.' Witloof patted his pocket. 'I collected it twelve years ago from the deck of a sinking ship.'

Cordelia dropped the useless brass key as Witloof stalked forward.

'But you *have* discovered something I didn't know,' he said, his eyes roving over the living doorway that had erupted in the Guildhall. 'The source of magic is not beneath

Stonehenge after all. You've saved me a journey halfway across the country.'

The Harpy clambered into the air. Lightning sizzled from its wings, chasing the Makers to the edge of the room.

Goose was left lying near the doorway, paler than ever. Cordelia darted forward, but a bolt of lightning drove her back, scarring the floor.

Witloof laughed.

'Stop!' Delilah cried, pushing Cordelia behind her.

'Ah, Delilah.' Witloof smiled. 'Won't you join me? We can destroy the Makers together, as we always planned.'

Delilah hesitated. For a moment, everything was still. The very air of the Guildhall seemed to bristle.

Then Cordelia saw Delilah's shoulders square.

'I won't wreck anything with you!' Delilah declared. 'It is far greater to create things than to destroy them. I am a Maker.'

Witloof's smile soured.

'You've picked the wrong side!' he sneered.

Delilah rushed at Witloof, fierce as a wolf protecting cubs. Before Cordelia could call out to warn her, there was a flash of glass and Delilah had frozen.

Witloof's knife glinted in his hand.

'Who's next?'

None of the children moved; fear held them in place. Witloof clapped his hands and the Harpy swooped off into the hallway.

Before Cordelia could think of a plan, an ice-eyed troop of Makers shuffled into the Guildhall, compelled before the Harpy's wings.

Cordelia saw her aunt and uncle, staring sightlessly. The Bootmakers, Cloakmakers, Glovemakers and the old Watchmaker hobbled slowly beside them. Cordelia felt her friends quail with dismay. Sir Hugo and Win appeared last, beside the king and the princess.

'The Leechglass worked quickly on them,' Witloof told the children. 'Though not as quickly as it did on this Bootmaker.'

He nudged Goose with his toe.

'Don't touch him!' Cordelia screamed.

But she was struck silent as the Harpy dragged a monstrous contraption into the chamber. It was a deformed glass dome, large enough to trap a man. A glass tank attached above the dome made the whole thing look like a huge, sinister hourglass. It had a disturbing gravity: Cordelia found it hard to drag her eyes away.

Witloof surveyed it proudly. 'I extracted all the magic I could from Peregrine's precious hidden places, to make this machine out of Leechglass.'

'You destroyed those places,' Cordelia growled. 'To make something evil.'

'This machine works the same way my pocket watch does,' Witloof went on, ignoring her, 'but it does not merely suck the magic from a butterfly to turn the hands of a clock. It extracts the magic from a different kind of creature and turns it into gold. An alchemist's ultimate goal.'

Cordelia was momentarily speechless. Then she croaked, '*There are other ways to make gold . . . greater and more terrible ways*. That's what you told me months ago.'

Witloof smiled horribly.

'Yes, I did, Miss Hatmaker. And I have perfected the machine, after years of experimentation. I stole the magic from those places to make the Leechglass dome . . . now all I need is magic strong enough to fuel it and I will make all the gold I desire.'

'You mean the Essence of Magic?' Cordelia said. 'That's why you needed Merlin's Map so badly!'

'Yes, indeed, Miss Hatmaker!' Witloof said. 'The Essence of Magic is the only fuel strong enough to power my machine. But do you know what the ingredient is? Do you know what creature contains the thing that can be turned to pure gold?'

'My father always told me that the human soul is the only –' Cordelia began. She broke off in horror.

'He told me the same thing once, long ago,' Witloof said. 'Let's see if he can finish teaching us that lesson.'

Witloof signalled and the Harpy dragged a wooden crate into the middle of the room. Ropes were tied round it: it had been hauled across the city.

'I have my first ingredient in here,' Witloof announced, yanking the ropes off. 'I've kept him prisoner for two months because I wanted him to be first into my Soul-jar.'

Witloof kicked the crate open and dragged a man out.

He was bound at the hands and gagged, thin and ragged. Cordelia stared.

The word came in a whisper.

'Father.'

Prospero Hatmaker was barely recognizable, but Cordelia would have known him anywhere. She hurtled towards him. They collided, tumbling in a heap against the crate. She tore the filthy rag from his mouth.

'Hello, littlest Hatmaker.'

His voice was cracked like dry land. His face was thin and dirty, but his eyes were brimming with a familiar shine. It was made of absolute love.

Cordelia was torn from her father's arms. She kicked in the air as her feet left the ground.

'*No!*' she screamed. 'Let me *go*!'

'CORDELIA!' Prospero cried.

'Put him in the Soul-jar,' Witloof ordered.

Cordelia tumbled to the floor. Massive grey wings unfurled as the Harpy lifted the heavy glass dome in its talons and swept Prospero inside with a cuff of its wing.

The dome clamped shut over him. He threw himself against the glass, then recoiled, burnt by the cold of the Leechglass.

Cordelia lurched forward, but talons dug into her shoulders and lifted her, helpless, off the ground.

'Now,' Witloof announced, striding over to the enchanted door. 'I will open the doorway.'

He reached into his pocket and drew out a slender bottle. A soft song was emanating from it, gentle and bright all at once, like dawn over the sea.

Cordelia was dizzy. The key was a song! She had been so swept up that she had forgotten Peregrine's explanation of how the keys worked: *The key is always something found in nature.*

'I worked out what the key was twelve years ago,' Witloof gloated. 'I hunted it over the ocean and stole it from the deck of a sinking ship.'

He strode to the door, brandishing the bottle.

'OPEN!' he commanded.

The doorway stirred, its vines writhing. But it remained closed.

'OPEN!' Witloof demanded.

The doorway of starlight and ivy seemed to get denser. The song got stronger, wilder. It made Cordelia's heart ache.

She looked to her father.

He stared steadily back at her, through the disaster of it all. He touched his nose and mouthed something.

Little Bear.

'Little Bear?' she whispered.

He nodded.

She tried to understand, but the facts were scattered like stars.

Little Bear had been her father's pet name for her mother. It was his favourite constellation – Ursa Minor – the one that showed you the way home, like Guinevere in the story . . .

'OPEN!'

Witloof's scream interrupted Cordelia's thoughts.

The ancient doorway stood rebelliously closed. A vine stretched out, wrapped itself round the song-bottle, and took it high above his head into the safety of moss and ivy.

'Prospero lied to me!' Witloof raged, turning on Cordelia. 'The song isn't the key after all!'

His face was suddenly an inch from hers. She struggled as the Harpy held her off the ground.

'*You* must have the real key after all!' he snarled.

Cordelia didn't have the key, but if he *thought* she did, she might have time to work everything out –

'*Give it to me!*'

'I *won't*!'

'Don't help him, Cor!' Sam howled.

Witloof strode over to Sam and, with a tiny flick of his glass knife, silenced her.

Cordelia's heart dropped.

The surprise on Sam's face became glassy.

'SAM!' Cordelia screamed. '*No!*'

The Glovemakers struggled, Charity struggled, Hop struggled, Tick even bit Witloof, but each fell silent, their faces vacant.

Tears ran down Cordelia's cheeks – would they freeze when Witloof cut her?

The knife was glinting in his hand. He raised it to her face. It whispered as it twisted through the air.

He held it an inch from her chin.

She could feel the cold coming off it.

'There is only one thing that will save your friends now,' Witloof said. 'You must open the way into the magic.'

'But I don't have the key.'

Even as she said it, she realized.

She did.

'Don't lie!' Witloof snarled. 'Your mother must have given it to you, if it isn't that blasted song! That's how the legend goes – the key is passed down from mother to daughter.'

From mother to daughter. Of course. Cordelia, remember those seven little gifts your mother gave you.

'All right!' Cordelia cried, struggling valiantly in the grip of the Harpy's talons. 'All right – I'll fetch it!'

Witloof's snarl broke open.

'Do it now! Unless you want to watch your friends and family freeze to death from the inside.'

'Then let me go,' Cordelia demanded, more bravely than she felt. 'I've got to get the key from – from its hiding place.'

Witloof's eyes narrowed.

'*I'll* fetch it,' he said.

'The key can only be carried by the keeper,' Cordelia invented. 'Otherwise it won't work.'

Witloof signalled to the Harpy. Cordelia was dropped to the floor. Her shoulders burned where the talons had gripped her.

She hurried across the Great Chamber, past her friends. Their glassy eyes stared as Witloof followed close behind. Cordelia picked up Win's bag of weather. She could feel it trembling.

'It's in the bottom of this bag,' she said.

'Get it quickly!' Witloof snapped.

She reached in and her hand closed over a jar. She pulled it out.

Snowflakes swirled inside it.

'That's not –' Witloof began.

Cordelia hurled the jar to the floor.

A snowstorm burst out in swirling white flakes.

Witloof lunged for her, a nightmare tearing through a lace curtain.

She skidded away, smashing the next jar without even looking at it.

A banner of colour exploded above her – a rainbow.

A third jar – great fists of ice crashed down in a deadly hailstorm.

And a fourth – she was swallowed by fog.

She ran into something solid – the wall.

'*Oof!*'

'I can hear you, dratted Hatmaker!' Witloof's voice was muffled, somewhere in the dense grey blanket.

But he could not see her. The fog was thick and pearly: Cordelia could hardly see her own nose in front of her face. The snow swirled down through the fog, muffling her footsteps.

She heard Witloof's breath, ragged with anger, getting closer. She crept sideways, quiet and quick.

'You know, Cordelia –' Witloof's voice was sing-song with victory – 'the longer you wait, the closer all the Makers come to freezing from Leechglass. If you want to save them, you'll *have* to open the doorway into the magic.'

She *did* have to open the doorway – it was the only way to save everyone. But it was exactly what Witloof wanted her to do, because it would give him the fuel to power his evil machine. The machine her father was trapped inside!

Cordelia listened hard – perhaps her father was calling out? Perhaps he could tell her what to do.

She could not hear his voice, but from somewhere in the fog the song from Witloof's bottle beckoned her. Going towards it felt like going home. Once again, her nose began to tingle.

Earlier, Sam had seen what Cordelia could not; she had pointed at her friend's face and said that her freckles looked different . . .

And the legend said that the one who held the key wouldn't see it, even though it was in front of their eyes . . .

A memory of her father touching each of her freckles lightly with the tip of his finger flashed in Cordelia's mind. *They could be part of a map*, he had told her.

For courage, Cordelia gripped the shell pendant with her mother's portrait. It was a fine portrait, so detailed it was possible to see the freckles on her nose – seven of them, in the shape of the Ursa Minor constellation, just like Cordelia's.

She could sense the great doorway beyond the fog. She walked forward and felt her nose meet leaves and roots and soft moss.

There was a primordial stirring, as though a constellation of stars was converging on her.

The vines fluttered, the roots moved, the moss parted.

The doorway was opening.

The vines curled back and Cordelia stepped through the enchanted doorway, on to the great spiral stairway leading down to the heart of Merlin's magic.

The vines curled back and Cordelia stepped through the enchanted doorway, on to the great spiral stairway leading down to the heart of Merlin's magic. The very air sparkled with ancient secrets.

'Harpy!' Witloof's voice shook Cordelia from her trance. 'Bring the pipe and pump!'

Cordelia turned. Witloof loomed behind her.

'You opened the doorway for me,' he sneered triumphantly.

'*No!*' Cordelia gasped. 'Not for you!'

She plunged down the stone stairs, but not before she yanked out the last storm jar from Win's bag: the Armada storm. It shuddered with a terrible strength.

The cork was stiff from centuries of stuckness.

Witloof's expression flared in alarm as he recognized what she held in her hands. He leaped forward.

'*Don't touch that!*'

She tugged the cork with her teeth.

He grabbed her hair, wrenching her head back.

The force budged the cork and the Armada storm blasted from the jar. Massive clouds that had been crammed into a jar for two hundred years finally had the chance to roar and storm.

Witloof was flung upwards on an explosion of air while Cordelia was hurled down the spiral steps. She crashed into the ancient tree stump. Carved into the wood was a tiny picture of a bear. She reached out and touched it, feeling its grooves beneath her fingertips.

Starry water trickled over her fingers. It was bubbling up from the middle of the stump.

'The Essence of Magic!' Cordelia could not hear her own voice above the deafening roar of the wind.

She scooped some into her mouth. It tasted the way flying dreams feel. Quickly, she filled the empty storm jar and ran up the steps.

A hurricane was howling round the Great Chamber, whipping paintings off the walls. The windows burst outwards in a great rain of glass and the Harpy was thrown into the very apex of the dome. Old Tudor plaster was scoured from the walls, bricks crumbled. It twisted down the spiral stairs and sucked the magic from the stump – up, up into a vortex of water, arcing in a starry column through the turbulent air.

As Cordelia reached the top of the steps, the enormous wind forced her sideways.

'*Goose!*' she screamed. He was lying frozen, staring into nothing. She fought through the storm to tip her jar of magic against his cold lips.

BOOM!

A thunderclap shattered the column of magic, which fell as starry rain.

Goose was coming back into his eyes.

'C-Cordelia!' he wheezed.

She flung her arms round him.

They were shoved across the floor by a violent gust of wind and collided with a frozen figure. It was Sam.

'GIVE THE MAGIC TO EVERYONE!' Cordelia had to bellow to be heard.

She poured some into Sam's mouth.

Sam came back, shivering with relief.

'Cor, ya beauty!'

Cordelia grinned. The tempest raged around them. They had to hold on to each other to avoid being blown away.

They tipped the magic on to Charity's lips. Sam slopped some into the Glovemakers' mouths. Goose got the idea, scooping handfuls for Hop and Tick. Cordelia splashed the last of it between Delilah's cold lips.

Everyone came back to themselves with shouts of joy.

As Cordelia raised her empty jar to refill it with the raining magic, she saw something that froze her, bone-deep.

The Soul-jar was working. The magic coming down in the form of silver rain had filled its upper tank. Something was happening to her father: he glowed, as if he was wearing his great golden soul on the outside of his body.

'QUICK!' Cordelia screamed, tearing across the floor. Her friends followed, linking hands. Together they were stronger than the storm that tried to sweep them off their feet.

Prospero's light was being torn from him, twisting away through tubes above his head.

Cordelia heaved with all her strength, the Leechglass burning her hands with fiery ice, but it was impossibly heavy. It wouldn't budge.

'Father!'

Suddenly, miraculously, the Soul-jar began to lift upwards. Her friends were helping: all of them, united, were able to lift what one could not.

The dome slowly tilted – Prospero got his arm out –

'*No!*' A screech ripped through the air.

Witloof was staggering through the storming chaos towards his wicked machine. Cordelia saw his furious maw distort as he screamed, '*Harpy!* Lower the dome! Keep it *closed*!'

The Harpy descended on the Soul-jar. The children couldn't match its strength: the dome began to close again.

'Father! *Quick!*'

The gap was narrowing.

Cordelia grabbed her father's thin arm and pulled.

Weak though he was, helped by Cordelia's sheer willpower, Prospero struggled out from under the glass.

Witloof lurched forward.

'*HARPY!*' he roared in fury.

The Harpy reared back fearfully as Witloof lunged.

It must have been a particularly strong gust that did it: the wind picked Witloof off his feet and swept him, like rubbish, along the floor.

He was thrust under the glass dome, just as the Harpy managed to clamp it shut again.

'*No!*' Cordelia yelled. Even Witloof did not deserve a fate such as this.

But the Harpy's eyes blazed with a kind of savage glee as it held the dome closed.

Something very strange began to happen to Witloof. Darkness was being drawn from him, sucked up into the dome of the Soul-jar, spiralling through the corkscrew tubes. He was becoming less substantial, somehow less *there*, by the second.

He yelled something, desperate, to the Harpy.

The Harpy simply watched him with lightning in her eyes.

The Essence of Magic bubbled and hissed in the fuel container; dark matter twisted through its glass tubes. The whole Soul-jar shook and smoked as it reduced a man into the purest version of himself, just as its inventor had intended.

Cordelia felt strong, safe arms close round her. She buried her head in her father's chest until there was silence.

'It's over,' her father murmured.

Cordelia poked her head out.

Witloof was gone.

Sitting in the middle of the Soul-jar was a small lump of lead.

The Harpy gave a wild cry and took to the air. It stretched its wings wide and swooped out of a shattered window into the sky, sweeping the enormous storm before it. The Armada storm was herded away, as though the Harpy was merely the shepherd to a flock of woollen clouds.

Inside the Guildhall, Cordelia stared at the fist-sized lump of lead gently smoking in the Soul-jar.

'But – but where did he go?' Cordelia asked, unable to tear her eyes from the place where Witloof had been.

'His machine was designed to turn the human soul into gold,' Prospero said. 'But, like every greedy alchemist before him, he's ended up with lead.'

'Y-you mean that's *him*?'

'It is him, distilled. What's left of his soul.'

Her father took her by the shoulders, steering her firmly away into the middle of the Great Chamber.

Cordelia saw the ranks of frozen Makers, staring icily at her and the young Makers.

'Come on!' she said. 'We've got to revive our families!'

The children and Prospero set to work dosing Witloof's victims with the Essence of Magic.

Because they were much more intent on curing everybody as quickly as possible, it happened that Goose was the one to revive Clodworthy Cloakmaker, and Bernard Glovemaker brought Nigella Bootmaker back to consciousness. Uncle Tiberius was restored by Charity Cloakmaker, and Hop Watchmaker rescued Mr Glovemaker. Vera and Violet were both gallantly given the magic by Tick, and Delilah Canemaker cautiously administered the magic to Aunt Ariadne.

By the time everyone was brought round, Glovemakers were stammering thanks to Bootmakers, and Hatmakers were gushing gratitude to Cloakmakers.

Cordelia restored Sir Hugo Gushforth, who buried his head in his hands and wailed.

Prospero dosed the king, and Sam tipped the magic into the princess's mouth. They came back to themselves with brays of surprise.

Delilah was carrying magic to Ignatius Bootmaker when the king caught sight of her.

'*Seize her!*' the king commanded. '*The Canemaker traitor is loose!*'

But Cordelia planted herself firmly in front of Delilah.

'*No!*' she bellowed back. 'She helped *save* us all! She deserves a second chance!'

Every Maker in the chamber looked round.

Cordelia hastily added, 'Your Majesty!'

The king seemed astonished that nobody was interested in clapping the Canemaker in irons. For a moment, it looked like Delilah might bolt for the door. But she straightened her spine and raised her chin.

'I was wrong to work for Witloof,' she said. 'Anger drove me like a whip drives a horse. But I realize now . . . thanks to these courageous Makers –' she indicated the children, scattered around the room – 'it is a far braver thing to work together than to break apart. Please, Your Majesty, let me join the Makers again.'

His Majesty studied her for a long moment.

'Very well,' he eventually boomed. 'I *would* rather like an impressive cane to wave about. Something gold with feathers on it!'

Nodding eagerly, Delilah hurried away to her family's old workshop.

Cordelia was about to follow when she found Win Witloof in her path.

'Did you use it?' Win asked. 'The storm?'

'Isn't it obvious?' Cordelia laughed, sweeping an arm around the storm-wrecked Guildhall.

The old Tudor mouldings had been scoured away, revealing what had been hidden beneath them for hundreds of years: the great standing stones around which the Guildhall had been built.

'If you hurry, you'll be able to see the storm sweeping away across the land,' Cordelia told Win. 'The storm that brought your ancestors greatness.'

Win smiled. 'Let it blow away. And it can take the name Witloof with it! From now on, I think I'll stick with Win Fairweather.'

'Well, Win Fairweather, all your weather was extremely useful,' Cordelia said.

'Did you like the haar?' Win asked eagerly.

'The what?'

'The haar. It's a type of sea fog,' Win explained. 'I collected it off the coast near Aberdeen. Was it good?'

'It was brilliant!' Cordelia confirmed. 'In fact, it might well have been the haar that saved the day!'

Although the Makers were restored, their spirits were shaken. Tick had hidden in his grandfather's jacket. Even when Aunt Ariadne and Uncle Tiberius saw Prospero, they could only cling to him and weep.

'They all need something to cheer them up!' Cordelia muttered.

'I got an idea,' Sam said.

She hared off to the Hatmaker workshop and came back leading a banner of fireflies.

'*Ooooh!*'

A soft gasp went up from the crowd.

The fireflies looped and swooped with liquid light as Sam led them through the Guildhall. She poured handfuls of sunlight into people's palms and they marvelled as the fireflies danced around them.

Prospero smiled. 'It seems we have a Lightbringer in our midst.'

'Lightbringer?' the king boomed. 'Someone is using magic without a royal charter!'

Sam gasped fearfully but Cordelia stepped forward. If Sam was going to be sent to prison, she would go too. They would go together, as sisters.

'Magic should belong to those who make it!' Cordelia declared. 'Everyone whose magic can make the world better should be allowed to decide how to use it, not just the man with the shiniest hat!'

The king's eyes bulged in surprise.

'Shiniest hat?' he blustered, adjusting his crown. 'Preposterous!'

Then the princess spoke up.

'Father, it's time to end that silly royal charter tradition. It was started by a *dreadfully* greedy king!'

The king looked mutinous for a moment, but then beckoned for more of Sam's sunlight.

'Very well, I'll scrap the royal charters,' he muttered, 'but I'll keep my shiny hat, thank you.'

Sam's hand was sweaty, gripped in Cordelia's. But her eyes were star-bright.

'I can make magic now, Cor!'

Goose nudged Cordelia and pointed.

Sir Hugo sat holding a single crumb of sunlight between his finger and thumb, gazing at it as though it contained all the wonders of the galaxy within it.

Princess Georgina sidled shyly up to him, staring at it too.

'He's finally got her attention!' Cordelia said.

With a heroic flourish, Sir Hugo presented Her Highness with the tiny piece of sunlight.

The princess seemed, if it was possible, even more interested in the light gleaming in Sir Hugo's eye.

Cordelia and Goose watched as the actor kissed the princess's hand. Fireflies spiralled around them in ecstasy.

'Would ya look at *that*?' Sam pointed.

Cordelia and Goose turned to see Goose's mother, Mrs Nigella Bootmaker, long-time enemy of Tiberius Hatmaker (who himself had uttered many a dreadful and sarcastic remark to the same Bootmaker), shuffle up to him. She held a speck of sunlight between her fingers.

'Tiberius,' Mrs Bootmaker murmured. 'I – I'd like us to be friends again.'

'*Again?*' Goose whispered.

For a moment, nobody was sure what Tiberius Hatmaker would do. Even he himself seemed uncertain.

Then he squeezed Mrs Bootmaker in one of his fiercest bear hugs ever.

'All right, Jelly!' Uncle Tiberius rumbled. 'Friends again!'

'*Jelly?*' Goose spluttered.

Cordelia hooted with laughter. She had never seen Goose's mother smile, let alone shriek with glee as she was spun through the air.

'This is for you, Goose.' Someone tugged his sleeve.

It was Charity Cloakmaker, holding out a small piece of sunlight.

Goose blushed ferociously.

Through the shattered windows of the Guildhall, light was rising. The Armada storm was blowing away Witloof's shadow ash.

Cordelia wandered to the magical doorway. She sat down, perched at the top of the ancient stone steps.

Her father came to sit next to her. She slipped her hand into his, relishing the familiarity of his fingers wrapped round hers. They were silent for a long while, staring down at the starry magic bubbling from the ancient stump.

'I think we should start a school here, in the Guildhall, and teach Making to anyone who wants to learn!' Cordelia said.

'That is a beautiful idea, Dilly. You are a worthy keeper of the key,' her father answered, touching his fingertip to each of her freckles. 'Just like your mother.'

He pulled her into a hug.

'That bottle of song Witloof had. Where is it?'

Cordelia heard the question through his chest. It trembled.

The doorway whispered its leaves, bringing the song-bottle down, entwined in a tendril of ivy.

'It's more than just a song, isn't it?' Cordelia asked as her father took it gently from the ivy.

Prospero held it to his heart like a flame to light a candle.

'Your friends are waiting to speak to you, my little Hatmaker,' he said, motioning to Goose and Sam, Buster and Bernard Glovemaker, Charity Cloakmaker and Hop Watchmaker, who stood smiling at her from a polite distance.

She scrambled up and scampered to join them.

'You made us be friends,' Bernard said, crushing Cordelia in a hug. 'We're so glad.'

Buster threw his arms round Cordelia too, and so did Goose and Sam, and Hop and Charity.

'We're *so* glad!'

So glad, so glad, so glad! The words murmured around Cordelia like good spells.

Violet and Vera stole towards them shyly. Tick detached himself from his grandfather and came dashing towards them, yelling:

'I'M GLAD TOO!'

Several nights later, the Armada storm had finally exhausted itself. It had blown over all the chimneypots in London, whirled round many weathervanes and dashed the clouds against the roof of the sky before sweeping them out to sea.

Cordelia and her father were sitting on the chimney of Hatmaker House, the night a great dome of stars above them.

Cordelia was wearing her mother's dress. It had been torn in the storm, but she had mended it with spiderweb. The stitches shimmered in the starshine, and Cordelia thought that mended things are so much more beautiful than perfect things.

She pointed to the North Star and traced the Ursa Minor constellation from it.

'That's the Little Bear,' she said. 'The one that showed Guinevere the way home when she got lost in the forest.'

Prospero smiled. 'Yes, it is. And when Merlin needed to make a key to his map, he gave Guinevere the key in the form of her freckles. Perhaps it was a little joke between them, that following Guinevere's nose would always lead her to magic.'

Cordelia wrinkled her nose, glad that it was its own kind of compass.

'Did Mother know she had the key to Merlin's magic?' Cordelia asked. 'And why didn't you tell me I did? It would have made everything so much easier.'

Her father wrapped his arm round her.

'I wanted to protect you. Bearing the key to Merlin's magic is a great honour – but also a burden. It is even a danger. I wanted to wait until you were old enough to understand it all.'

'I *am* old enough!' Cordelia protested.

'That was my mistake. You have proved yourself more than capable.'

Cordelia stuck her chin up. Her father ruffled her hair.

'You cleverly followed my map and found the library. And you helped protect the magic in a much bigger way than I ever expected you'd have to.'

'Even Peregrine didn't tell me I had the lost key,' Cordelia said.

She felt a flash of sadness when she thought of Peregrine, carried away in the arms of the river.

Earlier that day, Cordelia and her father had ventured up the Fleet's tunnel to find that the Library of Maps had been completely destroyed by fire and river. The collection of maps had been burned or scattered.

'It's all right,' Cordelia had said bravely, standing in the empty ruins of the library. 'The maps that survived the fire are out there now, ready to be discovered. Perhaps one day someone will pick up a strangely shaped rock and get a certain twitch in their nose and it will lead them somewhere magical.'

Now, on the rooftop, as the stars twinkled down on them, father and daughter linked hands.

'Peregrine didn't know you held the key to Merlin's magic,' he told her. 'It was a deeply kept secret in your mother's family. When I was younger, I became interested in the legend of Merlin's magic. I'd just been made a Mapmaker – my old schoolteacher named me as his successor – and I was determined to work out the secret of the key. With a friend of mine, I discovered the truth: the key is a person. We never discovered the true location of Merlin's magic, though. Merlin's decoy of Stonehenge had us all fooled.

'Around the same time that we realized the key was a person, I began to understand that my friend was interested in this for all the wrong reasons. He had developed a desperate, all-consuming obsession with making gold. It began with the desire to regain his dwindling family fortune and became a dangerous fascination with the idea that the Essence of Magic might be turned into the purest gold ever seen. I feared what would happen to the person who held the key if my friend discovered her identity.

'I vowed to discover her first. I trawled through old records and studied ancient paintings and deciphered scrolls, and eventually I worked out the location. I travelled to an overgrown cottage on the Cornish coast, and found an old lady living there, on the edge of the wild ocean.

'I warned her that her secret was close to being discovered, that there was somebody out there who might do her harm. I vowed to protect her with all that I had. She pointed into her garden, where her granddaughter was up a tree, eating apples and singing . . .'

Prospero's voice trailed away. Father and daughter both looked down at the tiny portrait of Stella Hatmaker painted on the shell necklace resting against Cordelia's heart.

Prospero pulled the small song-bottle from his pocket. Cordelia heard the song coming faintly from within it. Her father gazed at it with an ocean-deep kind of longing.

'Loving your mother taught me what life is for – the simple purpose of having a soul is to love with it. Loving turns your soul to gold,' he said. 'I discovered that all at once, in an orchard at the edge of an ocean.

'I lied to my friend – said we'd made a mistake: the key was a song, not a person. I tried to convince him that he'd been on the wrong path, and that alchemy wouldn't bring him the gold he craved. I told him the song was long forgotten, that our path to Merlin's magic was at a dead end. But, as your mother and I crossed the oceans, travelling the world together, I could feel my old friend like a shadow at our backs . . .

'Twelve years ago, when the storm struck our ship, all I thought of was your mother and you, your safety. Months later, when the reality of it all was becoming clearer, I recalled strangenesses about that shipwreck I couldn't explain: the ship on the horizon that seemed to be following us, the storm striking from an empty sky, the howl of a Harpy on the wind . . . I searched for answers for years . . . Then, when I was sailing home a couple of months ago, I heard the howl of a Harpy once more, and I knew I was in danger.'

'Jack said it tore you into the sky –'

'It did. It carried me to the Bleak Isle, somewhere in a raging cold sea. It was a fortress of rock and ruination: Witloof's hideout, where he tampered with the darkest magic. I was trapped, unable to escape. When Agatha came, that brave little bird flying through storm and magic to find me, all I had to give her was the necklace. I sent it back to you as a sign I was alive. And to remind you who you are.'

They were silent for a while, and the song twined around them.

'Witloof's got some form of glory now, if that's what he wanted,' Prospero said. 'He's been put in a small glass cabinet in the British Museum. For centuries, people will be able to admire him. They might even say to themselves, "What an exemplary piece of lead!" '

Cordelia couldn't quite bring herself to smile.

The song wrapped itself round her shoulders like a cloak and she felt a little better.

She laid her hand on the bottle. 'It's a part of her, isn't it – this song?'

Prospero looked far out into the sky. Cordelia could see stars sprinkled in his eyes.

'Yes, it is.' Constellations trickled down his face. 'I searched for years, hoping I'd find her. I thought she might still be alive. But Witloof separated her song from her body, and kept only what he needed. What he *thought* he needed.'

The song grew mournful.

Cordelia said, 'She's in her song, though, isn't she? So you *did* find her.'

'Yes, but now that I have, I realize it's time to let her go.'

Cordelia looked at the small bottle. No matter how much she yearned to keep it close and cared for, it was too small a vessel for such a beautiful song. This song was made for oceans and wide skies.

She put her hand gently over her father's.

Together, they opened the bottle.

With a joyful gust, the song rushed out.

It surged around them. For a moment, everything made sense to Cordelia, as though the whole world was woven together with song.

Then the song swirled upwards, eager to greet the great swathe of stars above it.

'She's everywhere now,' Cordelia whispered. 'So she'll always be near us.'

Her father nodded and pulled her tight to his chest.

'And she's here.' He laid a hand over Cordelia's heart. 'So she'll always be with us.'

The air was cold and bright and tasted of adventure.

And sawdust.

Cordelia, Sam, Goose and Jack Fortescue watched as the mast went up.

It climbed the sky above the dockyard and eventually came to a stop, pointing directly to the heavens.

'BRILLIANT!' Goose yelled.

Cordelia and Sam cheered. Jack hollered. The shipbuilders clapped and whistled. Captain Hatmaker climbed down the side of the half-made ship and jumped to the ground beside Cordelia.

'She's going to be a beauty, Dilly!' he said. 'What shall we call her?'

Cordelia gazed at the beautiful curve of the hull, the shining deck and the towering mast.

Before she could come up with a good enough name – one that captured the sweet urgency of a prow cutting through water and the wildness of a big wind in the sails –

'We can't be late for the portrait!' Aunt Ariadne came hurrying across the dockyard.

'But there's someone missing,' Cordelia objected.

'Who are you talking about, Dilly dearest? It's only the Maker families sitting for the new portrait,' Aunt Ariadne told her. 'I saw Clodworthy Cloakmaker on the way here; he said they'll be at the Guildhall promptly. And your family will be there already, Goose. Jones is taking Great-aunt in her chair. Even Miss Canemaker has brushed her hair.'

'But there's someone missing!' Cordelia insisted. 'We're waiting for him to arrive.'

'Who on earth do you mean?'

Cordelia and Goose grinned at each other.

'He's a member of our family and he isn't here,' Cordelia said.

'He needs to be included,' Goose added.

Cordelia pointed across the dock. A galleon was mooring at the wharf.

'There – that's the ship he's coming in on – the *Maiden's Promise*. She's just docked!'

The deck of the *Maiden's Promise* was filled with people whose hungry faces suggested they hadn't seen land for a very long time. One of them broke away from the crowd, and before the ship's huge ropes had been secured round the bollards, a thin figure was swinging from the rigging on to the quayside.

Sam gave a little cry, like a bird whose feathers were made of pure hope.

And she was running.

The Hatmakers followed and, when they reached the opposite wharf, they found Sam in a jumble of arms and tears, hugging a lad so ferociously it looked like she'd never let him go.

'It's Len Lightfinger, Sam's brother,' Cordelia explained to her family. 'The princess gave him a royal pardon to thank Sam for bringing light back into her heart. She sent for him to be returned to England at once.'

Cordelia smiled at the general outpouring of delight, and at her family's amazed faces. Sam and Len were holding on to each other like they had just discovered buried treasure.

Cordelia looked back at the Hatmakers' new ship across the dock. One day soon, the wind would sing through the sails and carry the boat across the oceans . . . and take her father with it. She was glad that Jack felt ready to go to sea again, but she felt a twinge of envy.

'The new ship is beautiful,' Cordelia said to her father. 'But I'm sad you'll be going away.'

Prospero swept her up in his arms. 'But you're coming with me next time, Dilly! We'll set sail on the spring tides – a new ship for new adventures!'

Cordelia felt an ocean swell of excitement lift her heart.

'I've thought of a name!' she cried. 'Let's call her *Little Bear*!'

As if in answer – faint on the air, but true as a whispered secret – Cordelia heard the murmur of a song.

It lifted her hair and made her nose tingle.

Glossary

Here follows a brief but useful list of ingredients most potent and valuable to an Apprentice Hatmaker.

Aurora Bush – ***Fructus aurora*** – The berries grown on this bush change colour through their ripening day, turning from pale orange to pink, purple and eventually blue. Hatmakers crush the unripe berries to make a dye, creating hats that change colour slowly, mimicking the breaking of dawn. Used in Transformation Hats, for wearers hoping to expand their horizons.

Bilious Goat – *Gāt grof* – A particularly gruff goat native to the Highlands of Scotland. This magnificently bearded beast is notorious for challenging rivals to headbutting

contests. Rivals include other goats, oddly shaped stumps, or humans who dare to make eye contact. Tufts of the beard used on a hat encourage the wearer to valiantly defend the helpless, though overuse may provoke a quarrelsome temper, leading to headbutting, which may in turn result in concussion.

Bombination Bee – ***Apis bomba*** – Large, round bee with an intense wing-hum. The buzz of a single bee inspires confidence, although hearing the hum of an entire swarm may cause overconfidence and bombast. A Bombination Bee's hum, captured on a tuning fork, can be transferred to a Confidence Bonnet for extra potency.

Cloud Velvet – ***Nimbus mollis*** – This beautifully soft, lilac velvet is made from the underbellies of clouds. Cloud Velvet becomes snagged on rocks on the high peaks of mountains and is collected by Makers using a special comb. Woven into a cap or bonnet, it promotes a sense of lofty serenity in the wearer, though care must be taken never to collect velvet from storm clouds, lest the wearer be affected by a tempestuous mood.

Cully Gull – ***Larus amicus*** – This affable avian is often found nesting in Ardourwood Trees. Its call of 'HAL-LOO HAL-LOO!' gladdens the heart. On seeing a fellow of its kind, the

Cully Gull becomes so delighted that it raises its crest very quickly, causing several of the bright yellow feathers to fly out. A Hatmaker may collect these feathers to use on all manner of Friendship Hats.

Ditty Beads – *Zingen zaad* – These beads are, in fact, dried Werble Flower seeds. The wind sings through the flower petals all summer, and by autumn the seeds are full of tunes that warble when they move. Often used on Song Bonnets, the seeds harmonize with the wearer's voice to make their solos more melodious.

Elysium Seeds – *Pituita paradisa* – Tiny, bright gold seeds from the Arcadian Aster. When touched by the morning sun, these seeds spring into fully grown flowers with a scent so heavenly it has been likened to walking on air. Elysium Seeds are used in special party hats: the wearer sprinkles a small bottle of sunshine on their apparently ordinary (but secretly seeded) hat, causing a meadow of flowers to spring spectacularly into being on their head.

Empyrean Crystals – ***Crystallum caelum*** – In ancient times, these clear, bright-blue crystals were believed to be pieces of heaven that fell to earth when the stars made holes

in the sky. These crystals are found on the slopes of Mount Ararat and can refract sunlight for use in alchemy.

Essence of Joy – ***Essentia gaudii*** – Found in all clouds and consequentially also in rain, joy is usually diffused enough to appear as silver linings. However, cloud or rain can be distilled by a skilled alchemist to obtain Essence of Joy, which is used in this more concentrated form for all types of Celebration Hats.

Evocation Shells – ***Cockle memoria*** – Found in the depths of the Morari Lagoon, these tiny shimmering spiral shells carry memory in their whorls. Used both to celebrate joyful times and to bring comfort and honour the remembrance of lost loved ones, these beautiful shells remind the wearer of the great spiral of life.

Fabula Flowers – ***Flos fabulae*** – Fabula Flowers grow on long, twisting vines that reach up to forty feet in height. The flowers are large, purple and frilly, and inspire the imagination of the wearer. Due to the rambling nature of the plant, the flowers can induce long-windedness unless paired with something to focus the mind, such as Pearls of Wisdom.

Flos Moth – ***Lepidoptera floris*** – With iridescent wings of many colours, and a sweet perfume that they trail through the air, Flos Moths are found wherever magical flowers grow in abundance. The Iceni tribe revered Flos Moths, believing them to be enchanted flowers come to life. A Hatmaker will never harm a Flos Moth, but it is possible to encourage them to flutter around a floral hat to wonderful effect.

Friendship Knot – ***Nodus amicus*** – A simple but strong knot, in which two ends (of ribbon, string or thread) are looped together to form a bond that will hold through thick and thin.

Fustian String – ***Filum fustium*** – Traditionally made in the Egyptian city of Fustat, near Cairo, this string is so strong it can hold together the wildest of claims, and tie together even the most precarious plans.

Gaudian Fern – ***Osmunda celebrare*** – A large and impressive fern, with fronds that unfurl triumphantly at daybreak. The leaves unleash a cheerful trumpeting sound as they unroll, celebrating the new day. A frond of Gaudian Fern will lend a sense of triumphal celebration to a hat.

Gladsome Rose – ***Rosa glathr*** – A deep-red rose, its scent gladdens the heart and its rich colour brings a sense of joy. It is a wonderful flower, inspiring the wearer to optimism and gratitude, two of the most empowering emotions.

Glamour Spider – ***Aranea grammatica*** – A spider with silver-tipped legs, she spins a web of such lustrous beauty that it catches looks of admiration, as well as flies. In Hatmaking, the web silk is used to stunning effect. However, the Hatmaker collecting the silk must be careful to distract the Glamour Spider with a drop of honey before harvesting, as a bite from this spider can cause intense self-obsession and may even result in a case of full-blown narcissism if not properly treated.

Insidious Ink Squid – ***Sepia esculenta sinistra*** – Ink from this squid was historically used to write letters of blackmail, conspiracy or treachery. It is a very wary creature, living in the darkest part of the Gloaming Ocean. One drop of its ink is used to temper the effects of any dye that might cause excessive buffoonery in sensitive people. It is important to use sparingly lest the wearer become paranoid and obsessed by conspiracy theories.

Jesterbell Flowers – ***Flos joculans*** – These tiny flowers are named because they are shaped like the little bells that jesters wore on their hats in medieval times. They tinkle merrily and give the wearer a sense of comical jollity that admirers are bound to find amusing.

Light – ***Lux*** – All forms of light are caught using either an Oculus Glass (fitted over a bowl or tray) or particular crystals such as Empyrean Crystals. There are, of course, infinite qualities of light. Below you will find the five main types used in Hatmaking.

~ **Dawn** – Excitable and abounding, this light is collected at daybreak. It is mostly used on Inspiration Bonnets, Big Idea Bicorns and Kindle Caps.

~ **Moon** – Gentle and mysterious, moonlight has different qualities (depending on the phase of the moon) and is most easily collected in the form of beams. Moonbeams collected during the waxing phase are excitable (and are used, for example, on Strengthening Hats), while those collected during the waning phase are pacifying (often used on Placid Hats). Beams from the full moon are strongest and are often used by opera singers and performers keen to hold sway over their audience.

~ **Star** – Soft and tingly on the skin, starlight gives hope when things feel dark and difficult. It is also used to give shimmer to evening wear, but fades if exposed to sunshine, so should only be worn after sundown.

~ **Sun** – The strongest of all the lights, particularly when collected at the zenith. Solid sunlight can be cut into shapes, much like gold leaf, and used to decorate hats to dazzling effect. A word of caution: if too much sunlight is used on a hat, the wearer may become hot-headed.

~ **Twi** – A blend of late sunlight and early starlight, twilight can be tinged pinkish, peachy, blueish or purplish, with occasional flashes of green. It calms the mind by fostering a deep sense of connection with nature, and is often twisted into the threads used to sew Sweet-Dream Nightcaps.

Lilt twigs – ***Lulte scrubb*** – The Lilt Bush is found growing on the south side of the North Downs. The young pink twigs are used to create a gentle, comforting fire, while the mature, dark-red branches create a stronger blaze. The twig fire imparts a lullaby-like mood, while the branch fire is more rousing. Both are used for transformational work in alchemy.

Luminant Mushrooms – ***Fungi illuminati*** – These mushrooms glow in the dark, growing wild in the Underearth Forest. Their pale, pockmarked caps resemble tiny half-moons scattered across the forest floor. Makers may cultivate these mushrooms by recreating their natural habitat; they will thrive in a dark box of very rich soil. They are said to promote inspiration and bright ideas.

Mesmeric Thread – ***Filum hypnoticum*** – Glamour Spider web that has been twisted with full moonbeams, beneath the whisper of Trancing Trees. Used on hats to captivating effect.

Murk Moth – ***Lepidoptera obscura*** – Moths that are attracted, unusually, to darkness (not to the light, as is normally the case). Deep indigo and very velvety, the fully grown moths lay eggs on the leaves of Umbra Trees. The silk produced by the worms is dusky and obscure, making it excellent for imparting mystery to garments. A garment made entirely of Murk Moth silk may prove difficult to see, however, and such garments are often lost at the back of wardrobes.

Mystique Bird – ***Avis kharisma*** – An ostentatious bird with great allure, the Mystique Bird has plumy white tail feathers that are used to lend intense panache to hats. However, the

effects of the panache only last about a day before it begins to fade. The panache eventually becomes tired and tedious, so the wearer should quit while the going is good. Removing the hat before the wearer becomes tiresome (exhibiting a tendency, for example, to repeat the same jokes or sing the same song four times in a row) is advised. In some cases, the hat may have to be forcibly removed, especially if the wearer has become attached to being the centre of attention.

Natterer Bat – ***Myopis nattereriae*** – Whiskers from a Natterer Bat will encourage a stoic wearer to be more expressive and talkative. Worn on a hat, the whiskers encourage witty conversation.

Noctus Knots – ***Næturhnútur*** – Complicated knots, said to be invented by the Icelandic elves. The patterns are complex and hypnotic, devised by the elves to distract and beguile unwary travellers, who would become so engrossed in trying to undo the intricate twists that they would fall asleep and would then be spirited away into the hills. Now used on nightcaps, Noctus Knots divert the wearer from distracting thoughts and draw them down into deep sleep.

Nodgrass – ***Notten græs*** – A very agreeable grass, happy

growing in many conditions. It is blueish-green and gets its name from the constant, gentle nodding of its shaggy seed heads. Used on Lullaby Hats and children's nightcaps, it is a most pleasant and soothing ingredient. When paired with something enlivening such as sunbeams, Nodgrass is excellent for use in Encouragement Tricorns.

Pomp Cotton – ***Bombaxia magnifica*** – Grown on the banks of the Nile, this exceptionally fluffy cotton must be harvested before it fully ripens, at which point it becomes so full of hot air that it detaches from the plant and floats away. Because of its extremely puffed-up nature, when used on a hat (either as woven cloth or in its natural flocculent state) it imparts an air of pride to the wearer. However, if it becomes wet, the wearer may become easily dispirited. Therefore, a Pomp Cotton hat should never be worn in damp weather.

Radiant Bay – ***Baca radiata*** – This impressive shrub from Italy is the favoured nesting site of Boor Pigeons. Radiant Bay on a hat (or, more traditionally, as a headdress) gives the wearer an air of regal importance, though if worn by an already prideful person, it may incite a feeling of superiority or even invincibility, stirring up jealousy in people around them.

Raving Owl – ***Bubo hootenanny*** – Small, fluffy-headed owls with a loud, loopy hoot. During a Parliament of Owls, packs of Raving Owls will often be found near the back, hooting distractingly and generally causing chaos. Their ear feathers are prized for Chuckle Caps.

Ribbon

Most ribbons used in Hatmaking are made from strands of silk, spiderweb, light, sound, plant or, occasionally, human hair. Depending on the desired effect, different threads are used in the creation of each individual ribbon.

~ **Affinity** – Made of friendly whispers and light from the waxing moon, these ribbons help to increase the wearer's empathy.

~ **Convivial** – Created by weaving together ivy tendrils and peals of laughter, they are used on hats worn to social gatherings and all sorts of revelry.

~ **Courage** – Often woven from Lion's Mane hairs and Titan Grass, Courage Ribbons bring bravery to timid hearts.

~ **Insipid** – Woven from Murk Moth silk and strands of Gloom Root, these ribbons are difficult to see and are therefore mostly used on hats for shy people hoping not to be talked to at parties.

- ~ **Quaggy** – Made from thin strands of twilight woven with thick stems of Marsh Orchid, Quaggy Ribbon imparts an air of mystery to the wearer. However, using too much can result in a perplexed wearer, who becomes mired in their own enigma, leading to confusion and (in extreme cases) complete stupefaction.
- ~ **Ravel** – Made from Tangle Spider silk and Flittering Flax stalks, Ravel Ribbons are usually used for dancing hats, although if a pair of dancers both wear hats featuring elaborate bows of Ravel Ribbon, they can become entangled with each other and may need to be separated by a third party.
- ~ **Running** – Small strands of ostrich feathers woven with March Hare tufts, these ribbons are mostly used on shoes, but they are sometimes added to hats designed to quicken the wearer's wits.

Schlafen Grass – ***Stipa Schlafen sonora*** – When this heavy-headed, nodding grass blows gently in the Bavarian wind, its fronds create a soft hushing sound that is very calming. Used in a nightcap, it is soothing and will encourage the wearer to return to sleep if they awaken in the night. Use on a daytime hat is not advised.

Selenite – ***Selenite*** – This is a beautiful translucent white crystal associated with the moon. It contains many qualities associated with the lunar body, including serenity, grace and clarity. Placing pieces of selenite on a hat on either side of the forehead will encourage perceptivity in the wearer, while one directly on the crown of the head (in the middle of a hat) helps to clarify questions that have previously been unanswerable. Selenite is often used in Thinking Caps.

Sloth Poppy – ***Papaver megalonychidae*** – A dark purple, heavy-petalled poppy whose flowers and seeds are used in nightcaps and Optimism Hats. The Sloth Poppy encourages the wearer to slow down and smile at the world, though overuse can promote such a laid-back attitude that it becomes difficult to get anything done.

Thundergoose – ***Branta tempestas*** – These storm-grey geese are said to clap thunder from their wings as they fly. Using these feathers on a hat would be ill-advised (making the wearer liable to excessive *Sturm und Drang*), but the eggshells may be safely used. A hatching Thundergoose egg creates a loud BOOM, but once the gosling is safely free, the shells may be collected and used on hats for encouraging vigour and vim.

Titan Grass – ***Stipula titanica*** – A tall, awe-inspiring grass, with strong silvery stems that can be woven into impressive structural shapes that may not be achieved with softer grasses. Titan Grass imparts a sense of stout-hearted determination to the wearer that can veer into mulishness if not woven together with something relaxing, such as a few strands of Nodgrass.

Toothy Fuchsia – ***Fuchsia dentata*** – Unlike its cousin the shyer Common Fuchsia, a Toothy Fuchsia will bite anybody who attempts to pick it. Due to this flower's assertiveness, it is useful in Confidence Bonnets. It is recommended that a person attempting to pick a Toothy Fuchsia should wear thick gloves. Smelling the flowers is, of course, not recommended. Too many Toothy Fuchsias on one hat will result in the wearer's behaviour becoming boisterous and their wit rather too biting.

Torpid Straw – ***Miscanthus defessus*** – From a pale green grass that grows only in quiet Welsh valleys. Walking or lying on fresh Torpid Grass can make a person sleepy. However, the dried grass has slightly different properties, and can be woven into straw hats that simply make the wearer less noticeable.

Tremulous Elver – ***Alga perterrita*** – An aquatic plant that sheds its tentacles like a gecko tail if it is frightened. Found in freshwater streams, stray tentacles can be mistaken for baby eels as they whizz through the water. They are difficult to catch and therefore highly prized. The wriggling tentacles lend great flamboyance to outfits, though care must be taken to pair them with something stabilizing, lest the wearer come unmoored from their centre of gravity and, simultaneously, their sense of reality.

Umbrella Bird – ***Avis abscondita*** – This extremely shy bird is a nondescript sort of colour, of medium height and build, with an unremarkable call. In fact, it is very difficult to describe. Its only remarkable feature is that it hides behind its feathers when it encounters a stranger, forming them into a cone shape around its body to completely conceal itself from view. This quality makes its feathers most useful in creating hats for those wishing to escape observation or scrutiny. The feathers are usually called upon for hats to wear when meeting nosy neighbours or overly inquisitive distant relations.

Vigil Weeds – ***Urtica vigilans*** – Poker-straight, dark green, soldier-like weeds with a potent sting in the stem. In a hat,

a small bunch of Vigil Weeds helps to keep the wearer alert, rustling at the first sign of danger.

Vitus Seeds – ***Salix velox*** – In Italian folklore, the Vitus Tree pulls up its roots and dances across the land from sunset on 15 June to sunrise the following day. If a Vitus Tree is caught unawares by the rising of the sun, it will be forced to root down wherever it is. On Vitus Night, Italian children leave out handfuls of compost in an effort to distract the trees and, come morning, people are used to finding them rooted in new places. The spiral-shaped seed pods are used on many dancing clothes, giving extra whirling capabilities to the wearer.

Zenith Nectar – ***Mel superior*** – Nectar from the Moonmel Flower, which only blooms at the full moon. As moonlight collects in the cup of the flower, it becomes syrupy and delicious. Depending on the moon phase and the month of the year, this nectar has different qualities. Blue Zenith Nectar is the rarest, but all Zenith Nectar adds dazzle and glamour to Makers' creations.

New Ingredients Discovered by the Proprietor of this Book

New Maps Discovered by the Proprietor of this Book

Acknowledgements

Much like a novice Mapmaker, I occasionally became rather lost and somewhat befuddled while trying to find my way through the magic of making this book! Luckily, I had many wise and wonderful people showing me the way when I strayed into difficulty, and I am immensely grateful to them for their passion, patience and guidance on this journey.

I would especially like to thank . . .

My editors at Puffin, Nat Doherty and Jane Griffiths, for helping me slowly discover the secret starlight ink on the blank page I began with!

Wendy Shakespeare (ably assisted by Bella Haigh) for your excellent signposts that always point me in the right direction, Daphne Tagg for spotting the places where I stumbled off the path, and Petra Bryce and Sarah Hall for nudging me back on to it!

Louise Dickie, Roz Hutchinson, Alesha Bonser and the whole fantastic team at Puffin for brilliant work spreading the word about Cordelia Hatmaker's adventures.

Paola Escobar, for creating an enchanting cover and stunning illustrations, and Emily Smyth for bringing Cordelia's world so wonderfully to life in the art and design of the book.

Claire Wilson, for being a wondrous spirit guide on this adventure, and an utterly stellar agent.

The authors and booksellers who have so generously supported and cheered my first steps along the path of writing books; I am very grateful to you all for welcoming me to your magical world.

My friends who have set me right when I've been going round in circles, and patiently listened to me rambling about magical maps. And my brilliantly supportive family, who have gently pointed out when I've been holding the map upside down.

Barney, my North Star.

Finally, I would like to say a huge thank you to the readers. Sharing Cordelia's world with you is utterly joyful, and I hope you've enjoyed losing yourself in her second adventure!

Read on to find out how Cordelia's next adventure begins, in

THE TROUBLEMAKERS

Chapter 1

'The stars are full of stories, Littlest Hatmaker. Following the stars will always lead you into great adventures.'

Cordelia Hatmaker stood gripping the great ship's wheel, the deck of *Little Bear* solid beneath her feet. She could *smell* adventure in the spring wind; it smelled of salt and sky laced with a hint of fresh tar. She gazed upwards, watching as the sky turned lilac and the stars appeared one by one. They spangled the rigging, winking with the promise of exciting escapades to come.

Her father, Prospero Hatmaker, stood on the deck beside her.

'But every adventurer needs a compass,' Prospero added. 'The *heart* is a compass. Follow your heart and you'll go wisely and wildly all your life.'

Cordelia put her hand to her heart. She could feel it beating, soft and steady in her chest – a living creature.

'Is that today's lesson, Father?' she asked.

Prospero grinned down at her. 'Today's lesson is this: be careful of the ship's biscuit! It doesn't taste like biscuits at all!'

Cordelia grinned back.

They were not out at sea yet. All through autumn and winter, Cordelia had witnessed the ship being built, coming together out of nothing. She'd marvelled at the magic of making such a thing: a beast to ride the sea, made of wood and rope and canvas. She had climbed through the ribcage of its skeleton, paid solemn respect to the heavy rudder, been caught up in the sinews of rigging criss-crossing the sky and amazed by the swags of sails that would fill, like lungs, with air. She knew the ship from bow to stern, from the lofty crow's-nest to the confident line of the keel. The figure-head was a perfect little bear with fur carved into wind-blown ripples.

The ship was made of Fleetwood, which skimmed swiftly across water. When the Master Shipwright, bobbing up from Greenwich on an important-looking barge, had come to inspect her, he had pronounced *Little Bear* 'the finest vessel of her kind' and had added, 'I'll wager she's the quickest too!' which caused Cordelia to glow with pride.

Tonight, *Little Bear* was quiet. After finishing the sticky job of tarring her hull, the shipbuilders had gone home, leaving Cordelia and her father listening to the lap and hush of the Thames just beyond the dry dock in which the ship had been built. In a few days, when the glistening tar had dried, the dry dock would be flooded with water and *Little Bear* would float out on to the wide river.

'Then all that's left to do before we set off,' Cordelia said, 'is add *provisions*. Meaning, food.'

'And water,' Prospero added.

'Yes,' Cordelia agreed. 'Water's very important for a sea voyage.'

The long-promised sea voyage! Now that the spring tides were rising, it was nearly time to set off.

Cordelia and her father were going on a voyage to collect Hatmaking ingredients for the magical hats their family made. Prospero had plotted a journey from England to the Canary Islands, where they would search for the freckle-leafed Vim Shrub and Songstress Snails, whose pearly trails warbled with silvery music. From the Canaries, they would sail due east to the coast of Morocco, where they planned to rummage in the sands for the tiny flashing whorls of Storm Nautilus Shells.

Soon there would be a much greater demand than usual for ingredients because next week, for the first time in two hundred and fifty years, King George was poised to declare that Making magical things would be unrestricted for everyone in England once again.

The king was to address Parliament to repeal the strict Maker Laws, which tyrant king Henry the Eighth had put in place to control magical Making, so that he would not fear his subjects using these skills to rise against him. Until now, only the six Maker families of London were allowed to create clothes using magical ingredients. But from next week *everyone* would be free to enjoy the delight of Making.

Cordelia loved feeling the tingle in her fingertips when she was making something magical, whether it be a bonnet to give the wearer confidence or a bicorn to inspire daydreams. She felt a trembling kind of excitement in her belly, thinking of all the people who would soon discover the wonder of Making magical things for themselves. When she and her father returned from their voyage, the hold of *Little Bear* would be bursting with magical ingredients to transform people's ordinary clothes into enchanted ones. Cordelia could not wait to set off.

However, just one slight shadow was cast over the bright adventure: the rumours of a dangerous band of pirates calling themselves the Troublemakers.

First, these pirates had kidnapped the daughter of an important politician. They'd snatched her from her boarding-school bed in the middle of the night and left nothing but their name scrawled across the wall as a sign that they'd been there.

Then there had been chaos at the Winter Ball, when several dignified lords had suddenly been attacked by their own garments, shrieking and howling when their boots suddenly made them leap and stamp as though their feet were on fire. Moments later, their hats clamped over their eyes and the wearers began bellowing swear words in multiple languages. Next, a Whistle-Wasp nest had been thrown into their midst from the gallery and the air had filled with the sinister whistle of thousands of wasps mingled with the cries of hundreds of revellers fleeing the scene. In the ruckus, several ice sculptures – not to mention Lady Trundlemonk's nose – had been broken.

London had barely had time to recover from the Winter Ball (victims of the wasp stings were still whistling) when the Troublemakers struck again. Imp Eggs were crushed into the ink of a self-righteous magazine called *The Quarterly Scorn* and, rather than the usual articles sneering about the latest fashions, accompanied by lectures on the importance of constant good behaviour, every single copy of the latest issue of *The Quarterly Scorn* contained nothing but rude words and fart jokes from cover to cover.

Days later, the king's horses were somehow fed Craze-Hay, which led to neighing chaos in front of the palace. Riots broke out regularly at chocolate houses across the city and Conquista Caterpillars were placed on hundreds of paintings in the Royal Academy, so that very serious portraits of noble ladies and gentlemen all appeared to have large bushy moustaches. The caterpillars proved impossible to catch and several days later hatched into large dazzling and distracting Bamboozler Butterflies that caused three carriage accidents on Piccadilly.

All throughout winter, the Troublemakers had gone on to create catastrophe and disaster across London, gloating about their actions in a morning newspaper called *The Rude Awakening*. Despite being the architects of some truly strange and spectacular acts of destruction, the Troublemakers had never actually been *sighted* doing their misdeeds. Cloaked in mystery, they were the subject of many rumours that grew wilder in the dark. Some people claimed that they were made of smoke and could walk through walls. Others insisted that they had the power of flight. One wild-eyed man was seen shouting at Speaker's Corner that the Troublemakers had 'dozens of devils doing their dastardly deeds'.

Prospero was hesitant to take Cordelia on a voyage across seas that could be infested with pirates such as these. Cordelia, however, had endeavoured to persuade her father that the Troublemakers were very unlikely to cross their path, seeing as how the ocean was very large and ships were very small. Though still a little reluctant, Captain Hatmaker had agreed that the *Little Bear*'s voyage should go ahead as planned.

'Besides,' Cordelia had said confidently, 'they're causing havoc in *London* – we'll be somewhere else!'

Prospero had pointed out that, although the trouble was being made in London, many of the magical ingredients being used to create the chaos were unusual and not commonly found in England.

'They must be finding them somewhere else,' he mused. 'And then getting them into London somehow.'

Cordelia was not concerned by this small detail – so long as the Troublemakers did not stop her from going on the long-promised voyage with her father aboard their beautiful new ship.

She had her own little cabin, with a bunk that swung gently from the ceiling on ropes to stop her getting seasick as she slept. The cabin had a round porthole with a circle of rippled glass in it. She liked to look out of it, imagining the sights she would soon see. Perhaps a triumphant sunrise over the blue Atlantic or the coast of a whole new continent.

Her father's cabin, which had glittering windows that stretched the width of the ship, contained a collection of maps and sea charts and instruments that he used to navigate the seas. The other cabins, pieced together inside the ship like a neat puzzle, contained bunks for all twelve members of the crew – everyone from the first mate to the cabin boy. There was a galley for the ship's cook, complete with a brick stove, and a large store for the food and water they would need for the journey.

One of Cordelia's favourite nooks on *Little Bear* was the Weather Pantry, which had been stocked by her friend Win Fairweather, who brewed all kinds of weather and bottled it in glass jars. Cordelia loved to run her hands over the weather jars, neatly stacked in their special cabinet.

Weather-brewing was not officially legal yet because it was a kind of ancient Maker magic that had been outlawed centuries ago, so the cabinet was cleverly concealed behind a wooden panel. The shelves hung on ropes so that the jars wouldn't be shaken about in stormy weather. In their secret cabinet, the Cumulus Bottles gleamed, the Wind Bags trembled on their pegs and the Breeze Strings danced.

'All you need do, if you're stuck in the doldrums,' Win had told Cordelia, catching a piece of Breeze String as it wriggled away across the deck, 'is undo one of these knots. It will unleash the strand of wind caught within, then you'll be underway again. You should save the Wind Bags in case you ever become becalmed.'

'*Becalmed*' meant that the wind had completely stopped blowing and the ship was drifting with nothing to fill the sails.

When Cordelia put her hand on a Wind Bag, she felt a belly of air straining at the cloth. She was proud of the Weather Pantry; it had been her idea to ask Win to provide a supply of weather for the voyage. No other ship had a secret store of weather on board.

This evening, Cordelia decided to practise climbing the rigging once more before they went home for dinner. She was determined to climb it as fast as the cabin boy, Jack Fortescue. He was as quick as a monkey, scampering up the ropes to the crow's-nest. Cordelia climbed more slowly, hand over hand, up the nets. She already had calluses forming on her palms from the rough ropes. She was very proud of her calluses.

She swung towards the rigging, up into a complicated forest of ropes and masts. The deck grew smaller as she climbed, her father below moving across it like a beetle as he went to check the bowsprit ropes. Cordelia climbed high enough to see the haze of the marshes beyond London, almost lost in the blur of twilight. A ship was coming upriver towards them, a heavy shape low in the water, laden with goods it was bringing to London from some far-flung place.

'Must be a merchant ship,' Cordelia murmured.

Suddenly a *splash* tore through the quiet tapestry of evening river sounds.

A wooden crate had gone over the side of the merchant ship as it glided by. The crate bobbed in the water, but the ship sailed on, heedless of its lost goods.

Cordelia was drawing breath to call 'CARGO OVERBOARD!' when she heard a thread of voice twist along the river.

'*Double, double!*'

'Double, double!' came a hissed reply.

And, quick as an eel through the water, a rowing boat nipped out from the riverbank into the current.

It was dangerous for a tiny boat to be out there in the

gloom, among the hulking ocean-goers. But the boat was nimble, the person rowing quick and strong.

As the merchant ship sailed onward, the rowing boat chased the crate left bobbing in its wake. Within moments, the boatsman caught it and hauled it aboard. Then, as quickly and quietly as before, the rowing boat slipped away into the shadows.

Cordelia was motionless in the rigging.

The river soon smoothed over as though no great hull had just cut through it and no shallow skiff had skimmed its surface. The whispers of '*Double, double*' dissolved in the air.

It had all happened in a few heartbeats, in that strange last light as the evening lost to the oncoming night.

But Cordelia was sure she had seen . . .

'Smugglers!'